A GIRL TO COME HOME TO

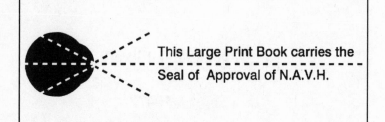

This Large Print Book carries the
Seal of Approval of N.A.V.H.

A GIRL TO
COME HOME TO

GRACE LIVINGSTON HILL

THORNDIKE PRESS

A part of Gale, Cengage Learning

GALE
CENGAGE Learning·

Detroit • New York • San Francisco • New Haven, Conn • Waterville, Maine • London

GALE
CENGAGE Learning®

© 2014 by Grace Livingston Hill.

All scripture quotations are taken from the King James Version of the Bible.

Thorndike Press, a part of Gale, Cengage Learning.

Thorndike Press® Large Print Gentle Romance.

The text of this Large Print edition is unabridged.

Other aspects of the book may vary from the original edition.

Set in 16 pt. Plantin.

LIBRARY OF CONGRESS CATALOGING-IN-PUBLICATION DATA

Hill, Grace Livingston, 1865–1947.
 A girl to come home to / by Grace Livingston Hill. — Large print edition.
  pages ; cm. — (Thorndike Press large print gentle romance)
  ISBN 978-1-4104-6613-6 (hardcover) — ISBN 1-4104-6613-2 (hardcover)
 1. Large type books. I. Title.
PS3515.I486G575 2014
813'.52—dc23   2013040993

Published in 2014 by arrangement with Barbour Publishing, Inc.

A Girl to Come Home To

CHAPTER 1

World War II
Eastern United States

The stars were all out in full force the night that Rodney and Jeremy Graeme came home from the war. Even the faraway ones were peeping eagerly through the distance, trying to impress the world with their existence, showing that they felt it an occasion when their presence should be recognized. And even the near stars had burst out like flowers in the deep blue of the darkness, till they fairly startled the onlooker, rubbing his eyes in wonder if stars had always been so large. It was early evening, scarcely six o'clock, but it seemed so very dark, and the stars so many and so bright.

"It almost seems," said Jeremy, "as if all the stars we have ever seen since we were born have come out to greet us now that we've come home. They've all come together. The stars that twinkled when we said our prayers at night when we were little kids, and seemed to smile at us and welcome us into a world that was going to be full of twinkling lights and music and fun. The stars that bent above the creek where we were skating, and seemed to enjoy it as much as we did. The stars that smiled more gently when we drifted down in the old canoe and sang silly love songs, or lay back and grew dreamy with unmade ambitions."

"Yes," said Rodney with a grin down at his brother, "the stars that blessed us with a bit of withdrawing when we walked home from church, or a party at night with our best girls. Right, Jerry? There must have been girls somewhere in your life after I left. There'd have been stars for them, too, of course. That's a swell thought that all those star fellows have sort of ganged up on us for tonight. Nice to think about."

"It seems an awfully long time ago, though, all those other things happening," said Jeremy thoughtfully. "Like looking back on one's self as an infant. After all we've been through, I wonder how we're going to fit into this world we've come back to."

"Yes, I wonder!" said Rodney. "I sure am glad to get back, but I've sort of got a feeling every little while that somehow we oughtn't to have come away till we'd finished the job and had 'em licked thoroughly so they can't start anything again."

"Yes, that does haunt you in the back of your mind, but anyway we didn't 'come' away. We were *sent,* and *had* to come. They thought we were more important over here."

"Of course," said the older brother. "And I'm satisfied, understand. Only somehow there's a feeling I ought to take hold and do some more over there yet. But I guess that'll wear off when I really get into this job over here they think is so important."

"Yes, of course," said the younger brother. "But there's this to remember: we aren't like some of the other fellows. I heard one fellow on the ship complaining the folks over home didn't understand. They hadn't any idea what we've been through. They've been just going on happily having a good time between their good acts of doing a little war work. But our family isn't like that. Our dad and mother understand. Dad's never forgotten his own experience in the other war. You can tell from their letters."

"Yes, of course," the older brother said, smiling. "Our family has always been an understanding family. But you're right about this world we're getting back to, I suspect. For a while it will be like going out to play marbles or hide-and-seek. The trouble is one can't go out to meet death without growing up. We've grown up, and marbles don't fit us anymore."

"Sure!" said Jeremy thoughtfully. "We'll just have to get adjusted to a new world, won't we? And somehow I don't see how we're going to fit anymore. I don't really have much heart for it all myself, except of course getting back to Dad and Mom and Kathie. But the others will seem like children. Of course you don't feel that way because you have Jessica. You'll get married, I suppose, if it really turns out that we get that job they talked about overseas. You planning for a wedding soon, Rod?"

There was a definite silence after that question, and suddenly the younger brother looked up with a question in his eyes. "I didn't speak out of turn, did I, Rod?" He looked at his brother anxiously. "You and Jessica aren't on the outs, are you?"

Rodney drew a deep breath and settled back. "Yes, we're on the outs, bud. Our engagement is all washed up."

"But *Rod*! I thought it was all settled. I thought you bought her a ring."

"Yes, I bought her a ring," said the older brother with a forlorn little sound like a sigh. Then a pause. "She sent it back to me a year ago today. I guess by now she's married to the other guy. I don't know, and I don't want to know anything more about it. She just wasn't worth worrying about, I suppose."

There was a deep silence with only the thunderous rumbling of the train. The younger brother sat and stared straight ahead of him, his startled thoughts taking in, in quick succession, the sharp changes this would make in his idolized brother's life, the things he knew in a flash must have been being lived down by Rodney all these silent months when they had not been hearing from each other. And then his comprehension dashed back to the beginning again.

"But the ring!" he faltered, thinking back to the bright token that had meant to him the sign of everlasting fidelity, the lovely, peerless jewel that they had all been so proud their Rodney had been able to purchase with his own well-earned money and place upon the lovely finger of the beautiful girl who was his promised bride. "What will you do with the ring?" Jeremy was scarcely aware he was asking another question. He had been merely thinking aloud. Rodney turned toward him with a look almost of anguish, like one who knew this ghastly thing had to be told, and he wanted to get it over with as soon as possible.

11

"I sold it!" he said gruffly. The brothers' eyes met and raked each other's consciousness for full understanding. And in that look Jeremy came to know how it had been, and how it had to be with Rodney. Rodney was four years older, but somehow in that look Jeremy grew up and caught up the separating years, and understood. It did not need words to explain, for Jeremy understood now. Saw how it would have been with *him* if he were in a like situation.

But after a moment Rodney explained. "At first I wanted to throw it into the sea. But then somehow that didn't seem right. It wasn't the ring's fault, even though it was of no further use to me. Even supposing I should ever find another girl I could trust, which I'm sure I never will, I wouldn't want to give her a ring that had been dishonored, would I? No, it would never be of any further use to me, or to anybody unless they were strangers to its history. Yet what to do with it I didn't know. I couldn't carry it on my person and have it sent back to my mother sometime after I had been killed, to tell a strange story she wouldn't understand, could I?"

"Then Mom doesn't know?" asked Jeremy.

"Not unless Jessica has told her, and I

doubt if she has. She wouldn't have the nerve! Though maybe there was some publicity. I don't know. I haven't tried to find out. There hasn't been a word of gossip about it in any of my letters. My friends wouldn't want to mention it, and any others didn't bother to write, so I've had to work this thing out by myself. After all, it was my problem, and I worked at it part-time between missions. It helped to make me madder at the enemy, and less careful for myself. What was the use when the things I had counted on were gone?

"And what was the ring that I had worked so hard to buy but a costly trinket that nobody wanted? So I found a diamond merchant who gave me a good price for the stone, more than I paid for it, and I was glad to get rid of it.

"That's the story, Jerry. It had to be told, and there it is. At first I thought I couldn't come home, where Jessica and I had been so much together, but then it came to me that there was no point in punishing Mom and the rest just because Jessica had played me false. So I'm here, and I only hope I won't be subjected to too much mention of the whole affair. Jessica, I'm sure, will be out of the picture, thank heaven! She spoke of being married in another part of the country.

"Certainly I never want to lay eyes on her again, of course, and perhaps in due time, with the help of a few more wars, I may forget the humiliation I have suffered. But I don't want pity, kid. I'm sure you'd understand that."

"Of course not," said Jeremy, giving a sorrowful, comprehending look. "But Rod, I don't see how she *could.* She always seemed to be so crazy about you."

"Well, let's not go into that. I've been through several battles since that thought used to get me," said Rodney.

"The little vandal!" said Jeremy. "What did she do? Just send the ring back without any letter or explanation?"

"Oh, no, she sent a nice little letter all right, filled with flowery words and flattery, to the effect that she was returning the ring, though she did adore it, because she thought I might want to use it again, and that I had always been so kind and understanding that she was sure I would see that it was a great deal better for her to frankly tell me that she had discovered she didn't care for me as much as she had supposed; and as she was about to marry an older, more mature man, who was far better off financially than I could ever hope to be, and she wished that

I wouldn't feel too bad about her defection. She closed by saying that she hoped that this wouldn't be the end, that she and I would always be friends as long as the world lasted. That we had had too much fun together to put an end to it altogether. Words to that effect, said in a flowery style, quoting phrases that had been supposedly dear to us both in the past, showing me plainly that they had never really meant a thing to her but smooth phrases."

"The little rotten rat!" blurted Jeremy. "I'd like to wring her pretty little false neck for her!"

"Yes, I felt that way for some time, but then I reflected that I didn't want to even give her that much satisfaction. She isn't worth so much consideration."

"Perhaps not," said Jeremy, "but all the same I'd like to class her with our enemies and let her take her chances with them."

The older brother gave an appreciative look.

"Thanks, pard!" he said with a wry grin. "Well, enough said. It's good to know you'll stand by if an occasion arises."

"Yes, brother, I'll stand by," said Jeremy solemnly, and then after a moment, "And what about Mom and the rest?"

"Oh, they'll have to be told I suppose, but

at least not the first minute. The time may come soon, but probably not tonight."

There was silence for several minutes, and then Jeremy spoke slowly, speculatively. "Ten to one Mom knows," he said. "You know she always had a way of sort of thinking out things and knowing beforehand what had happened to us before we even got home."

"Yes, that's true. Dad always said it was her seventh sense. That she sort of smelled 'em out ahead of time. Still, I don't see how she could this. However, it's all right with me if she has. I guess I can take it. Gosh, I hate to tell her. I hate to be pitied."

Another long silence, then Jeremy said, "Yes, I know. But I guess you can trust Mother."

"Yes, of course," said the older brother, lifting his chin with a brave gesture. "Yes, Mother's all right. Mother's wonderful! And it ought to be enough for any fellow to be getting home to her without worrying about some little two-timing brat of a gold-digger."

Jeremy flashed a quick look at his brother. "Was that what she did? Was it money?"

"Yes, I figured that was what did it. A guy I met in the navy mentioned his name once and said he was just rolling in wealth. Had something to do with the black market he thought, though when I came to question closer, he wouldn't tell any more. He said he guessed he oughtn't to have mentioned it. Seems the fellow is an uncle of a buddy of his on his ship, and he was afraid it might get back to him that he had been talking. Well, what difference did it make? She'd thrown me over. Why should I care what for?"

"But Rod, we're not exactly poverty-stricken. And as for you, Jessica knew Uncle Seymour left you a nice sum. You had a good start in life for a young man."

"My shekels wouldn't hold a candle to what a black market man could make now," Rodney said, grinning.

"No, I suppose not," said his brother with an answering grin. Then there followed a long silence, the brothers thinking over what had been said. Rodney had perhaps been more confidential with Jeremy than ever before in his life, and the younger brother had a lot to think over.

Rodney had dropped his head back on the seat and closed his eyes, as if the confidence was over for the time being, and Jeremy stared out the window unseeingly. They were not far from home now, another half hour, but it was too dark to notice the changes that might have come in the landscape. Jeremy was interested, after his long absence from his own land, in even an old barn or a dilapidated station they passed. Anything looked good over here, for this was home.

But there were adjustments to be made in the light of what Rodney had just told him. He had come home expecting a wedding soon, and now that was all off, and there was a gloomy settled look of disappointment on the face of the brother who had always been so bright and cheery, so utterly sure of himself, and what he was going to do. Was this thing going to change Rod? How hard that he not only had the memory of war and his terrible experiences at sea, but he had to have this great disappointment, too, this feeling of almost shame — for that is what it had sounded like as Rod told it — that his girl had gone back on him. The girl whose name had been linked with his ever since they had been in high school together. What a rotten deal to give him! Good old Rod! And he had always been so proud of Jessica! Proud of her unusual beauty, proud of her wonderful gold hair, her blue eyes, her long lashes, her grace and charm!

Jeremy searched his own heart and found that for a long time he himself had never cared so much for Jessica. Perhaps it was because she had always treated him like a younger brother, sort of like a little kid, always sending him on errands, asking favors of him, just a sweep of her long lashes and expecting him to do her will, do her errands, give up anything he had that she chose to want, like tickets to ball games. Well, he thought he had conquered those things, because he had been expecting ever since he went overseas that she would sometime soon be his sister-in-law, and he wanted no childish jealousy or hurt feelings to break the beautiful harmony that had always been between his brother and himself. The family must be a unit. And so he had disciplined his feelings until he was all ready to welcome his new-to-be sister with a brotherly kiss.

But now that was out! And Mom didn't know anything about it yet? Or did she? Could a thing like that fail to reach their mother? If she didn't know, how would she take it? Had she been fond of Jessica? He tried to think back. He could dimly remember a sigh now and then, a shadow on her placid brow. When was that? Could that have been when Rod first began to go with Jessica? But Mom had later seemed to be quite fond of Jessica, hadn't she? Jeremy couldn't quite remember. He had been more engrossed in himself at that time. About then was when he got that crush on Beryl Sanderson, the banker's daughter. Of course that was ridiculous. He, the son of a quiet farmer, living outside the village, on a staid old farm that had been in the family for over a hundred years, without any of the frills and fancies that the modern homes had. And she the daughter of a most influential banker, who lived in a great gray stone mansion, went to private schools, then away to a great college, dressed with expensive simplicity, and never even looked his way. Beryl Sanderson! Even now the memory of her stirred his thoughts, although he hadn't been pondering on her at all, he was sure, since he went away to war. Well, that was that, and he wasn't mooning around about any of his childhood fancies. He had a big job to do for his country, and there wasn't time for anything else then.

Suddenly Rodney broke the silence. "How about you, kid? Did you pick up some pretty girl across seas, or was there a girl you left behind you? Come, out with it, and let us know where we both stand now that we're getting home."

Jeremy grinned. "No girl!" he said.

"No kidding?" said the older brother, turning his keen eyes a bit anxiously toward the younger man, with a pleasant recognition of the goodly countenance he wore, his fine physique, his strong, dependable face. There was nothing of which to be ashamed in that brother.

"No kidding," said Jeremy soberly. "Not after the line of talk Mom gave me before I went away. She didn't exactly hold you up as a horrible example of one who had got himself engaged before time, but she did warn me that it was a great deal better to wait for big decisions like that till one was matured enough to be sure."

"Hm! Yes, well maybe Mom felt a little uncertain about what I'd done, though she never batted an eye about it. Of course I went away so soon after Jessica and I thrashed things out, and Mom was always fair. She never jumped to conclusions nor antagonized one of us. Probably she didn't want to have me go away with any unpleasantness between us. She took her worries, if she had any about us, to God. She was that way. She had a wonderful trust that God could and would work *any*thing out that she couldn't manage. Mom was wonderful that way. It somehow strengthened me a couple of times when I had a close call, just to remember that Mom was probably on her knees putting a wall of her prayers around me, maybe right at that time."

"Yes, she's been a wonderful mom," said Jeremy thoughtfully. "That's why I don't want anything to upset her now. I gotta go slow and let her know I haven't got away from her teaching. But say, aren't we coming into our station? Isn't that the old Clark place? Yes, it is. Now it won't be long before we're home. Boy, but I'm hungering for a sight of the old house and Mom and Dad and Kathie and even old Hetty. Won't it be good to eat some of her cooking again? I'm hungry enough to eat a bear."

"Here, too," said Rodney, looking eagerly out the window. "But a bear wouldn't be in it compared with Hetty's fried chicken. Nobody ever fried chicken to beat old Hetty. Maybe we ought to have let 'em know we were coming. It takes time to go out and kill a chicken and cook it."

"Have you forgotten, brother, that they have an ice plant in the cellar? Ten to one Mom's had chickens galore, frozen and ready to fry, just in case. You know Mom never got caught asleep. She's probably been getting ready for this supper for the last two months. She won't be caught napping."

"No," said the older brother with solemn shining light in his eyes. "Well, here's our station. Shall we go? It's time to get our luggage in hand."

"Here, I'll reach that bag, Rod. You oughtn't to be straining that shoulder of yours, remember. You don't want to go back to the hospital again, you know."

And so, laughing, kidding, eager, they arose and gathering their effects, trooped out to the platform.

Casting a quick glance about, they made a dash toward the upper end of the station, and using the tactics known to them of old in their school days, they escaped meeting the crowd that usually assembled around an arriving train. They cut across a vacant lot and so were not detained but strode on down the country road toward their home. That was where they desired above all things to be as rapidly as possible. That was what they had come across the ocean for. Mother and home were like heaven in their thoughts, and at present there was no one they knew of by whom they were willing to be delayed one extra minute.

They were unaware, as they hurried along with great strides, of the eyes of some who saw them as they dashed around the end of the station, and pointed them out, questioned who they were. For though the uniforms of servicemen were numerous, in that town as well as in others, they shone out with their gold braid and brass buttons and attracted attention as they passed under the station lights.

"Well, if I didn't know that man was overseas in a hospital, I'd say that was Rodney Graeme," said one girl stretching her neck to peer down the platform behind her. "He walks just as Rod did."

"You're dreaming," said another. "Rodney Graeme has been overseas for four years. Besides, there are two of them, Jess. Which one did you think looked like Rod?"

"The one on the right," said the first girl. "I tell you he walks just like Rod."

"I guess that's wishful thinking," said Emma Galt, an older girl with a sour mouth, a sharp tongue, and a hateful glance.

"That other one might be Rod's younger brother, Jerry," said Garetha Sloan.

"Nonsense! Jerry wasn't as tall as Rod; he was only a kid in high school when Rod went away."

"You seem greatly interested for a married woman, Jess," sneered Emma Galt.

"Really!" said Jessica. "Is your idea of a married woman one who forgets all her old friends?"

But out upon the highway the two brothers made great progress, striding along.

"Well, we beat 'em to it all right," said Jeremy.

"Okay! That's all right with me," said his brother. "I'll take my old comrades later. Just now I want to get home and see Mom. I didn't notice who they were, did you?"

"No, I didn't wait to identify anybody but old Ben, the stationmaster. He looked hale and hearty. There were a bunch of girls, or women, headed toward the drugstore, but I didn't stop to see if I knew them. I certainly am glad we escaped. I don't want to be gushed over."

"Well, maybe we've escaped notice. You can't always tell. We'll see later," said Rodney. "But there's the end gable of the house around the bend, and the old elm still standing. I was afraid some storm might have destroyed it. Somehow I forget that they haven't had falling bombs over here. It looks wonderful to see the old places all intact. And a light on our front porch. Good to see houses and trees after so much sea. And isn't that our cow, old Taffy, in the pasture by the barn?"

"It sure is," said Jeremy excitedly, "and my horse, Prince! Oh boy! We're home at last!"

They did the last few laps almost on a run and went storming up the front steps to meet the mother who according to her late afternoon custom had been shadowing the window, looking toward the road by which they would have to come if they ever came back. Not that she was exactly expecting them, but it seemed she was not content to let the twilight settle down for the night without always taking a last glimpse up the road as if they might be coming yet before she was content to sleep.

In an instant she was in their big strong arms, almost smothered with their kisses, big fellows as they were.

"Mom! Oh, Mom!" they said and then embraced her again, both of them together, till she had to hold them off and study them to tell which was which.

"My babies! My babies grown into great men, *both* of you! And both of you come back to me *at once*! Am I dreaming, or is this real?"

She passed her frail, trembling hand over eyes that had grown weary watching out the window all these months for her lads.

"This is real, Mom!" said Jeremy, and he hugged her again. "And where's Dad? Don't tell me he's gone to the village! We can't wait to see him."

"No, he's here somewhere," said the mother's voice, full of sweet motherly joy.

"He just got back from bringing Kathleen from her day at the hospital, nursing. He went out to milk the cow. Kathie, oh, Kathie! Father! Where are you? *The boys* have come!"

There was a rush down the stairs, and the pretty Kathleen sister was among them, and the kindly father, beaming upon them all. It was a wonderful time. And good old Hetty came in for her share of greeting, too.

And then the boys hung their coats and caps up on the hall rack, in all the glory of gold braid and decorations, dumped their baggage on the hall table and chair, and went to the big living room where the father had already started a blaze in the ever-ready fireplace that was always prepared for the match to bring good cheer.

Then as they sat there talking, just looking at one another — even old Hetty having a part of the moment — smiling, beaming joy to one another, somehow all the terrible impressions, so indelibly graven in the consciousness of those fighters who had returned, were somehow softened, gentled, comforted by the sight and sound of beloved faces, precious voices, till for the time the past terrible years were erased. It seemed almost like a look into a future where heaven would wipe out the sorrows of earth.

Then, softly, old Hetty slipped out into the kitchen. She knew what to do, even if Mrs. Graeme had not given that warning look. So many times, dark days, when there had come no expected letters, and news was scarce and bad when it did come, these two good women had brightened the darkness by making plans of what they would do, when, and if, the boys did come suddenly, unexpectedly.

Hetty hurried to the freezing plant and got out her chickens. All the children home now, all the family together at last. And Hetty was as happy over the fact as any of the family, for they were her family, the only family she had left anymore.

And presently there was the sweet aroma of frying chicken, a whiff of baking biscuits at the brief opening of the oven door, the fragrant tang of applesauce cooking. Oh, it was going to be a good supper, if it *was* hastily gotten together. There would be also mashed potatoes and rich brown gravy, Hetty's gravy, they knew of old. And there were boiling onions, turnips adding to the perfume. Celery and pickles. They could think it all out in anticipation, and Mother Graeme could smile and know that all was going on as she had planned. Little lima beans. Her nose was sensitive to each new smell. There would be coffee by and by, and there was a tempting lemon meringue pie, the kind the boys loved, in the cold pantry. The boys would not be missing anything of the old home they loved.

They had asked about the horse and the cow and the dogs, the latter even now lying adoringly at the feet of their returned masters, wriggling in joy over their coming.

They had heard a little of the welfare of near neighbors, a few happenings in the village, the passing of an invalid, the sudden death of a fine old citizen, but by common consent there had been no mention yet of the group of young people who had been used to almost infest the house at one time, when the boys were at home before the war. Of course many of the men and a few of the girls were in the service, somewhere, and there was a shadow of sadness that no one was quite willing to bring upon their sweet converse, in this great time of joy. Jeremy, sitting quietly, watching his mother's sweet, happy face, suddenly realized that she had not ventured to tell them about any of their old friends and comrades, and he wondered again if she knew what had befallen Rodney. He wished in his heart that the matter might not have to be mentioned, at least not that night. There would be time enough for the shadow of a blighting disappointment to one of their number, later, but not tonight. Not to dim the first homecoming. They were there, just themselves. It was almost as they used to be before they grew up, when they were a family, simple and whole. Oh, that it might be that way for at least one more night before any revelations were made that might darken the picture!

He gave a quick look toward Rodney, sitting so quietly there watching his mother. Was Rod wondering about the same things? Of course he was. Somehow he and Rod always seemed to have much the same reactions to matters of moment. And this surely must have been a matter of moment to Rod.

Good old Rod! These first few days might be going to be tough for him. He must be on hand to help out if any occasion for help should present itself. People were so dumb. There were always nosy ones who asked foolish prying questions and would need to be turned off with a laugh, or silence. A brother could perhaps do a lot.

It was just then it happened.

The blessing had been asked. That seemed this time such a special joy to be thanking God for bringing them all together again. Father had served them all heaping plates of the tempting food, and Rod had just put the first mouthful in his mouth. Jeremy watched him do it. And then the doorbell rang, followed by the sound of the turning doorknob, the opening of the big front door, the entrance of several feet, the click of girls' heels on the hall floor, just as it used to be in the past years so many times. For all their young friends always felt so much at home in their home. But oh, why couldn't they have waited just this one night and let the home folks have their first inning? Just this first night!

A clatter and chatter of young voice, as Kathleen sprang up and hurried into the hall.

"Oh, there you are, Kathleen," said a loud, clear voice that Jeremy knew instantly was Jessica's. "Oh, you're eating dinner, aren't you? Never mind, we'll come right out and sit with you the way we've always done. No, don't turn on the light in the living room, we'll come right out. Of course we've had our dinners before we came, but we simply can't waste a minute, and no, we won't hold you up. I know you must be hungry —"

Jeremy's quick glance went to Rodney's face, turned suddenly angry and frowning. Yes, he had recognized the voice. His reaction was unmistakable.

In one motion as it were, Rodney swept his knife and fork and napkin and plate from the table as he sprang stealthily to his feet and bolted for the pantry door, carrying with him all evidences of his former presence at the table. Only his mute napkin ring remained to show there had been another sitting there at the right hand of Mother Graeme. Then quickly, quite unobtrusively, the mother's hand went out and covered that napkin ring, drawing it close to the other side of the coffeepot, entirely out of sight from the door into the hall by which the bevy of guests seemed about to enter. It was then that Jeremy came to himself and realized that this was his opportunity. He swung to his feet and grasped the chair that stood by his side where his brother had been sitting, giving it a quick twist, and placing it innocently off at one side, where any unsuspecting person might sit without noticing that it had but a moment before been a part of the family circle of diners.

Jeremy came forward courteously and met the guests as they entered, ahead of the disturbed Kathleen, who had done her best to turn them aside and failed. But no one would ever have suspected that Jeremy was playing a graceful part, or that he was at all anxious about the present situation. Rodney was definitely out of the picture, that was all that mattered. The pantry door was closed, and there was not even a shadow of the passing of a blue coat with brass buttons, gold braid, and ribbon decorations.

Jeremy glanced at his mother, but she was coolly welcoming the guests, seating them around the room, not saying a word about Rodney's absence. Perhaps she hadn't even noticed yet that he was gone. But you never could tell. Mother was a marvelous actress.

CHAPTER 2

Out on the road going slowly by, two old men were jogging along, as much as an ancient Ford could be said to jog, even in war times, and as they passed the car standing in front of the Graeme house, they even slowed down their war jog and stared at it as they were passing.

"Ain't that the car Marcella Ashby bought off that Ty Wardlow jest afore he left fer overseas? Seems like there ain't another one jest that make an' color in these parts. And I seen her driving by awhile ago with Emma Galt an' Garethy Sloan, an' another gal. It looked very much like that highflier who married that old gray-headed ripsnorter of a so-called stockbroker from the West, her that useta be Jessica Downs. Poor old Widow Downs done her best by that gal, but she was a chip off the old block, I guess, and couldn't get by with that temper'ment she inherited from that flighty ma of hers an' her good-for-nothin' pa, Wiley Downs. He was jes' naturally a cussed young'un from a three-year-old up, when they all thought he was so sweet and cute. Well, he was cute all right. I never did see no sweetness about him though, did you Tully?"

"Not so's you'd notice it," answered Tully glumly. "I know he was anythin' but sweet when I knowed him in school, and I guess his teachers all felt the same way. And that Jessica, she had every one of his traits, including that washed-out yella hair that she flung around sa proudly, 'zif she was the only one who had any. Oh, she was sorta pretty, I'll admit, but she had sly eyes, and I always wondered how it was that Rod Graeme ever took up with her. I sort of figured that his pop an' mom was almost glad ta let him go to war jesta get him away from that little gold-digger. Well, she does seem like a gold-digger, doesn't she? How she shelved Rod Graeme and took up with an old man just because he was said to be rollin' in wealth."

"Oh, she's a gold-digger all right, Tully," said Jeff Springer, turning out for the car they had just been discussing. "They do say that old guy, Carver De Groot, is rich as they make 'em. Ur leastways that's the talk. Though I'm wonderin' what she came back here fer, if that was her in that car with the other gals. I heard tell it was some likely that the Graeme boys might be comin' home soon on a furlough."

"Yep," said Tully. "They hev. I seen 'em jest a little while ago. They got in on the late train and shied off across the meadow as if they was tryin' to escape notice. Beats all how shy some o' them heroes are."

"Well, mebbe the gals seen 'em," said Jeff, "an' they've come here to find out if it's so."

There weren't many in the town who could beat Jeff and Tully figuring out what had happened and what people were going to do about it.

"Well, I don't see what she'd wantta come back here fer," said Tully thoughtfully. "She's married all righty, fer I heard that Marcella Ashby went out to the weddin', an' it ain't so long ago, neither."

"Yep. But then, there's such a thing as *di-vorces*, ya know."

"Shucks!" said Tully. "No gal brought up in this here town would think about gettin' a *di*-vorce. Why, it ain't considered *respectable* here."

"Well, you needn't tell me that gal Jessica would ever stop anythin' she *wanted* ta do fer respectability's sake. It ain't in her."

"Mebbe not," said Tully speculatively, "but it would any of those Graemes. You know that, Jeff."

"Yes, I s'pose so," reflected Jeff, "that is, of course, Mom and Pop Graeme would feel that way. But that ain't sayin' the boys would feel that way *now.* They've been ta war, ya know, an' they do say that war changes men a whole lot. You can't jus' say fer sure them Graeme boys feels that way now, ya know."

"It may be so," said Tully unbelievingly, "but I don't believe it. I've knowed them Graeme boys since little up, an' I never saw a look or an act that would lead me ta believe they would think a *di*-vorce would be right. Not them with their bringin' up. Not them with a father an' a mother like they got."

"Well, that's so, too," said Jeff thoughtfully. "There's a great deal in what's before you. Your forebears mean a whole lot, even in these days. Well, mebbe you're right! But if that's so I can't figger out what that ripsnorter of a gal has gone there fer."

"Look here now," said Tully protestingly, "I didn't say nothin' about that highflier gal bein' against *di*-vorce, did I? *She'd* prob'ly be *fer* it, I s'pose, but that ain't sayin' what she could do about it, bein' as one of the parties was a *Graeme.*"

"Well, I hope yer right. I sure do, Tully! It sure would be a contest worth watchin', and I'm somehow bettin' on the Graemes my own self, if you ast me. I sure hope I'm right."

They drove on down the highway, and their voices were lost in the distance.

But inside the Graeme house the contest had already begun.

It was such a pity that Jeff and Tully couldn't have been present to see the start.

It was Jessica who opened the first round, with a quick glance around the table, taking in the place where Rodney should have been and wasn't, and not even a napkin ring in sight to mark where he had been.

Her eyes came back quickly to Mother Graeme's face with a quick suspicious glance. She had always felt that there was not full harmony between herself and Mother Graeme even in the days when she was the acknowledged fiancée of Rodney and supposed to be under the advantage of a blessing and the full acquiescence of his parents. She had none of her own to worry about. Just the one quick glance, searching to see if the mother had somehow managed to spirit away the desirable son in the brief space of time. Then her face melted into a sweet, tender look, for she was very versatile and well knew what kind of a look she should put on to deceive these elect people.

"Oh, dear Mother Graeme!" she said tenderly, meltingly. "It's so good to get back to you. I have come to believe that there is no mother in the whole wide world as good and dear as you are."

Mother Graeme looked at her with an inscrutable, unbelieving smile that showed this false girl's words had not gone even skin deep into her heart. But even her son Jeremy couldn't be sure just what his mother felt about it when he saw.

"There are a great many mothers in the world, Jessie. You haven't been away long enough to have seen them all, child." And then Mrs. Graeme turned away and greeted the other girls graciously.

Mom is a perfect lady even though she's never been much out of Riverton in her life, decided Jeremy as he watched the quiet poise of his lady-mother. And then he noted that her brief acceptance of the gushing compliment had been enough to put the showy admiration out of running, and Jessica turned quickly to her next interest, which was really what she had come for. It began with another quick survey of the table, dwelling on each vacancy where another might have sat, and then she addressed a remark to the whole table. "But where is *Rodney*?" she asked, letting her eyes touch each face tentatively and coming back decisively to Jeremy. "I was told that he had come home also. Surely he hasn't left already?"

Jeremy caught the question midway before anyone else could answer, the way he used to snatch the football out of the very teeth of the enemy when interference hadn't been suspected from his direction.

"Rod had to go out," he said quite casually, as if it were a thing to be expected and not at all as if he were apologizing for his absence. And he noted that their mother did not look astonished at his words, and not even Kathleen seemed surprised. Strange. Even his father, after a quick sharp look at Jeremy, went right ahead with his eating and kept his genial family atmosphere intact. He had a great family, Jeremy reflected. And oh, but they must surely know that something was wrong. Didn't they know that Jessica had married somebody else? Or hadn't she married him yet? Maybe she didn't get married. Maybe she had got over that and had come out after Rod again. Well, if she had, he personally would devote himself to seeing that she did not get him.

After what she had done to Rod, she was less worthy than he had thought her long ago, not fit for such a prince as his brother. He would keep out of this as far as he could, but if it came to a showdown he would go out for Rod in a big way and save him, even from himself, if she should prove canny enough to lead him so far afield as that.

So Jeremy devoted himself to the other girls, asking them questions about their families and what they had been doing for the war during the years of his own absence overseas.

But presently, as Rodney did not appear and time went on while Jessica watched the younger brother, she became quite intrigued with him and broke into his conversation with vivacity. "Do you know, Jerry, you've quite developed," she said patronizingly. "You're really a man now, aren't you?" And she lifted her eyes with that long appeal from under golden lashes that he used to watch her give to his older brother and wonder at so long ago. It fairly sickened him now, the memory of it.

He grinned his slow, indifferent grin. "Well, I guess that's what was intended I should be, wasn't it?" he said. And then he turned to his sister and said, "By the way, Kath, we met an old crush of yours in New

41

York as we came through, Richard Macloud. He asked after you and wanted to be remembered. He's going back in a few days now and is slated for some big job, the powers-that-be aren't saying what just yet."

Jessica gave full attention to Jeremy during this brief conversation and took a hand at once.

"Do you know, Jerry, you look very much like Rod. I hadn't noticed before, but of course now that you're older, the resemblance is very marked. You're even taller than he is, aren't you?"

"Oh no, he's an inch and a half taller," the younger brother answered with a gleam of amusement. But he did not further pursue the subject. Instead he turned to his mother and began to ask questions about her old neighbors, women his mother's age who used to give him cookies when he was a child. He told one or two amusing stories of things that happened long ago.

Jessica was watching him and deciding that when his brother was not present there would at least be Jerry, and he really seemed to be worthwhile. In fact anybody in uniform was interesting to Jessica.

Meanwhile Jeremy kept wondering what Rod was doing, or going to do, and was Hetty giving him more chicken out in kitchen, and would she give him coffee? Rod hadn't had his coffee yet, and he knew he was hungry and anxious for a cup of real home coffee. And what would Rod do if these tormenting callers continued to stay far into the night? Could he possibly steal up to bed without being heard and lock his door and go to sleep? Or was it thinkable that he himself could help out somehow by making an excuse to get Rod's coat and hat out of the front hall and throw it down the back stairs? There were complications any way he saw it. And it certainly wouldn't be a good thing for these callers to go out the front door again and pass those two identical overcoats and caps hanging there together. They would know in an instant that Rod hadn't gone out of the house, that he had merely been hiding somewhere. Well, perhaps that was what Rod wanted, to let Jessica know definitely that he did not wish to see her.

However, as he talked, he continued to work away at the problem in his mind and wonder if this was possibly where his own helpfulness and initiative should work in.

So presently he brought the conversation around to talk of people he had met overseas, and he spoke of one he was sure was known to them all. "Just wait!" he said

43

springing up. "I think I have a snapshot of him upstairs. I'll get it. It was taken just after he came back from his most dramatic mission and won a lot of honor."

He went hurrying out, snatching the two overcoats and caps from the hall rack as he passed them and bore them upstairs, striding to his room, and dropping them on a convenient bed out of sight. Then he plunged his hand even in the dark into the collection of hand luggage, located his own bag, which he knew carried some photographs, and hurried back downstairs, producing the picture, with a few others but taking care he did not show them any in which his brother figured. Let that highflier girl forget Rod if she could. Rod definitely wanted none of her; or if Rod only *thought* he didn't, and there was a doubt, there was no doubt in Jeremy's mind about whether *he* wanted that girl for a sister-in-law.

Now, Jessica was accustomed to getting all the attention there was from every man within her charmed circle, and she didn't like it that Jeremy divided his attentions so thoroughly, so she set herself to achieve interest in this new man who had only been a kid before he went away and had turned man overnight as it were. But Jerry wasn't interested. Perhaps if he let her know he wasn't she would get tired and go home.

At last Jessica looked straight at Jeremy. "When is Rod coming back?" she asked directly, and her eyes demanded the truth.

Jeremy laughed lightly. "That's hard to say," he answered. "Men don't usually confide little matters like that."

Without really repeating her own words, Jessica turned to the quiet mother and managed to shift both her glance and her question to her, as if she were the one she had meant to interrogate in the first place.

Mrs. Graeme met the shifted glance with an odd quietness and answered promptly, calmly. "He didn't say when he would be back."

Jessica seemed a bit perplexed at the answer and the calm demeanor. She shifted her sparkling nervous fingers so their load of glittering diamonds would shine directly into the lady's eyes, and asked impertinently, "Where did he go, Mrs. Graeme?" in the tone of one who has an undeniable right to ask.

"He didn't tell me," said the mother quietly.

There followed a deadly moment of silence in which it was evident that the visitor was a trifle disconcerted. Then Mrs. Graeme lifted a sweet smile and asked quite casually, "Is your husband in Riverton with you, Jessie?"

Jessica's cheeks flamed into crimson above the lovely makeup, and her eyes went down to her glittering fingers nervously. "Why, no, Mrs. Graeme," she answered indifferently. "He's too busy. His business engrosses all his time. He seldom goes anywhere away from home."

"Oh," said Mother Graeme, "then I suppose you're not remaining here long."

"Well, I don't know just what I shall do," flashed Jessica angrily. "I'm quite free to stay as long as I please if it suits me. Depends upon how interesting you folks can make it for me. But I certainly do want to see Rod."

"Yes?" said the calm mother voice. Then after another instant's silence, she said, "What a pity Mr. De Groot couldn't have come with you, just for once. Your old friends would certainly like to meet him."

What a mother! commented Jeremy in his heart. *She certainly is tops. Then of course she has known about the break between Rod and Jessica, perhaps for a long time, and never breathed a word of it to Rod! Even called her husband by his name! Rod needn't have worried lest there would be a scene. Mother never would permit a scene. She isn't*

46

a day older than when we were little kids, and she always kept her hand on everything! Bless her! And Dad follows right along with her!

He cast a quick look toward his father, and saw him eating quietly along, enjoying the festive dinner, not seeming to question what had become of Rod. Not being upset nor allowing any tenseness in the pleasant home atmosphere since these old-time friends suddenly dropped in upon them so unexpectedly. Just taking it as if it were an everyday happening.

"Jeremy," said his mother pleasantly, "take this coffeepot out to Hetty and ask her to make a little more coffee. These friends will have a cup of coffee with us surely, even if they have had their dinner."

Jeremy arose promptly, smilingly, took the coffeepot, and vanished kitchenward.

Then arose Jessica, scowling. "I think we should be going," she said sharply. "I want to find Rod."

"Oh," said Marcella Ashby, whose car they had come in, "but how will you find him? You don't know where he's gone."

"Oh," said Jessica scornfully, "we'll just scout around until we find him. I imagine he'll not be hard to find. Will he, Mr. Graeme?"

Father Graeme looked up with an inscrutable smile. "I wouldn't know, Jessie," he said. "Rodney has always been a bit unpredictable, and there's no telling now, since he's been off to war on his own."

Jessica turned angrily and marched toward the hall door looking back to say, as Jeremy came in with the coffeepot, "No coffee for me, thank you. I'm going out to find Rod."

But suddenly Marcella spoke up. "Speak for yourself, Jess. I'm staying for coffee. I haven't had any of the Graeme coffee in ages, and there's nobody else in Riverton can make coffee like old Hetty."

Jessica paused angrily. "Oh well, then give me your keys to the car. I haven't any time to waste. I can pick you up later when I'm ready to go back to your house." It was spoken quite haughtily, as if Marcella might be a sort of hired servant.

"No, you don't get my car keys," said Marcella, reaching out to accept the cup of coffee Mother Graeme made haste to pour for her. "I'm not running any risks like that. You always do make a car act all haywire. And besides, I know the hours you keep. I'm not going to wait around here and make everybody stay up entertaining me nor walk home without the car."

"Oh, very well," said Jessica disagreeably.

"Next time I'll *hire* a car of my own or get a gentleman to accompany me."

So Jessica stood pettishly in the doorway, staring down the hall, wondering what had become of the coats and caps she had seen on the hat rack when she came in. And there she stubbornly stood while the rest of the party lingered drinking their coffee in a leisurely manner, reluctant to leave the pleasant old home and the charming family circle that had once been so dear to them all.

CHAPTER 3

Out in the pantry, Rodney, boiling with rage, slammed his plate down on the pantry shelf and scowled. What right did those girls have to come here the first night he was at home and barge into the dining room? Yes, they were old friends, most of them, but they ought to have better sense. And *that* girl! What was her idea in coming? He and she had nothing in common anymore, and he didn't want to see her ever again. Rotten little double-crosser! And then presume to think she could smile and smooth it all over and be just as good friends as ever. Not on your life he wouldn't.

He didn't know what the family would think of his having run away, when perhaps Mom didn't know anything about it all and wouldn't understand. Though he could usually depend on his family to stand back of him whatever he did. And of course those others. He didn't know what they would think about him, and he didn't much care. Had any of them seen him go? He thought not, for the hall wasn't exactly in line with where he had been sitting. But he was most troubled about Mom. Of course she might have heard some gossip and might have got on to the fact that there was a break between him and Jessica. Still, he hadn't meant to have it come to her knowledge in such a way as this. But since it had come, it had, and he would have to take it and get it over with, no matter what. Of course, if Jessica had carried out her threat and got married, Mom would certainly have heard some gossip, but he was definitely not going to be friends with Jessica, not even acquaintances if he could help it. He thought of the hours of peril and danger through which he had lived, and of how he had all this time also battled with the thought of her disloyalty to him, disloyalty to the tender vows of everlasting love she had uttered before he went away, and how many times he had writhed in their memory as he went forth to fight the enemy! He had thought over all the precious times of their youthful association, her professed overwhelming love for him, which she had so utterly repudiated afterward, all those treasured looks and touches of her hands and lips! No, he had torn them from his consciousness, flung them away to some foreign breeze in a strange land, renounced them forever, erased them from his memory. And now that he had come back to a pleasant homeland, did she think that he could smooth them all over and be *friends*? Could she think that for a smile from her he would take her back into his friendship? No! A thousand times *no*! He was done with her forever. If she forced him ever to have to see her again or speak to her, he would certainly make her understand clearly that he had no faith in her whatever. Not even if she should repent and say she was sorry and want him back would he ever love her again. For, strange to say, the separation and the peril and her own disloyalty had utterly killed all the love he used to think he had for her. And suddenly, sitting there in the pantry, he saw that it never had been real love but only imagination. He had taken her lovely image, beautiful features, a flawless complexion, gorgeous hair that seemed so like the crowning of a young saint, and upon those outward forms he had built up a character for her that was not really hers.

And now, was it possible that he could ever be *glad* that all this happened and that her action would, in a way, set him free from what — if it had gone on as he had planned — would have been a galling life of torture for him? Disillusionment had come early and in a hard way at a hard time. But how much better that it had come now instead of after they were married and he was doomed to a life that would have been worse than imprisonment or death. Come back to her and be good friends? Well, she could guess again. He was done with her forever. He didn't ever want to see her again, and *wouldn't* if he could help it. But if he had to see her again under circumstances where he couldn't help it, he would make her understand once and for all that he was finished.

Just then Hetty tapped softly at the pantry door. "Mr. Roddy," she whispered softly, using his old pet name by which she used to call him when he was a child, "I'se got some more good chicken for you, an' some mashed taters real hot, an' some o' them yeller turnips you useta love so much, an' nobody won't know you'se here. They all think you'se gone away."

Cautiously, Rod shoved away the chair he had braced under the latch of the door and held out his empty plate, grinning sheepishly.

Silently the old servant filled his plate with

choice pieces and much hot gravy, added a cup of coffee and an extra understanding grin, and Rod attacked his second helping with much gusto. Somehow he would have to make his peace afterward with his mother, but after all, Mom always understood, and maybe she never had cared much for Jessica anyway. He tried to think back and began to see a glimmer of half disapproval in the past. Well, anyway, it was good to be at home, and his hunger was getting appeased. Good old Hetty, who had always understood, too! Now, whenever those stupid visitors departed, he could come out of hiding and be none the worse for wear.

As he finished off the last breast of chicken Hetty had brought him and started in on the applesauce and hot biscuits, he grinned across the kitchen at Hetty as she hovered just outside the dining room door with her ear trained near to a hearing crack and an interested eagerness on her kind old face.

He lifted his hand with a summoning gesture, and Hetty stole noiselessly across the smooth kitchen floor with a questioning look.

"Who's in there, Hetty?" he asked. "Anybody I know?"

"Dey sure is!" said Hetty in her low, soft

voice. "Dere's Miss Emma Galt an' Marcel' Ashby. I reckon dey come in her car. And there's dat rattle-pated Miss Jessie wif her fingers all dolled up in di-mon's. 'Rings on her fingers an' bells on her toes,' like de old hymn useta say. An' she's usin' her tongue for bells for she's done mos' all dat talkin' like she always done when she useta come ta see you. An' she come ta see you dis time, too, leastways dat what she says, an' now seems like she's goin' away ta hunt you up. It's my 'pinion you all bettah get ta bed 'fore she gits back, or you'll git caught fer sho."

Noiselessly shaking her sides with laughter, old Hetty rolled softly away and took up her stand at the crack of the door again, until finally she came back to report that they were all getting ready to go, and pretty soon he could go back and finish his dessert with the family.

But Rodney was taking no chances. He waited patiently for Hetty's signal. He even opened the pantry window a crack to wait until he heard the car driving away.

The cold air came in refreshingly against Rodney's hot forehead, and the quiet out-of-doors seemed to make him understand that he must be patient. He ought to know by this time that those girls never left when they got to the door but just stayed and talked and talked. Well, this draft was getting chilly. He reached out and drew the window shut, and straightway his mind jumped back to the present situation and what he was going to do next. Well, if those unwanted guests ever took themselves away definitely, he must go out at once to the dining room and make his peace with his family. It was going to be a bit embarrassing of course, but after all he had been through in the war, why should he mind a bit of embarrassment? It certainly would be great to get his family alone again.

Eventually the group in the dining room gathered themselves in the hall to leave, and Kathleen went to the door with them. The rest of the family remained seated in silence until Kathleen came back and sat down. They waited even then a second or two till the sound of the retreating car driving away came to their ears, and then Father looked up with a comical twinkle in his eyes.

"Now," he inquired mildly, "is it perfectly safe to ask what this is all about? And does anybody know what suddenly became of Rodney?"

They all burst into laughter, and the sweet homey sound of it reached to the kitchen, even as Mother Graeme reached out and tinkled the little silver bell for Hetty to take the plates and bring the dessert.

"Do you know what this is all about, Son?" asked the father, appealing to Jeremy innocently.

"Why certainly, Dad," answered Jeremy jovially. "It simply means that someone was about to come in that Rod didn't want to see, and he scrammed. That was perfectly natural, don't you think?"

"Well, yes — how do you say it? 'Could be'? But there was more than *one* somebody here. *Which* one?"

Jeremy grinned at his father. "Do you have to ask that? Wasn't it obvious?"

The father sat thoughtfully for an instant, and then he said slowly, nodding his head half amusedly, "Yes? I suppose you are referring to the glittering one. If that's so, I wouldn't judge Rod *would* want to see her. A girl that would turn down a single real good stone for a display like that! I'm not surprised! I somehow thought that Rod would find out what the girl was before it was too late! Well, we've got nothing to worry about in her loss. And now, where's Rod?"

"He's right here in my kitchen," said Hetty, appearing on time with her tray in her hands and beginning to gather up the plates. "Dat boy ain't ferget what ta do

57

when he's hungry, no mattah who barges inta de dinin' room."

"Oh, so he's up with the program, is he, and doesn't have to be waited for while he catches up on the first course?" said the smiling father.

"No sah, he ain't behind. Fact is, he's had somethin' like three good-sized helpin's of the fust co'se."

Mother Graeme's smile and Mother Graeme's eyes thanked faithful old Hetty.

"I knew he'd be all right in your hands, Hetty," she murmured quietly as Hetty took her plate away.

"Yes, ma'am, I knowed you'd be sure o' that," answered Hetty happily.

It was just then that Rodney came grinning out of his hiding with a quick apprehensive glance toward his mother's beloved eyes, a wink and a grin toward Jeremy, answered by a salute from the brother in true military style.

"Pretty slick, old man," said Jeremy in an undertone as Rodney sat down.

Rod grinned like the sun shining from behind a thunderhead. Then with a courteous smile toward the family he added in his most pleasant voice, "Sorry folks, I couldn't take time to say excuse me!"

And that understanding family only smiled

comfortably. That was the great thing about that family, whether they understood or not, they always took startling things with a smile, quite as if they expected them.

But Jeremy was sure by this time that his mother understood. Just how much she understood, or how it had come about that she knew anything about it, didn't matter. Mom was all right, and she would never bungle things by throwing a monkey wrench into the works.

So the happy silence settled comfortably down upon this reunited family, and they were just getting ready to savor the joy of it all, when there came another interruption.

But this time it was not the sound of the doorbell but the rattle of a latchkey in the lock, and they all looked up astonished. Evidently Kathleen had locked the door after the guests left, but who had a latchkey? Their eyes went around the circle, a question in each face, and Rodney sprang to his feet as if for another flight. This was an evening of surprises. Who was using that latchkey?

There were only three outside the immediate family who had a latchkey to that front door. One was Hetty, of course, for the rare occasions when she took her day off and went out to spend it with some of her old friends. The second was Mrs. Graeme's brother now overseas on confidential business for the government and not likely to return for some months. The third key was in the hands of the widow of a distant cousin of Mr. Graeme who had spent some weeks with the family, professedly on business connected with her late husband's will. She had recently departed for another city and had neglected to return her latchkey. Her departure had been a great relief for the family, and they had not anticipated her soon return, so when they heard someone walk into the door after Kathleen had locked it they could not understand it.

But Cousin Louella Chatterton was stealthy. She came quietly, for she loved surprise effects, and it also gave her the advantage of hearing words not intended for her ears. So she stood silently observing them, and not a thing missed her sharp eyes.

Suddenly Rodney subsided and dropped easily back to his chair again, slickly as if he had not intended otherwise.

"Yes, Rodney, it's no use for you to attempt to slide away," said Cousin Louella. "I was too quick for you. You can't get by with a thing like that with me. I know what I'm about."

Rodney grinned. "Could be," he said mischievously. "I haven't seen you in a good many years, but you certainly sound to be in good form."

"Take care, now, Rodney!" said the lady, stiffening up as if Rodney were a child of three. "You needn't try any of your impertinence on me. I know what you have just done, and I have come in for the distinct purpose of telling you just what I think of you. Of all the rude things for a young man still in the service to do, I think what you have just done was about the rudest. And you presuming to wear all those ribbons of honor on your breast and then running away when ladies, some of your oldest friends, came in to welcome you! I'm surprised. I really think this ought to be reported to your chief officer and you disciplined for it. What are we coming to when the men we have sacrificed for, and given bonds for, and sent munitions to, come home and perform like that? And the worst of it was that one of those girls was the girl who used to be your former fiancée, or maybe is yet for all I know. Though I have heard rumors that she is about to marry someone else. Did you know that, Margaret? Had you heard there was any break between your son and that lovely girl with the wonderful gold hair that he used to be so crazy about?"

Rodney went white, his black brows drawn in a terrible frown, but nobody but Jeremy saw him, and he looked quickly away toward his mother. How would she take this announcement?

But Margaret Graeme was a thoroughbred, and she lifted calm eyes to the unwelcome relative and answered in a low, quiet voice without a quaver in it, "Why certainly, Louella, that engagement was broken long ago, soon after Rodney went away to war."

"It *was*? But Margaret, you *must* be mistaken about that. You know I was here for a long time and no one ever said *a word* about it to *me*."

"Why should they, Louella? It wasn't a matter that any but the two concerned had any right to talk over. Won't you sit down and have a piece of Hetty's lemon pie and a cup of coffee with us? Jerry, bring that chair over here by me for her."

"Well, yes, I don't mind if I do have a cup of coffee," she said in a parenthesis, "but Margaret, *who* broke it, Rodney or the girl?"

Then before the gentle-voiced mother could reply, Rodney spoke up haughtily, "That's not a matter for outsiders to discuss, Cousin Louella," he said, and Jeremy, listening, caught the look that Rodney must have worn when he went out after the enemy and felt like cheering for him.

It was then that the wise, quiet father put in his voice. "Cousin Louella, did you ever succeed in getting in touch with that lawyer out west who had had to do with that property that you were so worried about when you were there last?"

The cousin turned, annoyed, and answered sharply, "No, I didn't, not yet. We'll talk of that later. You know, Donald, I hate to be interrupted when I'm talking about something else, and I'm not through with this matter yet. I want to know the truth about this before I speak of other things. Rodney, suppose you tell me the whole story, and then I shall know what to answer when I'm asked."

Then Rodney sat up straight and faced the curious cousin sternly in most decided tones. "I've nothing to say, Cousin Louella, and I should think if anybody asked you impudent questions like that, the only answer would be to say it was none of their business."

"Oh, but Rodney! That would not do at all. If the engagement is broken, why did that girl come here to see you tonight? Does she want to make it up?"

"I really don't know," said Rodney in a cold voice. "She couldn't have known that I was here, unless some lousy sneak who had seen me get off the train told her. Even Mom didn't know I was coming."

"Oh, *I* told her," said the cousin serenely. "I met her as I was coming away from the post office where I had stopped for a package. They sent me a notice that it had come for me postage due, and *I* told her."

"Oh, *you* told her," said Father Graeme. "And how did *you* know, Louella?" His face was grave and his voice very stern.

"Why, the taxicab driver told me. He saw the boys as they went across lots from the station, and he was eager to tell me. And later, coming out of the post office I met Jessica, and she said she wondered if Rodney had come home yet, and I said, yes, he had."

"Oh," said the master of the house. "Well, now, Louella, if you've got that off your chest I think you and I will go into the other room and talk over that matter of business."

Mr. Graeme took his last bit of pie and the last swallow of coffee and arose with finality. But the persistent guest sat still, her full coffee cup in her hand, and shook her head with firm determination. "No indeed, Donald. I intend to finish this lovely pie and coffee before I talk business, but I certainly have to get a little more data about this broken engagement."

The she took her first bite of her pie, and the children by common consent arose from the table and followed their father from the room, wearing amused and angry looks, if one can combine those two adjectives.

And there were only Margaret Graeme and Louella left at the table, while Louella took another bite of the pie and cast an eager inquiry toward her hostess. "Now, Margaret, they've gone, and you'll tell me all about it, won't you? I feel terribly hurt to have been left out of this important happening of the family. When did you first find it out, and weren't you *terribly* disappointed and grieved?"

"No, I'm sorry you feel that way, Louella," answered Rodney's mother. "I don't feel that it was so important a happening. It was just a youthful high school attachment, you know, and things of that sort are better ignored, don't you think? No, I wasn't disappointed. I knew if it wasn't the wisest, best arrangement all around it would work itself out, and we were all quite satisfied that it did. But I do feel that it is a thing of the past and not to be brought into our conversation again. And now, Louella, what plans have you made? Are you to be in this region long, or do you have to go right back? And where is your luggage? I ought to have asked you if you didn't want to go upstairs and freshen up. Did you come right here from the train?"

"No," said Cousin Louella coldly, "I went to the inn first and left my things and then took a taxi over here. You see, I had no idea of course if you would be home or gone perhaps to Florida."

Louella finished her coffee hurriedly and rose. "Thanks for the coffee. It just touched the spot. And now if you don't mind, I'll run on. I've a room at the inn, and there are people I want to see who may be waiting for me, so I better go at once. As for the business, it can wait, or I may find a lawyer who can help me. No, don't call a taxi, *I'll* phone the inn to send their cab for me, and don't disturb yourself for me. I'll be seeing you again before I leave, that is, if I get time. Good night!" And Louella walked angrily to the telephone in the hall and sent for her cab. It was not long before she was gone and the family was rejoicing in her departure. Then Mother Graeme gathered her children around her and beamed on them, and Father Graeme poked the fire into brilliancy again, drew down the shades as for a blackout, turned out the lights in the hall, locked and chained the front door, and in every way made sure that no more callers would seek welcome that night in the Graeme home.

"Maybe it's selfish," he said as he came smiling back to the library again, "but I declare if we can't have one evening with our children to ourselves after all these long months of anxiety and waiting, I'll do something desperate!"

And the children lifted proud, happy eyes.

"Thanks, Dad. That's what we wanted!" said Jeremy.

"Here, too!" said Rodney.

"And Mom, if anybody else tries to break into the family sanctum, let's make them have an examination on what topics of conversation they are going to select to talk about before we pass them in," said Kathie.

"That's all right by me," said the smiling lips of the mother in her best imitation of the present-day slang. And then they all burst into a joyful round of laughter, and the mother had to wipe some happy tears away before she could hold hands with her two boys, seated on the floor one on each side of her.

And then began the happy converse that

they had been anticipating all the way across the sea.

Chapter 4

If the Graemes had been able to look in on
their last caller in her comfortable apartment at the inn and seen the luxurious ap-
pointments, the elaborate little evening
repast that was being set out for her expected guest, they would no longer have
been under the impression that she was
hard up financially. She had spared nothing
to give the right touch of festivity to her setting, including candles on the little table,
set in readiness.

She hurriedly changed into a charming
outfit, gave just the right touch to her hair
with an artificial rose that dropped at-
tractively to one side. Then she took up her
position in a comfortable chair with one of
the latest bestsellers, the kind of book that
was the rage in the fashionable world. A
glance at the clock and she settled herself
for at least five minutes of pleasant relax-
ation.

But in less than five minutes her telephone rang. "Is that you, Louella?" asked the dashing voice that answered her acknowledgment of the ring. "This is Jessica! You are back? Okay. We're on the way. Be there in five minutes."

And it was less than five minutes when Jessica marched in followed by her three friends and sat down to sip tea and eat cakes and bits of sandwiches and confections. But Jessica did not waste much time. "Well, what did you find out?" she asked with eyes that pierced the eyes of her hostess. "Did you find out where he is? Was he there?"

"Why certainly."

"Where was he?"

"Sitting at the dinner table, enjoying his meal with the rest of the family," said Louella with satisfaction. She adored playing such an important part and being able to prove her prognostications. "Did *you* go out and look for him?"

"I certainly did," said the vexed Jessica. "I went simply everywhere that he used to go, to all his old haunts, or telephoned where it was too far, and none of the people had even heard he was coming home. But do you mean he was there *all the time*?"

"I shouldn't be at all surprised. He had that home atmosphere about him, in spite of his uniform. I doubt if he had been any farther away than the garage or even just the pantry. Of course I don't know, but I just have a hunch," said Louella.

"But didn't he act as if he knew that I had been there?"

"My dear, he didn't act at all. He just sat there and glowered. In fact when I entered silently with my key and watched them all an instant before they saw me, I think he had heard me and was on the point of leaving the room quite suddenly, and then when he saw it was only I, he sat down in his chair and began to eat again. But he certainly was in a poisonous mood. He was as rude as he could be to me, declined to answer any of my questions, and positively shut me up. Said if anybody asked me any questions about you and himself, I might tell them it was none of their business."

"Oh, *really*?" asked Jessica with a defeated look on her handsome face. "Well, I suppose I might as well give up and go back west and work things out some other way."

"Not at all, my dear," soothed Louella. "I should say from what I used to know of Rodney in his youth that the outlook is very hopeful."

"*Hopeful?*" said the younger woman, astonished. "Why, you have just given me to understand that he is very angry with me and doesn't want to see me. I don't see anything hopeful about that."

"Then you can't know Rodney very well. Don't you understand that the very fact that he is angry at you and doesn't want to see you shows that he is still deeply in love with you, and you will have no trouble at all in getting back his admiration when once you get really face-to-face with him and have a good talk? I'd be willing to wager that you with your beautiful face and your graceful ways can easily win him back to love you more than he ever did before."

It was then that Emma Galt plunged into the conversation. "But Jess is married, Mrs. Chatterton. You forget that. And Rod was brought up with very strong moral ideas about the sanctity of marriage."

"Fiddlesticks for any moral ideas nowadays," said Louella grandly, as if she were empowered to speak with authority on the new moral standards of the present day.

"But you don't realize at all, Mrs. Chatterton, how intensely those Graemes feel on moral questions. Those boys have very strong ideals and real conscientious scruples about things. They were brought up that way, and it has taken deep root in them," said Marcella.

Louella smiled. "Piffle for their conscientious scruples! You seem to have forgotten that those boys have been to war. You will probably find that out when you come in closer contact with them. I don't fancy many conscientious scruples can outlive a few months in the company of a lot of wild young soldiers or sailors off on their own. And remember *Rodney* has been away from his hampering, narrow-minded parents for at least three years!"

Then up spoke Marcella Ashby again. "I think that is perfectly terrible, Mrs. Chatterton, for you to call those dear people narrow-minded. All the years while we were growing up, they have been the dearest people to us all. Their house was always open to give us all good times, and they never showed a bit of narrow-mindedness. They were ready to laugh and joke with us all and spend money freely to give us enjoyment."

"Oh yes, children's stuff, picnics and little silly games and nice things to eat, of course, but did they ever have dances for us or cards or take us to the theater or even let us play kissing games?" spoke up Jessica. "No, indeedy. Everything was very discreet and prim, and of course we are no longer children and times have changed. You couldn't expect people like the dear old Graemes to be up to date. They are old people and can't understand the present-day needs of young folks. But I think myself that it is quite possible that the boys may have changed. They've been out in the world and seen what everybody is doing. I don't believe for a minute that Rodney would be shocked at all if I told him I'd made a big mistake in marrying a man so much older than myself, and that I was going to Reno to get a divorce as soon as I've finished up a few matters of business here in town. Isn't that what your idea was, Mrs. Chatterton?"

"Well, yes, I think myself you'll find those boys, at least Rodney, is much more worldly than his folks give him credit for, and I feel sure Jessica, if you give your mind to it, that you can win him back."

And then they went into a huddle to plan a campaign against Rodney Graeme.

And even as they plotted, with the devil whispering advice secretly to them and only Marcella Ashby of their number protesting at their plans, the Graeme family was kneeling in a quiet circle about the fire in the library. Father Graeme thanked God for the return of his children and petitioned that they might be guided aright in the days that were ahead, that none of them should be led astray from the way in which the Lord would have them go, and that His will might be done through them all, to the end that they might become changed into the image of His Son, Jesus Christ, and be fit messengers for the gospel of salvation.

And he prayed also for the rulers of their beloved land that they, too, might be led by the Holy Spirit to make right laws and decisions, and to govern the beloved country as God would have it governed, and that all spirit of unrighteousness might be put down, and any mistakes inadvertently made might be overruled, and the land saved from mere human guidance or acts ordered by warped judgment.

And he prayed for his boys, who had been so graciously spared from death or torture or imprisonment, that they might understand that God had thus spared them so that they might be the better fitted to do His will in the life that was still before them, that they might live to serve their Master even more fully than they had served their country.

As they rose from their knees and brushed away tender tears that had come to all eyes, the plotters were just starting out on their second attempt to start their campaign.

"Now," said Father Graeme as they stood

a moment thoughtfully before the fire, "I think these boys should get to their rest at once, and especially this wounded shoulder needs to have complete rest. Besides, if thoughtless friends are contemplating any further raids on the household tonight, it seems to me that would be a good way to head them off. Just let us get to bed as quietly and quickly and as much in the dark as possible, and when and if they come again, let them find it all dark. I suggest if they ring the bell and continue to ring, that you let them wait until I can get my bath-robe on and go down and meet them. I think perhaps I can show them that any further visits tonight will not be acceptable to anyone."

He grinned around on them pleasantly, and they all responded gratefully.

"All right, Dad!" said Rodney happily. "This has been our family's own night, and we don't want it spoiled in any way. You don't know what it's meant to me to hear you pray for us all again and to know that we are back together again, after so many terrible possibilities."

"Here, too," said Jeremy huskily. "You got me all broken up with that prayer, but perhaps tomorrow I'll be able to tell you all about it. What a memory I had of your prayers when I was out on a mission meeting bombs and knowing the next one might carry me up to God, and I wanted to go from my knees to meet Him, so my heart knelt as I flew along, and perhaps that was how I came through. I felt God there!"

The testimony of the two boys stirred them all deeply, and they lingered in spite of themselves, and then suddenly they heard a car coming.

"That wouldn't be our friends, would it?" asked the father anxiously. "Perhaps you better all scatter as swiftly as possible. Here, Mother, you take this tiny flashlight. I don't want you to fall. I guess the rest of you can manage in the dark, can't you? I'll wait a minute and make the fire safe for the night."

Swift embraces, tender kisses, and they scattered silently, and when Marcella's car arrived before the door the house was dark as a pocket and silent, too, everyone lying quietly under blankets and almost asleep already.

"Why the very idea!" said Jessica sharply as she clambered out of the car. "They *can't* have gone to bed this early, and they wouldn't have been likely to go out anywhere this first night."

"You seem to have forgotten that Rod was wounded and has been in the hospital for some time," said Marcella.

"Nonsense!" said Jessica. "Anyhow I'm going to ring the bell good and loud. I guess they won't sleep long after that."

CHAPTER 5

Three girls were grouped together in a pleasant corner of the Red Cross room sewing as if their very life depended upon their efforts. One was running the sewing machine, putting together tiny garments for the other two to take over and finish. The second girl was opening seams and ironing them flat and then finishing them off with delicate feather-stitching in pink and blue, binding edges of tiny white flannel jackets and wrappers with pink and blue satin ribbon. The third girl was buttonholing scallops with silk twists on tiny flannel petticoats. They were making several charming little layettes for a number of new babies who had arrived overnight without bringing their suitcases with them, and these three girls had promised to see that the needy babies were supplied before night. And because these three girls were used to having all things lovely in their own lives, it never occurred to them to sling the little garments together carelessly. They set their stitches as carefully and made their scallops as heavy and perfect as if they had been doing them for their own family. Others might sling such outfits together by expeditious rule, but they must make them also beautiful.

"Aren't they darling?" said Isabelle Graham. "I feel as if I were making doll clothes and I'd like to play with the dolls myself. They say that a couple of these poor little mothers have wept their hearts out mourning for their husbands and they haven't taken time to get anything ready for their babies. The husband of one baby's mother has been reported killed, and another one is taken prisoner. A terrible world for a little child to be born into."

"Yes," said an elderly woman coming over from a group across the room to take the measurement of the hems the girls were putting into the little petticoats, "I think it's a crime! Bringing little helpless babies into a world like this. And all because their silly mothers couldn't wait till their men came back from fighting. It's ridiculous!"

Alida Hopkins shut her pretty lips tightly on the three pins she was holding in her mouth, ready to set the measurement of the little petticoat she was working on, and cast a scornful look at the woman.

But the woman pursued the subject. "Don't you think so, Alida?"

"I don't think it's any of my business," said Alida with a little laugh. "It certainly isn't the poor babies' fault, and they're here and can't go around without clothes in this freezing weather, so I'm here to make clothes for them. Beryl, have you got any more of that lovely white silk twist? I've an inch more scallops to make on this petticoat, and I don't like to change color."

"Oh yes," said Beryl Sanderson, fishing in her handbag for the spool and handing it out. "I have a whole lot at home. I bought it before they stopped selling such things. I thought it might fit in somewhere."

"Well you certainly were forehanded," said the critical woman sharply. "But I wouldn't waste real silk twist on baby garments for little war foundlings. It won't be appreciated I tell you. Better save it for your own children someday."

Beryl smiled sweetly and covered the rising color in her cheeks with a dimple. "Well, you see, Mrs. Thaxter," she said amusedly, "I haven't reached that need yet, so I guess we'd better let this little war baby have the benefit."

Mrs. Thaxter cast a pitying, disapproving glace at the girl, pursed her lips and tossed her head. "Oh, well, I guess you're as improvident as the rest," she said sharply. "I thought you had better sense."

"Improvident?" laughed Beryl. "Why should I provide for children I don't possess and may never have and let some other little child suffer?"

"Hm!" said Mrs. Thaxter. "I guess they won't do much suffering for the lack of a few needlefuls of buttonhole twist." And she marched off to the other end of the room with her head in the air. Her departure was announced to the room by little rollicking ripples of laughter from the girls she had left.

"Shhh!" warned Beryl softly. "There's no need to make her angry, even if she is an old crab. Do you know she has worked all this week cutting out garments, worked hours over time?"

"Yes," said Bonny Stewart with a twinkle, "and ripped every last worker up the back while she did it. I was here. I heard her, and believe me it was the limit!"

"Well, I guess she's pretty upset that her Janie got married without letting her know before her soldier went away. And now he's got himself killed and Mrs. Thaxter has to keep telling Janie 'I told you so' all the time," said Isabelle with a trill of a laugh.

"Oh, but he didn't get himself killed, he's only a prisoner. Hadn't you heard?" said Celia Bradbury, drawing her chair over to join the group and getting out the little pink booties she was knitting. "The word came last night from the War Department. Janie called up and told my sister. She's in her Sunday school class. She's very hopeful that he will get home now."

"Being taken prisoner by the enemy is almost worse than death these days," commented Beryl sadly.

"Yes, I think this war is *horrid,*" said Bonny with tears in her voice. "I don't see why somebody doesn't put a stop to it."

"That's what they are trying to do, child," said Beryl with a smile.

"Yes, I suppose it is," answered Bonny. "But say, did you know both the Graeme brothers came home last night? I was on the train. I saw them, and they're perfectly stunning in their uniforms. Not all the servicemen get killed or taken prisoner. Say, Beryl, didn't you used to know those Graeme boys?"

"Why yes," said Beryl looking up interestedly. "I went to high school with Jeremy. He was a fine scholar and a swell person. I didn't know his brother so well; he was older than I and out of high school, in college, but I've always heard good things about him. They've got a wonderful mother and father. My mother has often told me nice little kindly things they've done for people who were in trouble."

"Oh, yes," said Alida with a half-contemptuous smile, "they're like that. Always doing good. Terribly kind but kind of drab and uninteresting."

"No," said Beryl suddenly, "they're not drab and uninteresting. My mother has told me a lot about them. She loves to talk with them. And certainly Jeremy was interesting. The whole school loved to hear him recite. He could make the dullest study sound interesting. He always found so much to tell that wasn't really in the books."

"You mean he made it up, out of his head?" asked Alida.

"Oh no," said Beryl, "he'd look it up in other books, the dictionary and encyclopedia, and sometimes several other books. He always told where he'd found it and who had written things about it. He studied up all his subjects that way."

"My word!" said Isabelle. "He must be a hound for hard labor."

"But he seemed to like it," said Beryl,

"and certainly the class liked it, and the teachers were crazy over him."

"I'll bet they were. It probably saved them a lot of work preparing for the class, and they likely lauded him to the skies. I suppose he's as conceited as they make 'em."

"No," said Beryl gravely, "he didn't seem to be. In fact, he always appeared to be quite humble, in spite of the fact that he was well thought of in athletics."

"Well, speaking of Jeremy Graeme," said Bonny Stewart, "he's going to speak at our church next Sunday night. I just remembered it was in the church paper that my sister brought home from Sunday school, and I happened to read it. It was headed 'Local hero will speak at the evening service'!"

"Hm!" said Mrs. Thaxter, appearing on the scene to make sure she had the right measurement for petticoat hems. "I guess you mean his older brother, Rodney Graeme. They wouldn't ask *that* little squirt to speak. He's only been in service a little over a year, and Rodney has been there three years. I understand Rodney did some notable things during his service."

"No," said Bonny firmly. "It was Jeremy. Definitely. I remember thinking what a strange name he had. And it said he had only been over there a few months over a year and was once reported missing but was saved in some unusual way. Say, girls, let's all go to our church next Sunday and give him a good send-off. Is he shy, Beryl? We won't embarrass him, will we, and spoil his speech? We might hide in the Sunday School room where he wouldn't see us."

Beryl smiled. "No, he isn't shy."

"Well, girls, will you go? You will, won't you, Beryl?"

"Why, I might," said Beryl. "I'll see what plans Mother has. Perhaps I'll go. But if I were you I wouldn't hide. He wouldn't mind your being there, I'm sure. He isn't that kind."

"But say, girls," said Isabelle thoughtfully, "wasn't that brother Rodney the one who was engaged to some girl with bleached hair? Jessica. That was her name. And she sported around with his ring on and made a great fuss over being engaged, and then after he went away she got married to some rich old man? Wasn't that Rodney Graeme's girl?"

"I'm sure I don't know," said Beryl Sanderson. "He always impressed me as a grave, quiet kind of man, the few times I ever saw him. The kind you would trust, you know."

"Oh, *that* kind. Well, a girl just looking for a good time wouldn't stick by a fellow like that, of course," said Alida. "Say, what's this Jeremy like? Awfully religious? Because if he is, I won't go Sunday. I don't care much for religion anyway. It always makes me cry and wish I'd never been born."

"I really don't know, Alida," said Beryl almost haughtily. "I only knew him in high school, but he seemed very cheerful then."

"Why, he'll likely just talk about the war I suppose," said Isabelle. "They all do. I adore to hear the fellows tell about their experiences, how many enemies they killed and all that and how they just got off by the skin of their teeth."

"Isabelle! You bloodthirsty thing! How dreadful!" exclaimed Bonny.

"Well, isn't that the way we're supposed to feel during this war? We're out to get the enemy as quick as we can and finish them up so they can't start anything again, not in our lifetime, anyway. Isn't that the idea?" said Isabelle.

"Well, anyway, girls you'll all go, won't you?" said Bonny Stewart. "I'll get some credit up in heaven for bringing so many to church, won't I? Come and meet at my house. It's near the church, and I know my way around, you know. I'm supposed to be a member of that church. Meet at my house, and we'll have a cup of tea and some little frosted cakes before we go over to the church. Beryl, why don't you invite Jeremy Graeme to come over along with you, and we can all get acquainted with him?"

"No," said Beryl with dignity. "He wouldn't want to go to a reception before he spoke, and anyway I wouldn't do that sort of thing. I'll be at church, I think, but I'm not sure I'll be over at your place, Bonny, beforehand. Mother has company, and I may be needed at home until time for church to begin. I'll look you all up if I can."

Then the noon whistle sounded and there was a general movement to put away work and go out to lunch. Beryl slipped away out of notice to think over what she had been hearing.

So, Jeremy had been doing notable things in the war and was going to speak about them. It would be interesting, of course, and she was sure she would like to hear him. Yet she recognized in herself a certain shrinking from seeing him again lest the grown-up Jeremy might disappoint her. For he had been one of her childhood's admirations, and she didn't want to think that he had failed to turn out the kind of man his boyhood had promised. She did not like to think her little-girl ideas of people had been wrong. Somehow they made a happy young background for the childish self she had been.

When Beryl reached home she went to her own room and sat down to think. Her mind was going back to her days at school and to the times when she was interested in this one and that. It was very plain to her as she thought back, remembering the boy they had but just a few minutes before been talking about. Presently she got up and went to her bookcase where there were several big books full of snapshots and photographs of her school days. She had scarcely looked them over since she graduated from high school. Yet she knew exactly where to find the ones she wanted. They were grouped together in the middle of the book, flanked on either side by other members of her class. And there was one a little larger than the rest, not really a photograph, just a page cut from the class yearbook. For some time she studied the pictures, and when she put the book away she decided that definitely she wanted to go and hear Jeremy talk and see if he had carried out the promise of his childhood. Then she put away the thought of it all and went to her appointment at the hospital where she was taking a friend's place nursing for the afternoon.

There was another woman interested in the one who was to speak in the Harper Memorial Church next Sunday night, and that was Louella Chatterton.

Louella had gone into the city to visit with an old friend, also to be near the lawyer whom she wanted to consult about some business matters, and as she was passing along the street a name on the advertising board in front of a church caught her eye. GRAEME. Why, could this be the Riverton Graemes? Louella about-faced and drew up in front of the church, studying the notice.

Lieutenant Commander Jeremy R. Graeme will speak in this church Sunday evening at 8:00 P.M. Come and hear the thrilling experience of this young serviceman. Come and bring your friends.

Louella read the notice over several times, and when she started on her way she headed for a drugstore where there would be a telephone. Seated in the booth she called up her number and asked for Mrs. De Groot, and when a voice responded she said gushingly, "Is that you Jessica? I've got the most exciting news to tell you. Can't you take dinner with me tonight? We can talk so

90

much better in my room at the hotel, with no interruptions, and meantime I'll be looking up details and be able to tell you more than I can give you now over the telephone."

"Oh! Louella, what *do* you mean? What is it all about? Has it anything to do with Rodney Graeme?"

"Well, yes, in a way. I've got to find out a little bit more about it, but I've got a scheme and it ought surely to give you an opportunity to meet him and have a good talk, which ought to clear the atmosphere, don't you think?"

"Well, yes, it might. But what *is* all this? How did you hear about it, and what is it really?"

"Why, it's just that he seems to be advertised to address an audience in the Harper Memorial Church, here in the city. I have seen the notice outside the church so that's how I know about it. He's a lieutenant commander, isn't he? I thought so. They've got the names mixed somewhat, but I know it must be Rodney. It says Jeremy *R.*, but that means nothing. Notices often get the names or the initials wrong, and anyway, even if it should be Jeremy, Rodney will probably be with him on the platform, and perhaps we can work it so he will come and sit with us. I'm sure this is a break for us. I knew I'd find a way for you to see him in spite of his stubbornness. I'll find a way yet."

"Where are you?" asked the fretful voice of the girl.

"Why, I'm down in the city at a drugstore phoning. No, I'm *not* in the village of Riverton. I'm down in the *city.* I've been staying all night with a friend I met out west, and I'm coming home tonight. Will you be at my hotel by six thirty? All right, I'll be seeing you then, and we'll fix something up."

CHAPTER 6

Kathie came in from a trip to the grocery, her arms full of bags, bundles, and baskets.

"Have the boys come down for breakfast yet, Mother?" she asked eagerly. "Because I've brought some simply wonderful fruit, and I know they will enjoy it."

"No, they are not down yet. I thought they ought to sleep a little while, as long as they seem to want to, now that they are at home and there is no one around to say 'Thou shalt, and thou shalt not.' "

"That's nice, Mother. Isn't it wonderful to have them both home again and have a chance to spoil them just a little? Only, do you know, they somehow don't spoil. I think that's a tribute to the way you brought them up. I do hope, perhaps, someday, somebody will think *I'm* a credit to your bringing up, too."

"You dear child! Of course they will. Kathie, you have always been a wonderful daughter," and the mother stepped over and stopped to lay a kiss on the sweet white forehead as Kathie was bending over the table to arrange a great dish of fruit.

"Look, Mother, *pink* grapefruit, Florida oranges, lovely red apples, and see these luscious yellow bananas. They have sunshine in their skins."

"Yes, aren't they beautiful? I'm so glad you found them. But there, the boys are coming down. They must have been waiting for you to get back. Tell Hetty, won't you? Tell her she better get the griddle hot. We're having buckwheats, you know."

"Yes, I'll tell her," said Kathie happily, and she skipped out to the kitchen. Her mother could hear her eager young voice calling to Hetty, "All ready, Hetty, put the griddle on!"

Then the brothers barged into the dining room, breathing joyous good mornings, and in the same breath Jeremy cried, "Oh, *boy*! What do I smell? Buckwheat cakes! As I live. Rod, what do you know about that? We're really home at last and going to have genuine buckwheat cakes. And maple syrup from the row of maples on the meadow lots! Can you beat it?"

"No, I can't beat it, brother. I can't even in my thoughts come up to it. Sometimes on far seas I have lain in sacks and dreamed of buckwheat cakes. I've seen the butter melting on their hot brown surfaces, I've closed my eyes and tried to think how maple syrup would fall from the old silver cruet and how it would taste as I put the first luscious mouthful in my mouth. I almost thought there was syrup on my lips, and I must be careful not to drop any on my uniform and get myself all sticky."

"Oh, Jerry, what a boy you are," said his smiling mother. "Sometimes I was terribly afraid you would be so grown up when you came home that I wouldn't feel you were my little boy who left me and sailed away to foreign lands, but you're just the same, Jerry. There! Sit down and begin. Do you want fruit first and cereal?"

"Not on yer life, Mom. I want a buckwheat cake the first off the bat, and no kiddin'."

And so amid laughter and joking, the morning began, with Rodney not far behind in his appreciation of the buckwheat cakes.

Though it was three days since that first night that the brothers had arrived, yet it seemed to them all as if they had just come. The long months and years of their separation were still sharply in their minds, and they had to savor every moment of their presence together again. Oh how they had feared and dreaded that home might be sorrowful, might be filled with disappointment, worry for fear of disablement or incurable illness, or a burden of sorrow and inability for their dear ones. That very morning as the loving mother had knelt to pray for the opening of the day, she had thanked the Lord fervently that He had brought her dear ones home safely, not lame nor blind nor stricken with some fatal illness. And so she had gone down to meet the day with her heart filled with wonder and her face shining with joy and the glory of the Lord. And those boys saw the glory and rejoiced in it.

The brothers were just beginning to feel really at home again, ready to kid each other and feel thoroughly as if they had not been away at all. Their mother was beginning to hold her breath every time the telephone rang lest it might be some new orders from Washington and the boys might have to go away again. Although they had told her that they understood their next assignment would likely be in the United States, but her mother heart kept turning wistfully to her Lord, just to help her trust. For all her petitions had to go through the permission of her Lord.

So it was a very happy family at that

breakfast table the third morning of their stay at home, and they were beginning to plan what they would do and where they would go and who of the old friends they must be sure to see first. Though at any mention of leaving home even for a few hours they all groaned.

"Mom, if I were going to live a thousand years, I'd like to make sure I could come home here every night to sleep. Just you try to sleep once in a sack overnight or on a ship that is being bombed and you'd know what I mean. I have great sympathy for the man who wrote 'Home! Sweet Home!', 'Be it ever so humble, there's no place like home.' And this is anything but a humble home."

"Dear boy!" said Mrs. Graeme tenderly with sudden tears of joy in her eyes.

"Please make that plural, Mom," urged Rodney. "I could echo every word of that sentiment."

"Dear *boys*!" said the mother, suddenly smiling brightly through more tears.

And it was just then that Kathleen sprang from her chair and stepped over to the window, then backed away. "Good night, Mother, don't cry! Look who's coming in the gate. Mop up your eyes and pretend you're laughing."

"What! Who?" said Rodney, springing to his feet and stretching his tall height to look out the window from the vantage of his place at the table.

"It isn't that girl again, is it?" he blurted.

"No, no, Rod," laughed his sister, "not quite so bad as that. It's only Cousin Louella!"

"Good night, it is indeed," said Jeremy. "And I was going to eat another plateful of pancakes, but this has to do me till tomorrow morning. I can't stand another session with Cousin Lou." He grabbed the last two cakes on the plate, emptied a couple spoonfuls of sugar on one, folded them neatly together, and scuttled up the back stairs, calling back in a sepulchral whisper, "Mom, if anybody asks for me, tell 'em I didn't say where I was going, just errands."

Rodney stopped long enough to get the last swallow of coffee before he departed, and he could just hear Cousin Louella's key in the front latch as he closed the back door, pulling on an old sweater and making his way to the garage where Kathie kept the old car.

"It's all right, Rod," said his sister, hurrying after him. "I put the chain on the front door last night, and the latchkey won't do any good. She'll have to ring and wait till somebody comes to open the door."

Rodney grinned. "Thanks awfully, Kath. You're a good angel," he said. "You might hang a handkerchief out your window when she leaves. I won't come back till she's gone." With another grin and a wave of his hand he vanished into the garage.

Kathleen hurried back into the house to save her mother from going to the door. "You aren't going to ask her to stay to lunch, are you, Mother? Because the boys won't come back if you do. I promised to hang out a flag for Rod when she's gone."

"No," the mother said, smiling "not today. I have to go down to the village on an errand. I can perhaps ask her to go along."

"But Rod's got the car."

"Oh, well, that's all right. I'll go later. You leave her to me. If I give her some work to do she won't stay long. I'll let her put those hems in my new aprons. You bring them down to me and I'll sit right here and sew them on. You can be dusting the hall and library and be near enough to hear any signals I send out. She will maybe like to take a walk with you."

"Not she," Kathleen said with a grin. "She always says she has sprained her foot when I ask her to take a walk. But you might try her going down behind the barn to see the little new colt. I have to take some feed down to the colt's mother."

Mother Graeme grinned mischievously, showing how much she resembled her two boys. "Okay," she said calmly, "I'll try her, but you just watch her face when I do."

So Kathleen walked to the front door, which was now open about four inches and being banged impatiently, indignantly back and forth against the chain.

Kathleen with firm hand closed the door, released the chain, and then opened it, so quickly that the indignant semi-relative was flung almost bodily into the hall.

"Why, the very idea!" said Cousin Louella indignantly. "Whoever put that thing on, I should like to know?"

"Oh, didn't you know we use the chain now?" asked Kathleen coolly. "I guess nobody thought to take it off this morning. Won't you come in, Cousin Louella? Mother's in the dining room sewing. Just go right in there. I think Hetty is going to sweep in the living room so it will be pleasanter sitting in the dining room."

"Oh, *really*?" said the cousin with a lofty insulted air. "Well, of course if your mother is there. But it was really the boys I wanted to see. More especially Rodney. Where is he?"

"Why, I'm not sure. He went out to the garage, and I think I saw the car go out. You know you can't keep track of the boys once they get in their hometown, after their long separation."

"Rodney wouldn't by any chance have gone to see his old friend Jessica, would he?" asked the cousin pryingly, with an insinuating smile, as if she had a secret that Kathleen probably understood.

"Why no," said Kathleen calmly. "I don't think he went there. I don't think he has much to do with her anymore. You knew she is married, didn't you?"

"Oh, yes, I knew she was married, poor dear. But I feel so sorry for her and for Rodney, too. Such a pity, a nice suitable match like that broken up. What a foolish boy he was to let that happen. Of course what he ought to have done was to have married her before he went away. Then this couldn't have happened. But I suppose your mother blocked that. She always was opposed to having her children grow up."

"I beg your pardon, Cousin Louella, I don't quite understand you. Mother had nothing whatever to do with the breaking of that engagement. And I don't think we ought to talk about it, do you? Rodney would be furious, and I shouldn't think Jessica would care for such comments. At least *I* wouldn't. She's a married woman, you know."

"Yes, poor dear, I'm aware of that. I feel so very sorry for her. But there are ways of getting out of a situation like that of course."

"Is that the way you look at it, Cousin Louella? I don't think so. But here comes Mother. See what pretty aprons she is making. Here, sit down in this little rocker in the bay window. I think the view of the yard all snow is pretty out there, don't you? And Hetty is making hot doughnuts. Shall I get you one, or do you think it is too soon after breakfast?"

"Yes, I certainly would like some doughnuts. But I'd want a cup of coffee with them. Wasn't there some left from breakfast that Hetty could heat up for me?"

"I'll see," said Kathleen, and she vanished grimly into the kitchen. "The *idea*!" she muttered to Hetty. "Doughnuts and coffee, when she probably ate a huge breakfast at the hotel. Well, perhaps she won't attempt to stay to lunch if I feed her now."

So Kathleen got ready three hot doughnuts and a cup of coffee and brought them on a tray to the guest-cousin and then vanished to her dusting lest more would be demanded.

Meantime Hetty was filling two large platters with doughnuts already fried and hiding them on the top shelf of the pantry, where no snooping relative could find them.

So the guest settled back in her rocker with her coffee and doughnuts to enjoy herself and see how much information she could pry out of Mother Graeme.

"Well, so it seems Rodney is becoming a public speaker," she said as she took a large, sugary bite of doughnut and began to rock slowly, balancing her coffee cup neatly on the arm of her chair, with a careful hand guarding it.

Mother Graeme smiled.

"Oh no, not Rodney," she said pleasantly. "He was pretty badly wounded you know, and until his shoulder gets better he has been distinctly ordered not to do anything for a while. They wanted him to broadcast from Washington, but the doctors said no, not now, so they are putting that off till spring, or even later if his condition is not good yet."

"But what possible harm could a wounded shoulder get from his just getting up and telling of his experiences? I think that's ridiculous!"

"Well, the navy doesn't think so," said Mother Graeme, smiling quietly.

"Well, I guess you'll find that a spirited fellow like Rodney won't be tied down that way by any navy, now that he's home. Besides, I guess you don't know he's going to speak next Sunday night at the Harper Memorial Church in the city. I saw the announcement myself today when I was in town. In front of the church. I certainly thought it was strange that you hadn't told me, but that seems to be the way I am treated by my family in everything. However, he's going to speak, even if you don't know it. These boys think now they have been off to fight that they have a right to run their own lives without consulting their parents. I presume that was it. He wouldn't want to decline an honor like that, in that big important church. There'll be a big audience there, and you ought to be ashamed to try and stop it."

"No, Louella, you are mistaken," said Margaret Graeme with an upward quiet look. "It is *Jeremy* who is to speak at Harper Memorial."

"Jeremy!" almost screamed the cousin. "You don't mean that they would ask the *younger* brother to speak and leave out the older, more experienced man who has been in the service so much longer? Why, Jeremy

is nothing but a kid, just a child. He couldn't speak."

The mother went quietly, patiently on with her sewing and let her guest rage on explaining why this could not be, but when Louella stopped talking to begin on her second doughnut she spoke quietly. "Why, you see, Louella, Jeremy has already done quite a little speaking on the radio and other places, and of course Rodney has also, for they have been through some great battles. But this Harper Memorial engagement came through a buddy of Jeremy's who is a member of that church, and he wrote home to his friends about Jeremy, so he had the engagement to speak there before he sailed for home."

"You don't *mean* it!" said the astonished cousin. "Well, that'll be quite a feather in Jerry's cap, won't it? And aren't you afraid it will create jealousy between the brothers, having Jerry speak instead of Rodney?"

"No, Louella. I don't see why it should. They don't regard it in that light at all. It's merely another duty in the winning of the war. Besides, the boys each have had experiences that may help someone. And now, Louella, I wonder if you wouldn't like to go down behind the barn with Kathie and see the new colt. It is very cunning and attractive, and Kathie is taking a pan of mash down for the mother. There is a nice path all the way down, and you won't get your feet wet."

Cousin Louella took her last swallow of coffee, and arose. "No thanks, I don't care for animals, and colts don't appeal to me. But I think I'll be going now. There are several people I want to see, and I have an appointment with a lawyer in the city this afternoon. Well, I'll be seeing you, as the young folks say. I suppose, Margaret, even if it's only Jerry that's going to speak, you'll all be going in to hear him, of course."

"Why, we haven't talked that over yet, Louella. There's a possibility it may be on the radio, and then everybody will be able to hear it."

"Really? Well, Jerry must be quite set up having such a fuss made over him. I suppose of course Rodney will at least go in with him, won't he?"

"I really wouldn't know what Rodney's plans are. But you needn't worry about Jerry. He doesn't get set up with things like that. He just wants to do the right thing."

"Oh, yes, Margaret, you always did think your children were models of every kind. Well, I'm sure I hope you won't be disappointed in them."

"No? Well, thank you, Louella. But I feel rather happy that both my children are saved. That's the only thing to be proud of."

"Yes, of course," said Louella. "Most parents are proud when their children get honor to themselves doing hard things and being courageous and all that and then get safely home without any very bad scratches. Yes, they are *saved* from this horrible war. I don't suppose they'll have to go back again, will they? So you really count them saved. Saved and *all* through with it."

Mother Graeme looked at Louella perplexed. "Oh Louella, you *know* I mean saved from something far worse than any war. I mean saved from sin — from eternal punishment. Saved for heaven."

"Oh! *That!*" said the cousin sanctimoniously. "Well, I guess you never can tell about that until you get there. Or course some do say that if you died in the war, you did what the Lord did. You died for others, and therefore you are saved. But your boys didn't *die,* so they wouldn't be saved on that score. I wouldn't count on that too much if I were you though. You might find out when you get over there that you were mistaken. It sounds rather far-fetched to me, and boastful."

"No, Louella, I won't find out. I'm not

mistaken and it's not boastful, because it's nothing the boys have done themselves, only their trusting in what Christ has done on the cross. The Lord has promised, and my boys have accepted the promise and believe in Him as their Savior. The Bible says, 'He that believeth on the Son *hath* everlasting life,' so I *know* my boys are saved. But Louella, you go and hear Jeremy and you will understand."

"Oh, *really*! Well, I *may* go, I'm not sure. If I can get my friend to go with me, I might go. It will be odd to hear him speaking in a big church. Little Jerry! Do you think he'll be embarrassed? Talking about himself and what he's done?"

Jerry's mother smiled. "No, Louella, Jeremy won't be talking about himself and his achievements. He'll be talking about his Lord and what He has done for Jerry."

"Oh!" said the cousin uncomprehendingly. "Well, I'm not sure I know what you mean, but maybe I'll go and see if I can understand. Well, good-bye." And Louella Chatterton went out of the house and wondered at herself over how very little she had been able to find out about Rodney.

Then came Kathleen with her duster in her hands, smiling at her mother.

"That was great, Mommie dear," she said,

coming over and kissing her mother on the top of her head. "You certainly did give her something to think about, although I don't believe that poor soul understood at all what you meant."

"Yes, dear, I'm afraid you're right," the mother said, sighing. "I was just thinking of the Bible verse that describes her. 'If our gospel be hid, it is hid to them that are lost.' "

"Oh, Mother!" said Kathleen solemnly. "Do you really think she is lost?"

"I'm not her judge," said the mother sweetly, "but she certainly is not saved yet and doesn't know what it means. But it isn't too late yet for her to believe."

"But I don't think she even wants to believe, Mother."

"A great many don't," the mother said with a sigh. "I guess we ought to pray more for her and criticize less."

"Well it isn't a bit easy to pray for anybody that has such a vitriolic tongue as our cousin," Kathleen said, laughing. "But say, I must run upstairs and put out my signal for Rod to come back."

Then there came a voice from the top of the front stairs — Jeremy calling to know the signs of the times. "Mom, has that old harridan gone yet?"

The mother smiled. "Why, Jerry, I thought you went with Rod. Yes, the coast is clear, son, but what kind of a cataclysm would you have precipitated if she hadn't gone yet and you had called those words down in time for her to hear? You know that would not have been an easy thing to live down."

"Oh," said the grinning young man, "but perhaps I wouldn't want to live it down."

"Oh, but you must, dear. For I was just about to ask you to help us to pray for that unpleasant cousin. You can't exactly feel that way toward her if you are going to pray for her."

"Hm!" said Jeremy thoughtfully. "I hadn't exactly thought of her as a candidate for prayer."

"Well, perhaps that's the reason she is that way. Nobody has been praying for her."

"Why this sudden anxiety, Mom?" asked Jeremy. "I never heard you mention her as a subject for prayer. What started you on this line?"

"Well, I don't just know, dear. We got to talking. She asked about your engagement to speak. She had seen a notice of it in front of the church. Only she thought it was Rodney, not you, who is going to speak. But I think she is coming to hear you. Perhaps you'll be given a message that will reach her heart."

"Say, Mom, you know how to go to the heart of things, don't you? But I'm afraid it would take more faith than I've got to get up a message to reach that woman."

"Oh, you wouldn't have to get one up, Jerry. If you did it would be powerless. That's the trouble with so much of the preaching, these days. Remember the Holy Spirit will do that for you. Just be sure you have your heart open to be led, and don't clutter up your mind with all your childhood's dislikes and prejudices. Just ask the Lord to show you what He wants for you. And then don't worry about it. You are well taught in the Bible, and the Holy Spirit can speak through you if you are fully yielded to Him. That's all. Now, what are you going to do, Jerry? Any plans?"

"Not 'specially, not today. I'm expecting a phone call tomorrow night, but till then I'm free to do anything I please, that is anything *you* please, Mom!"

Mom Graeme's eyes grew misty. "Dear boy!" she said. "To think I have you home again. To think I have you *both* home! If I only could be sure it was to stay."

"Well, Mom, it might be you know. That is it might not be far away. There's something in the wind, but we'll let you know as soon as we find out."

A sweet, tender look came into her eyes, a kind of a light as if some great hope were shining in her heart.

They were still for a minute, and then the mother spoke again. "Jerry," she said, "tell me something. Rodney isn't quite happy, is he?"

"Well, I'm not sure. No, I don't know as he is, not exactly the way he used to be."

"Do you think it's that girl? That Jessie?"

"I'm not sure, Mom," said Jerry, looking troubled. "I don't want to force his hand."

"Of course not," said the mother. "But I wanted to find out what your reaction is to the whole thing. Do you think Rod is mourning for that girl?"

"No, Mom, I don't think so. I was afraid that might be the matter with him when we first talked it over, but after that gal appeared on the scene I saw he wasn't grieving after her. And didn't you take notice how happy he was when he came back from the pantry and settled down to eat his pie? No, Mom, I don't think he's grieving. I don't think he has been anything but *mad* for a long time. I think he has sorted her out with the enemy, and I don't believe he's in any further danger from her. Except, of course, she can annoy him. But he's had experience enough fighting the enemy, not to be caught napping now. After all, Mom, he's your son, and he has eyes to see a whole lot."

"Yes," said Mom thoughtfully, "I could always trust Rod. Of course —" She hesitated thoughtfully an instant. "Of course, I was troubled when he first began to go with Jessie. She didn't seem up to him, but I realized he was a young boy, and then a good deal of their intimacy probably came from the girl. Some girls seem to be born that way, or else, well, she didn't have much upbringing, I'm afraid."

"That's it, Mom. Now you've reached the point. I don't think you ever knew what her mother was, or you would have done something about it sooner. However, I guess there's no harm done. And a fellow has to grow up sometime and learn how to judge the world. Besides, you'll have to remember this, Mom. Rod has been to war. He wouldn't pick out the same girl now that he would before he went through the service. Of course if she'd have been half decent and hadn't gone back on him herself, he'd have been true to her, because he wouldn't think it was right to do otherwise. And that's partly it now, he couldn't believe at first that

Jessica had done this to him. He knew he was true to her. And when he finally reached the stage where he accepted the truth, it made him angry. It took the heart out of him so much that he flung himself into this war business, not caring what became of him. It was partly what made him such a wonderful fighter. Mom, I guess God has everything worked out for all His children. He sees they need some hard going, and when He can trust them to take it right He gives it to them. Isn't that right, Mom?"

Mother Graeme looked at her boy, who such a little while ago was just her little boy, her mere baby, as she heard him utter these words of wisdom, and wondered. Then her face blazed with that rare smile that she sometimes wore that suggested nothing else but glory in her face. And then after a moment of deep thought, as if she were receiving a revelation, she said, "Oh, my dear son, God has been wonderfully teaching you, too. You are speaking thoughts I never knew you could understand. My boy. My *two* boys! How proud I am of them, proudest of all that you have been taught of God. Thank you for telling me that!"

And then Hetty came in with her brooms and sweeper and cleaning cloths and announced that she was going to clean the living room if that was agreeable to the family, and the conference between mother and son broke up.

CHAPTER 7

It was the next afternoon that Jeremy met his old admiration, Beryl Sanderson.

He had wondered about her and almost decided that before he had to go away from that region he would perhaps call on her, just a brief call of greeting as an old schoolmate. But he wasn't at all sure that he would. Before he ever decided to do anything like that he would have to find out all about her. Maybe she was married or engaged. Maybe she had moved away. Certainly he did not wish to bring either himself or her into the limelight by making too pointed inquiries about her. No, he would go slowly. He had nothing to lose by going slow, and perhaps nothing to gain. Nevertheless he kept thinking he would like to meet her again and see if she was as interesting as he had thought several years ago. But he wasn't bothering himself about it yet. It would all come in good time, if it came, and perhaps would only upset him and make him discontented if he should discover that she was definitely not for him. One night as he knelt beside his bed before retiring, the thought of this girl had come to him, and he had definitely laid the matter before his Lord.

"Lord," he prayed, "this is a matter I can't very well do anything about. I don't want to make any mistakes. So I'm laying this in Your hands. If You want us to meet, please make it plain. If not, please help me to put her out of my thoughts. I leave it with You."

It was a habit he was forming, to leave important matters, or even trifling ones, to his Lord. And each time he did it, somehow the matter seemed to be settled for him without his worrying about it.

That was two days ago that he had made that prayer, and he had scarcely thought of her since.

Today Rodney had asked Jeremy to drive with him to see the family of a buddy of his who had died in combat overseas. He was a stranger to them of course, but he had been close to their son, and he could tell more than anybody he knew, of the last days, even the last few minutes of his friend's life, and he felt he ought to go as soon as possible. So he had asked Jeremy to drive him, and after the call was made they would go to the hospital where Kathie was working today and bring her home.

So Jeremy had agreed, not realizing that Rodney's call would lead him into the region where the Sandersons lived. When he did draw up at the curb and let Rodney out, he saw that the Sanderson house was not more than a block and a half ahead. Still it did not matter. It was not in the least likely that he would see Beryl, and if he did, why worry? That was something entirely in the Lord's hands now.

So he sat quietly behind the wheel and waited, gazing idly about the pleasant surroundings, thinking how glad he was that the girl of his fancy lived in such a lovely spot. She was the kind of girl that it seemed to him fitting that all should be quite perfect around her.

It occurred to him to make the contrast between this sort of life and the places where he and Rodney had been in their war service. It was good that fine, sweet girls and women had places like this street and these attractive houses where they could be cared for and safe. So good that these nice people were not subject to some of the terrible things that had happened to beautiful homes abroad. There had been no bombing in his own blessed country, thank the Lord. Not yet, anyway.

It was just at that point he looked up and saw her coming straight toward him, just walking briskly down the sidewalk, not at first noticing him at all. But then suddenly she stopped and looked straight at him, a little rosy glow in her cheeks, a sparkle of welcome in her lovely eyes.

"Jeremy! Jeremy Graeme! It is really you, isn't it? I am so very glad to see you."

She put out both her hands with a real welcoming gesture, and Jeremy sprang out of the car and took both her hands in his, and there they stood looking down and up at each other and reading great joy and deep interest in each other's eyes.

Somehow they didn't have many words at first to express their joy in finding one another, but something in the touch of their hands spoke, something in the glance of their eyes, and presently the words came.

"What are you doing over here, Jeremy?" she asked, her cheeks brightly rosy now. "I don't think I ever saw you over here before."

"No," faltered Jeremy. "I often wanted to come. I always liked it over this way. But I never seemed to have time, and then I went across."

"Yes, I know," said the girl. "I've been

reading about some of the things you did over there, some of the decorations you've had. But what are you doing here today? Don't tell me you have friends over this way that I don't know about."

"No, I have no friends over here, unless I can count you one," said Jeremy, smiling.

"You may," said Beryl. "Go on."

"Well, you see my brother wanted to call and see the mother of one of his friends who died over there. He asked me to drive him over. He has a wounded shoulder. He's in there now." He nodded toward the big brick mansion before which they were standing.

"Oh," said Beryl, "you mean Carl Browning? How wonderful! Poor dear Mrs. Browning. She knows so little about Carl's death. It will be great for her to talk with a young man who knew him well. I've heard about your brother. He was quite distinguished, too. But I understood he was badly wounded."

"Yes, he was, but he's recovering rapidly, especially since we got home, and he's had Mother to take care of him."

"Yes. I imagine that would make a difference for all wounded men. And is he in there? I'd like so much to meet him. I wonder if you couldn't both come into my house for a few minutes after he comes out."

"Why, we'd love to, I know, but we're supposed to go to the hospital after my sister Kathie who is doing some nursing today, and it's almost time. Perhaps another time, if we may."

"Oh, of course! And I shall want to meet your sister, too. It isn't far to the hospital from here. Couldn't you bring her down here and all come in for a little while, just till we get to know one another?"

"Well, we might work something out. Why couldn't you get into the car with us and drive over after Kathie, and then you come over to our house to dinner with us? I think that would be swell. Mother would be delighted to meet you. I used to tell her a lot about you when we were children in high school. Will you come?"

"Oh, wonderful! Why, of course I'll come!" and then those two suddenly discovered that they were still holding hands, with bright cheeks flaming, bright eyes glancing, like a whole battalion of homecomings. And it was so, suddenly standing apart consciously that Rodney saw them first as he came out of the house of mourning.

"There's Rod now," said Jeremy, thrilling at the thought that Beryl Sanderson had just been holding hands publicly with him and she didn't seem to mind at all.

Then Rodney stood beside them inquiringly.

"Rod, this is Beryl Sanderson. You know, I've told you about her, and she's going with us over to the hospital to get Kathie, and then she's coming home with us to dinner."

"Swell!" said Rodney, looking with fine appreciation at the sweet face of the girl his brother admired. "Why, that's great! I've wanted to get acquainted with you, and I'm sure Dad and Mother will be terribly pleased. Say, getting home is something real, isn't it, Jerry?"

Soon they were all in the car speeding away to the hospital after Kathie, who presently looked at the new girl with shy interest. Oh, Kathie had seen her before, had known who she was in school days of course, although Kathie was younger than Beryl, but she added her invitation to the new girl to stay to dinner with the Graeme family.

"You know Mother always likes to have lots of company. She always did, and we're just delighted to have you. I've known all about you and often admired you in the past."

"Why, you dear," said Beryl. "You don't mean to tell me you are the little girl who used to come to school and go home with your brother? I often watched you and thought you were lovely."

"Well, this seems to be a sort of a mutual admiration society, Jerry. What do you think of that? All of us friends in a hurry."

From there they went on making a brisk acquaintance and all of them liking one another.

The road lay through the town of Riverton on the way to the Graeme farm, and who should be walking down the street as they drove through town, entirely engrossed with their guest, but Jessica De Groot and Alida Hopkins, slowly window-shopping by the way and turning to look sharply at each car that passed them.

"Why, who was that with the Graemes, Jess? That girl? Haven't I seen her before?"

"That, my dear naive little Alida, is Beryl Sanderson, the exclusive daughter of the great banker Sanderson."

"Well, but didn't you know her in school once? Wasn't she in our high school for a time before her father bought that big stone mansion on Linden Shade Drive?"

"She certainly was, my lamb."

"But she didn't speak to us, Jessica."

"No, she certainly did not. She's too much of a snob. She never did have anything to do with me, you know, and of course just now she was entirely too much taken up with those two navy men to know that anybody else existed. She's too snooty for words, Alida. I'm glad she didn't see us. I would have frozen her with one of her own cold looks if she had tried to speak to *me*. Of course I used to be a poor girl when she knew me, but now I'm even above her class financially, I suspect, so what does it matter?"

"Well, I wonder if that's what Rodney has on his mind now."

"Oh no, lambkin," said Jessica, "guess again. *She* belongs to little brother Jeremy. I used to watch them in school. He was just nuts about her."

"But they never went together at all in high school."

"Oh no, Mama wouldn't have approved, you know. She's a very carefully brought up girl."

"But who was the other girl in the car?"

"Why, that was Kathleen Graeme, the boys' sister. She certainly has grown up fast."

The girls passed on to other topics, now and again recurring to the Graeme family, in one way or another, and finally ended up at the hotel where Cousin Chatterton was temporarily abiding, because there was

124

almost always some interesting information to be got out of Cousin Louella, after any brief absence. If she didn't really have further information, she could always invent some, which was almost as interesting.

And this time it was interesting, if not exactly accurate.

"Yes, girls, I really have some news for you. I went over to see dear Margaret Graeme this afternoon and uncovered a bit of information sort of unawares. That is, I walked in on it when there was a private conversation between two members of the family going on. They didn't know I had come in. I found out that the Graeme boys are likely to stay in this country permanently, or at least for a time. There is some notable position being suggested for them. I didn't discover just exactly what it is, but I think — now you mustn't say anything about this of course outside, for it is a family affair, and of course I always try to be loyal to my family. But you, Jessica, were at one time almost family, so I know you won't say anything, but I think — mind you, I don't *know* for sure, I only sort of *think* whatever this job is, it may have something to do with Naval Intelligence. I'm not sure that I know exactly what that is, so I may be incorrect in my judgment, but I just thought it had to do with spotting spies in this country, or else teaching young navy men just before they go over what will be expected of them in going among the enemy. But anyhow it sounded interesting, and if I work judiciously I can find out a great deal that you might like to know. Of course I know I can trust you girls that you won't betray me. I would never be forgiven by the Graemes if they dreamed I was reporting things I'd overheard. But you know those Graemes are so terribly shy and retiring, afraid of publicity, that is, that often I'm quite ashamed of them. Everybody knows that I am related to them, and of course I'm expected to be kept informed of their moves, and it's so embarrassing to have to say, 'I'm sorry, I haven't heard yet what the decision is,' or something like that. So I'm simply forced to obtain my information by backhanded means. And I don't like it at all. I'd much rather be treated like one of the inner circle and be told frankly everything and not made to appear as one who is not honored with the confidence of those near and dear to me."

"Of course," said Alida in a pitying tone.

"But I imagine you with your cleverness," put in Jessica, "can really obtain a wider scope of information than even if you were wholly in their confidence. Sometimes these underhanded ways are more productive than a closer relationship. Oh, you are clever, Louella, and no mistake. Do you know what I would do if I were you? I'd get a connection with some rather outspoken daring magazine or newspaper and then write some spicy little articles anonymously that would set people wondering and get them all agog. You could really sway governments that way, and if you made the right contacts you could make oodles of money. Believe me, I know. I haven't been asleep all the time since I got married, and my husband is as smart as a whip. Perhaps I'll put you on to two or three matters, if you stick by me long enough, Louella. And believe me, my clever friend, life isn't just made up of catching the right man and making him fall in love with you. It's nine-tenths of knowing what to do with him when you've got him, and how much you can make out of him."

"Now, Jessica, that sounds very worldly indeed. I never would have suspected you of having been at one time almost a member of this dear, silly Graeme family. And now, my dear, since you don't seem satisfied to be utterly done with those innocent dears, I have a little scheme for you, and it has to do with your attendance at that church service in Harper Memorial Church next Sunday night. I would suggest that you plan to be there, and to perhaps sit in the top gallery. Get Alida to go with you, and keep a watchful eye out for Rodney. I'm almost positive he's going to that meeting and will probably sit in the gallery himself. He seems to want to keep in the background at present. And if you and Alida should be sitting nearby, it will be easy to slip over and sit beside him and get to talking. I can put you on to two or three matters that Naval Intelligencers ought to be able to answer without a suggestion that there was anything out of order in your asking questions, or their answering them, especially if it was done under the guise of a very loving old friend, merely wanting to get near Rod's work, because of old times. And my dear, I'll write two or three questions for you, which if you could write up the answers you get, I could get you good pay for the articles. You would be just the one to write them, for you are clever enough to disguise your intentions, both in asking the questions and in writing them up, anonymously of course, afterward. Think it over, my dear, and I'll see what I can do. And now, really, I must go. I have an appointment at the hairdresser's."

"Well, that sounds most interesting. I certainly could use a little extra money," said Jessica, "even though I am married, and if I couldn't win the personal attention I'd like from my old beau, at least I could find a way to punish him for his indifference."

And so the meeting ended, and the girls went out to talk it over. Not that Alida was a very wise adviser, but she certainly could gush and encourage anything that sounded like a lark, or an interesting intrigue.

CHAPTER 8

"Dad," said Kathie quietly the next morning when her father came downstairs a bit early to attend to something in the barn, "wouldn't there be some way to get that key away from Cousin Louella? I was worried to death all last evening while that lovely Sanderson girl was here, lest Cousin Louella would barge in on us again and butt in on all the conversation. Dad, she is simply impossible!"

"Yes, I know," said Father Graeme. "I have been thinking about that. I'll get the key. There's no reason why she should have a perpetual right to open our door without notice. I'll see to that today. But don't say anything to anybody about it yet. I don't want your mother worried."

"Yes, I understand, Dad. Thank you so much. You don't know what a trial she has been. I'll be kind to her when we meet, but it's awful to have her turning up in the most embarrassing times. You know how she comes right into the room when we are having family prayers and sits there scorning us. She takes no pains to hide her dislike of it. She told me the other day that she couldn't understand why we hadn't protested against such old-fashioned ideas. She said nice people nowadays didn't flaunt their religion in the faces of outsiders."

"Poor soul!" he said with a sad little smile on his kindly face. "Poor soul! She certainly needs praying for, and the day may come when she'll be glad to have some religion to flaunt, even if it is old-fashioned. Don't worry, Kathie, I'll see to it."

Father Graeme came in very soon, ate his breakfast, and then took the car and went down to the village.

"The boys won't be down for a while," he said as he went out. "Let them sleep as long as they want to. They've had to do a lot of getting up early over there in the war. I'll be back by the time they want to use the car."

Kathie flashed a twinkle of a smile at her father. She knew what he was going out for, although she couldn't imagine how he was going to work it. Sometimes there were things that only Dad could accomplish. Things that were difficult, yet Dad could always manage to get them done without definitely offending anyone.

As he drove down the street into the glory of the morning, he began to think over the night before, and it gave him great comfort that a girl like Beryl Sanderson had come to their home and seemed to be so glad to be there and to like his boys and his girl so much. He thought it all over, recalled the lovely smile she wore, the sweet unspoiled look of her, the happy way in which she entered into the conversation, the reverent way she bowed her head during the blessing at the table, with not a trace of sneer on her lovely face afterward. She had stayed for the evening and entered into the family life as if she had been one of them, as if she had real sympathy for the things they liked and did and said. And Mother liked her, too. He always knew when Mother liked a girl. Yes, she was the right kind. How was it that her boys hadn't found Beryl before? He recalled also that he had met her father a few years ago and liked his attitude on certain questions in the presbytery. He was a right-minded man. On the whole Beryl Sanderson had made a good impression on Father Graeme, and he hoped in his soul they would see more of her. She was like a breath of fresh air in a stifling atmosphere, after that other girl with the bleached hair that

Rod used to go with. He prayed in his heart that they would not have to see more of her. Well, of course they said she was married now, but that didn't seem to mean a thing in these days when there were almost as many divorces as marriages. He hoped with all his heart that his two sons had not come to feel lightly about marriage.

Thinking these thoughts, he soon arrived at his destination, a place to which he did not often go, the hotel where Louella Chatterton was staying for the present.

He parked his car and went to the desk, asked if Mrs. Chatterton was in, and being told that she was, sent up his name. He was informed that she would presently come down, as she was planning a trip to the city that morning, so he sat himself down to wait, well knowing that he must have patience, for he had had experience in waiting for Louella before and knew that she would not hasten.

When she arrived he made haste to come toward the elevator to meet her. "Good morning, Louella. I hope I didn't interrupt you seriously, but I shall not keep you long. I came to ask you for my house key, which I loaned you over a year ago, you remember. And now the time has come when I need it, so I thought I would stop by and get it."

Now Louella made her mind up that he had come to invite her to dinner perhaps, and she had come down all smiles. The dinners at the Graemes' were always good and cost her nothing. So the little matter of a latchkey did not interest her. The interest when out of her eyes.

"A key?" she said meditatively. "Oh yes, a key. I believe you did give me a key. I thought of course you meant me to keep it. Let me see, what did I do with that key? I think I may have brought it east with me. I'm not sure. I'll have to look through my things and see." Louella gave an obvious glance toward the clock as if she had no time now to look it up.

"Oh, yes, you brought it with you," said Father Graeme. "You used it to open our door the night the boys came home and walked right into the dining room, don't you remember?"

"Did I? But no, I think you are mistaken. I think the door was not locked."

"Yes, the door was locked, Louella. We always lock it at night, and we heard the key in the lock before you came in. I'm sorry to ask you to go back upstairs and get it now if you are in a hurry to go out, but I really need that key this morning."

"Oh!" said Louella with annoyance in her

voice. "What's the hurry? Wouldn't it do if I brought it over this evening?"

"Sorry, no, Louella, I need it this morning. Would you like to have me go up to your room and try to find it for you? I really want it now, if you please."

"Oh, no, of course not," snapped Louella. "But wait! Maybe I have it in my purse."

She opened her man-size purse of bright red she was carrying under her well-tailored arm and rummaged through it, and there right in the compartment with her change was the key, just where her cousin was sure she would find it.

"Well, of course, here it is, if you must have it, but I shall feel rather lost without it. Giving this up makes me feel that I have no family anymore." She managed a break in her voice. "But — how long will you need it? Perhaps I can call tomorrow and get it again. Will you be through with it by that time?"

"I'm afraid not, Louella. My family is all home now, and we need our keys. But I am sure you will always be able to get into the house if you ring the bell or even knock. Thank you, Louella, and now I won't keep you any longer. You have a nice day for your city trip. Have a good time. Good-bye." And Father Graeme lifted his hat and bowed himself out. Louella looked after him angrily and began at once to plan how she could get that key back. Perhaps she could bribe Hetty to give her her key. The very idea! Give a servant a key and take it away from a blood relation, at least a relation by marriage!

There was no denying that Louella was very much upset about that key, and she decided to get it back at the first possible moment. As she climbed into the bus that would take her to her lawyer's in the city, her mind was occupied with the problem of how to get that key back, and also incidentally to get a little more information concerning the doings of the Graeme boys.

The best way to do that would be to go there this afternoon and get Margaret by herself. She could always get things out of Margaret Graeme if she worked it in the right way. She was sure she could get that key. Margaret was softhearted, and if she showed that she was really hurt by not having that key she was sure she could get it.

So she hurried through her business with her lawyer and took the return bus that would go by the Graeme house. That would not waste so much time.

So, Margaret Graeme, fresh from a nap, and her heart at rest because her two boys were at home, took her sewing and went downstairs to sit by the library fire and wait for her family to drift back from their various wanderings and interests. She was no sooner comfortably seated than the doorbell rang twice, sharply, aggrievedly, and Margaret sat placidly as she heard Hetty go in a leisurely lope to the front door.

"Well, you decided to come at last, did you?" came Louella's sharp, faultfinding voice. "Where were you? Up in the third floor? Because I should think you'd arrange to be downstairs in the afternoon when calls are likely to come, or else get somebody to look after the door when you decide to go up to the attic and take an afternoon nap."

Then Hetty's indignant tones boomed out. "No ma'am, I wasn't taking no nap. I nevah takes no nap. An' I wasn't up in the third stoh'y neither. I was right in the kitchen, just liftin' out some chicken thet was 'bout to burn, an' I come as quick as I could."

"Oh, yes, I suppose you'd have an alibi. You never did learn how to be respectful."

"No ma'am, I don't have no Al Lebi. I don't eben know him. Ain't been no man at all around here."

"Well, never mind. Don't talk forever about one thing. Just answer the door sooner the next time. Now, where are the family?"

Hetty in her haughtiest manner shut the front door definitely and then turned toward the caller. "Mistah Graeme, he has went to a special meetin' of the presbytery. De young gemm'l'men tuk him down to de chu'tch, an' dey'll went after him when he's done de meetin'. Meanwhiles dey'll go roun' an' about an' call on dere frien's. Miss Kathie, she's off ta her hospital work, an' M'is Graeme, she's settin' in de li'bry. You can went in if ya like." And Hetty sailed nonchalantly into the kitchen.

With a sniff of disapproval, Louella marched into the quiet atmosphere of the library.

Margaret Graeme looked up with a pleasant smile. Not quite so pleasant perhaps as that smile would have been if the person arriving had been one of her boys or her girl. But she had heard most of the dialogue between Hetty and Louella and was prepared with quite a pleasant welcome, a little bit troubled, perhaps, and worried lest Louella might stay longer than would be pleasant and that she might insist upon staying until the boys got back, and that would be altogether unfortunate. She didn't want her sons to have anything to mar the sweetness of home. Especially if it should so turn out that they had to go back again to the horrors of war. She must be cautious. She must be quiet to be guided. *Oh God, help me!*

Perhaps it was a petty trial to bring to the great God for help, and yet Margaret Graeme had learned through long years that there is no trial so petty that may not work out to unpleasantness and even sin if allowed to sway the spirit. Mrs. Graeme had learned through long years how to keep that spirit of hers placid, unruffled by little things. She was always looking to her Guide for strength.

It is a pity that Louella could not have learned from the same Teacher, for she would have been a much more welcome guest if she had.

"Well!" she snapped from the doorway. "Here you sit as quietly and contentedly as if all the world was moving in oiled grooves according to your plan. Guests may come and ring at your doorbell and pound on your knocker, and that lazy so-called servant of yours opens the door when she gets good and ready. Really, Margaret, if I were in your place I would dismiss that Hetty before the day is over. I'm sure I could get you a servant who would be far superior to her at her best, and for less money, I'll warrant you. The trouble with Hetty is that she doesn't know her place. You spoiled her, and she thinks she can do anything she pleases."

"Good afternoon, Louella," said Margaret Graeme. "Won't you sit down by the fire? I know it isn't a very cold day, but yet there is still a little sting of winter in the air. And throw aside your coat, won't you? Then you won't be chilly when you go out again. Did you walk over?"

"*Walk? Me?* Mercy no. I never walk if I can ride. I came on the bus of course. I came after my key. It worries me not to have it on hand when I want to come over here."

"Your key?" asked Margaret. "What key, Louella?"

"Why, my key to this house. Don't you remember you gave it to me when I was living here, and I've kept it ever since? And this morning Donald came over and asked me for it. Where is he? He said he had need of it. He didn't say what for, and I told him I would come over and get it. Is he here?"

"No, Louella, he isn't here. He went to a meeting. I don't know when he will be back. He may stay for the evening session."

"Well, then won't you go upstairs and look in all his pockets and get that key for me? I haven't much time just now, and I can't be easy without that key. It has been in my inner consciousness so long it seems a part of me, and it gives me a feeling of belonging to a family."

"Oh, I'm sorry, Louella. But you see we need that key. There aren't keys enough to go around, and when we have a guest for a day or so, it is rather embarrassing not to have a key to give them. Donald has been going to ask you for it ever since you were here the other night, and he has just put it off."

"Well, that's ridiculous!" said Louella. "You can always get Hetty's key. She doesn't need a key anyway. Or you can get another made from one of yours. I insist, Margaret, that you get that key for me, and hurry up. I have other calls to make."

"I'm sorry, Louella," said the sweet Graeme mother firmly, "but I just wouldn't know where to look for that key. And anyway if Donald asked you for it, he likely had a reason. Besides, Louella, you don't need a key now that you are not staying here. Forget it, Louella, and let's have a nice talk. Are there any pleasant people staying at the inn now?"

"No!" snapped Louella. "None that I care for. I tried playing bridge with some of them

141

last night, but do you know Margaret, they cheated! Yes, they actually did. And then they charged me with not being honest. But of course they were strangers to me, and if I were going to stay here long I certainly should change my hotel. And that's another reason why I want that key back. Won't you please go upstairs and try to find that key for me?"

"Why, no, Louella, I wouldn't like to do that when Donald went after it. There must have been some reason why he wanted it. But really, Louella, there isn't any reason why you need a key. Especially if you are expecting to go home soon. It wouldn't be of any use to you. By the way, Louella, you hadn't seen Rodney since he was a very little boy until the other night. He was away in service when you were here before. Didn't you think he looked well? And did you notice how much he looks like his father?"

"No, I hadn't seen him in a long time, but I'm sure I couldn't tell who he looks like. He was so horribly cross and rude to me that night I couldn't bear to look at him. I can't see how he could possibly look anything like his father, for Donald never looks cross at anybody. He is always placid and polite."

"Well, I'm sorry, Louella," said Rodney's mother. "You just didn't understand. It happened that someone had been in just before you arrived, and it had upset him very much, and when you asked him those questions it simply made things worse. You didn't understand, of course, and wouldn't have hurt him for all the world if you had known. You were always kindhearted when you understood."

"Well what is it? Why don't you explain? You can't expect me to be kindhearted if I don't understand."

"No? Well, what is it you want explained?"

"Well, I would like to understand, first, just why this ideal engagement was broken?"

"I'm sorry, Louella, but I don't believe I would have a right to explain those matters. You see they are not mine to explain. Isn't it enough to say that the engagement is broken and that Rod is entirely satisfied about it, but he doesn't like to have that girl flung in his face continually, nor to be asked questions. After all, it is his affair, and nobody else has a right to know all the details. I don't know them myself, and I've never asked. Boys don't like to have their intimate affairs talked over, and I've never asked him a thing. I felt that he had a right to his own privacies, and I would rather have him *give* me any confidences he wants to give than to have him feel that I have been trying to dig them out of him."

Louella shut her thin lips tight and pursed them while she shook her head, disapprovingly. "Now Margaret Graeme, you know perfectly well that you had no right to take that attitude. You should have insisted on making Rod tell you *every*thing. After all, that is the way to encourage deception. And you have just deliberately encouraged Rodney in deceiving you. I certainly am glad I came in that night and brought the matter out in the open, even if Rodney didn't like it. And furthermore, I'll do all I can whenever I see him, in trying to make him see that the way he has treated and is treating that lovely girl is all wrong, utterly unmanly, just the part of a scoundrel!"

Mother Graeme gathered up her knitting and tucked it into her knitting bag and then looked at her visitor more indignantly than Louella had ever seen that placid cousin-in-law look.

"Louella," she said, and her voice was firm and angry, "what in the world do you mean? What an outrageous thing for you to say! You certainly will have to explain those remarks, or we cannot talk together anymore. I will not have my son maligned."

"Oh, yes, your poor little son!" taunted Louella. "Yes, of course you would defend the poor child. After all, if he has been able to fight in a grown-up war, I should think he could do his own defending."

"Now look here, Louella, I'm not trying to defend my son, because there is nothing to defend. I am trying to find out what you meant by saying that he has, and is, treating his former fiancée outrageously. What right have you to say that? Who has been talking to you? Where did you get any reason to speak like that?"

"Why, I got my information from the lady herself. She told me herself when she came into the dining room the other night Rodney took his dishes and dinner and marched out of the room without speaking to her, and that he did not return while she was there. She said you told her that he wasn't there. At least Jerry did, and that she couldn't find out anything about him from any of you. And she said she knew he must be there for his coat and cap had been hanging in the hall when she came through. Besides, he was there at the table eating pie when I came in."

"I see," said Mother Graeme. "So you have turned detective. Just why are you doing that, Louella? Is it merely out of curiosity? I didn't know that you were especially curious." Mother Graeme was growing quieter, more self-controlled.

Louella brindled indignantly.

"Really!" she huffed. "Since when did you take up this offensive way of talking? I certainly wouldn't know you, Margaret! But then I have heard that even a dog who is very gentle will snarl and bite when her offspring is attacked."

Margaret Graeme arose quietly, laid down her knitting bag on the little table by her chair. "That will be about all, Louella. Excuse me. I'll get us a cup of tea. Perhaps you will be less excited after that."

"Excited! *I*, excited! I should say it was you who is excited."

But Mother Graeme had gone out and closed the door definitely. She had not heard what the annoying guest had said.

When Mrs. Graeme returned she was carrying a tray. Two steaming cups of tea, lemon and cream and sugar, a plate of cookies and another of tiny sandwiches. Mother Graeme had a theory that she often put into practice. "When in trouble always feed the troublemaker." She was working her theory now. She put the tray down on the little table, removed her knitting bag, and drew up a chair for the cousin.

"Now," she said cheerily, "let's have a good time and stop arguing."

"But I wasn't arguing," said Louella belligerently. "I was just *telling* you."

"Lemon or cream? I can't ever remember which you take, Louella."

"Lemon!" snapped Louella. "I can't imagine how anybody can take cream. That's why so many people have to reduce, they take too much cream. And lemon is so much smarter."

"Here are napkins, Louella."

Louella accepted a napkin and thereby lost her line of argument.

"Help yourself to sandwiches, Louella."

"Are those cookies made by your mother's recipe?" asked the guest, her mouth filled with delectable sandwiches. But Louella never praised anything if she could help it.

"No," said Margaret Graeme. "I don't think they are made by mother's recipe. I had loaned out my recipe book. I think this was a recipe Kathie got over the radio the other day. Have a cookie and sample it."

"Thanks!" said Louella and took a generous bite. "Yes, this seems very light and tasty. I always thought your mother's recipe didn't have enough shortening in it. This seems better. Light as a feather. I wish you'd give me half a dozen of these to serve with

147

five o'clock tea when someone comes in to call."

"Why surely," said Margaret Graeme pleasantly, wondering how long this unwelcome guest was planning to stay and what subject she could start next that would be argument proof. But the guest did not wait for a subject. She had one right up her sleeve, the real reason for her coming.

"By the way, what are the boys going to do now? They don't have to go back overseas again, do they?"

"They haven't received their orders yet," said the mother.

"Do you mean they don't know? But I understood they knew before they left the hospital. I heard they had a good job provided for them and they were done fighting."

"Oh," said the mother, "just where did you hear that, Louella? It's strange they wouldn't let us know, if the matter is decided yet."

"Do you really mean that you *don't* know yet, or are you just trying to put me off again? Because, really, I don't think that's very kind of you, Margaret, to keep me in ignorance when practically everybody else knows and is talking about it."

"The next time they tell you that, Louella,

suppose you ask them where *they* got their information. Because there really has been no word come yet for the boys. In fact, they didn't expect it for a month yet. They were sent home for a good rest, and they will not be told the decision about their future work until they go down to Washington and have a thorough physical examination to see how they have progressed since they left the hospital on the other side."

"Oh, how perfectly silly! Those boys are in fine physical shape, don't you think, Margaret? Their mother certainly ought to be the best judge."

"I don't think I'd be the best judge, under the circumstances. You know I wouldn't understand all that they've been through and what reactions I should look for. It's the navy's responsibility you know, not mine. And whether I thought so or not wouldn't make any difference to them. The boys belong to the navy, and they have to do as the navy says."

"But I thought they were out for good. Mrs. Hopkins says her boys are home definitely to stay. And she says they were practically in the same company with your boys. She says her boys said they heard overseas that your boys were slated definitely for something else. Something over here, they said."

Margaret Graeme looked at the cousin thoughtfully. "I'm afraid I wouldn't know," she said quietly.

"Oh, now Margaret, don't be so close-mouthed. You know perfectly well you just don't want to give out information."

"I'm sorry, Louella, I've told you the truth. But if you don't choose to believe me I've nothing further to say. Won't you have another cup of tea? Another cookie?"

"No, Margaret, I've had plenty. And besides, I feel very much hurt at the way you are treating me. I know perfectly well you're not telling me all you know. I feel very much offended at your attitude."

"I am sorry, Louella, that you take it this way. I have no intention of refusing to give you any facts that I have a right to give, even though I feel that your attitude of demanding to know everything about the family is unjustifiable. However, in this case I do not know what the boys are going to be ordered to do and shall probably not know for several weeks. And by the way, here are the cookies you asked for. Take the sandwiches, too, if you like. Good-bye."

Louella accepted the neat package done up in paper napkins and took herself out of the picture.

Margaret Graeme turned thankfully away from the door, grateful that this trying relative was gone before her family got home.

On her way back to the hotel, Louella remembered that she had neglected to ask whether the whole family were going out Sunday night to hear Jeremy speak. Well, never mind. She would insist that Jessica carry out the plan of sitting in the gallery. She felt reasonably sure this plan could only succeed.

CHAPTER 9

But Rodney did not sit in the gallery, as Louella had been sure he would do, confirmed in this belief by Margaret Graeme's statement that the boys did not care to be in the public eye and be lauded for what they had been in combat. And so Jessica sulked in a dark corner of the gallery without a gallant to comfort her lonely state.

She had not taken any of the girls with her because she felt her part in the drama she was expecting to play would be more effective if she went alone and slid unawares, as it were, into the vacant seat beside her former beau. But just before the meeting began, the other girls of her "gang," as she called it, came into the church and, finding no seats downstairs, went grumbling up the stairs to find her. They could not understand why she had put them off and refused to go with them. And so when they had found her, they squeezed into a seat across the aisle from where she was sitting, in behind a post where they could scarcely see the platform, and sat staring around them.

"Say, are you sure Jerry is going to speak here tonight?" whispered Emma Galt to Alida Hopkins. "He isn't down there on the platform, and there are quite a lot of people sitting up there behind the pulpit."

"Yes, Jerry is speaking all right. I saw his name on the church bulletin board outside the church as we came in. Didn't you?"

"Sure!" said Isabelle. "Wait! Some more are coming. There! There he is! The last one. And see. Down there, coming in the middle aisle. That's Rodney Graeme, isn't it? And who are those girls with them? As I live, isn't one of them that Beryl Sanderson? It surely is! And who is the other one, oh boy! Gaze on that outfit. I'll bet she's some swell friend from New York. Girls, we made a big mistake. We should have come early and sat down in that front row of seats."

"You couldn't," said Alida. "There's a rope across the aisle. Those seats are reserved. Look! They're opening the aisle. They're escorting those people into those reserved seats. Why, look! Isabelle! Isn't that Rodney Graeme with them? And who *are* the girls? Beryl Sanderson and who else? I never saw her before. I *wonder* who she is."

153

Isabelle leaned forward and looked, whipped out her little old-fashioned opera glasses, which she had lately inherited from an old aunt, and stared at the group being seated.

"Yes, that's Rodney and Beryl all right. And wait. I know who that other girl is. She *is* from New York. She's been here before to visit Beryl. Her name is Diana Winters. Well, that's some setup. Just how do you suppose Rod got in with them? For the love of Mike, won't Jess be angry? This is what she gets for following the drivel of that poor old gawk of a cousin of the Graemes. That's what I told her when she insisted on going to that poky old hotel to call on her. I think that woman's a flop, and everything she tries to do is silly."

"Oh, keep still, Isabelle. That old man is looking at us. He wants us to stop talking."

"Well, this church doesn't belong to him. I shall talk if I like, and he can't stop me. There! There! See they've given those reserved seats to the Graemes. Say, I think this is a rank trick the old girl played on us, bringing us to a church to sit away up in the gallery where we can't possibly see anything or hear anything. Let's go downstairs and get a better seat."

"There aren't any seats, Isabelle," said

Emma Galt, leaning over Alida to speak to her. "I stood up and looked, and I just now heard that usher who passed down the other aisle at the end tell that old man that there wasn't even standing room left down there. We better sit still. At least Jerry has a good strong voice, and I'm sure we can hear him."

"Not unless you girls can stop your talking," said the old man, leaning forward and looking at them sharply.

That made Isabelle angry, and she was about to tell the old man what she thought of him, but suddenly the organ rolled into attention and fairly thundered, and not even Isabelle could be heard over that. Then all at once everybody began to sing:

It may be in the valley, where countless
    dangers hide,
It may be in the sunshine that I in peace
    abide;
But this one thing I know, if it be dark or
    fair,
If Jesus is with me, I'll go anywhere.

It was an old song, and most people in the audience knew the words. They had sung it in the primary class long ago, and it was still familiar in their different churches. But it was wonderful how the audience took hold of it and swung it along, setting a keynote for the meeting that was to follow.

The little crowd of indifferent ones in the gallery whose whole plan for the evening had gone far astray looked only bored. They did not care for this style of music. It seemed to them childish, belonging to an earlier age when men prated of sin and salvation, and Jessica sat back with a sigh of disgust. Jessica had distinctly not come here to listen to religious songs, even if they were so well sung that they filled the air to the exclusion of other thoughts. What did they have to sing such songs for?

But with scarcely a word from the platform the throng drifted into another:

We have an anchor that keeps the soul
Steadfast and sure while the billows roll,
Fastened to the Rock which cannot move,
Grounded firm and deep in the Savior's
  love.

Jessica, with another audible sigh, looked toward her gang across the aisle and curled her lip. She was all but ready to go out of this silly, childish gathering. What did she come here for anyway, to listen to a young boy who just a few days ago was nothing but a high school student declaiming? How much more of this did she have to sit through? If it wasn't for these obnoxious people who had crowded in beside her and shoved her even against her protest all the way to the inside end of the seat, making it impossible for her to leave without climbing over them, she would leave at once.

And then came another tiresome song. How perfectly pestilential! Probably this was somehow a workup to get the younger boys ready for going overseas. There was no telling. But how could a thing like that help anybody to be patriotic? They ought to sing "The Star-Spangled Banner" or some really patriotic song. Who in the world arranged a stupid program like this anyway? She wished they had asked her what to sing. Even though it was in a church they were entertaining a returned serviceman, weren't they? Why go so ultra religious?

There is a Shepherd who cares for His
  own,
  And He is mine;
Nothing am I, He's a King on a throne,
  But He is mine.

The melody was carried as a solo by an exquisite voice, but everybody seemed to know the song and the choral accompaniment of humming voices was rather wonderful.

There was not much time for Jessica to be thinking about leaving, for the program hurried along almost breathlessly, and somehow even the sneering gang *had* to listen.

Suddenly seven servicemen in uniform marched up to the platform and it was announced that instead of having the scripture read, these seven men would recite it, as each had experienced it overseas.

Then each spoke, with heartfelt accents, what was evidently a truth each had felt.

"The angel of the Lord encampeth round about them that fear him, and delivereth them. Psalm 34:7," said the first, a tall marine.

"We will rejoice in thy salvation, and in the name of our God we will set up our banners: the Lord fulfill all thy petitions. Now know I that the Lord saveth his anointed; he will hear him from his holy heaven with the saving strength of his right hand. Some trust in chariots, and some in horses: but we will remember the name of the Lord our God. Psalm 20:5–7." This was the word of a corporal in the army.

Then came a private on crutches, his face emaciated, his skin sallow, his eyes with haunting memories hidden by a great light.

It was whispered about among the audience by some who recognized him that he had recently escaped from a prison camp after two years' confinement, and his contribution, spoken in a clear, ringing voice was, "Praise the Lord, O my soul . . . The Lord looseth the prisoners. Psalm 146:1, 7."

Next came two navy men. The first a tall fellow with a clear voice and many decorations, and he spoke a ringing word like a testimony: "He that dwelleth in the secret place of the most High shall abide under the shadow of the Almighty. I will say of the Lord, He is my refuge and my fortress: my God; in him will I trust. Surely he shall deliver thee from the snare of the fowler, and from the noisome pestilence. Psalm 91:1–3."

Then, without a pause, his companion went on, "He shall cover thee with his feathers, and under his wings shalt thou trust: his truth shall be thy shield and buckler.

"Thou shalt not be afraid for the terror by night; nor for the arrow that flieth by day. Psalm 91:4–5."

Then followed a young army officer. In a steady voice, like an official oath he was taking, he said, "In Thee, O Lord, do I put my trust; let me never be ashamed: deliver me in thy righteousness. Into thine hand I commit my spirit: thou has redeemed me, O Lord God of truth. My times are in thy hand: deliver me from the hand of mine enemies. . . . Be of good courage, and he shall strengthen your heart, all ye that hope in the Lord. Psalm 31:1, 5, 15, 24."

And next came a navy flier with a kind of ringing triumph in his voice: "I love the Lord, because he hath heard my voice and my supplications. Because he hath inclined his ear unto me, therefore will I call upon him as long as I live. Psalm 116:1–2."

"It is better to trust in the Lord than to put confidence in man. Psalm 118:8."

The gang in the gallery listened astonished. They could not laugh, they could not sneer, for those words were too solemnly, too earnestly spoken, from men who obviously had been but lads so short a time ago. They bore marks in their faces of having been through fire and flood and death, and even worse than death. For just an instant, while those boys were speaking, even Jessica got a little glimpse of what the war must have meant to these men who but recently were to her just so many more to dance and flirt with. Now they were living souls who had been through something of which she had no concept. She was frightened. Her impulse was to turn and flee, but she had

160

not the courage to do it.

And then there came another surprise. Another soldier in uniform stepped up beside the seven, and they all began to sing, a double male quartet.

Be still, my soul: The Lord is on thy side;
　Bear patiently the cross of grief or pain;
Leave to thy God to order and provide;
　In every change He faithful will remain.
Be still, my soul: thy best, thy heavenly
　Friend
　Thro' thorny ways leads a joyful end.

Be still my soul: thy God doth undertake
　To guide the future as He has the past,
Thy hope, thy confidence let nothing shake;
　All, now mysterious, shall be bright at
　last.
Be still, my soul: the waves and winds still
　know
　His voice Who ruled them while He dwelt
　below.

The voices were beautiful, and the words were distinct. The audience was very still as the singing went on to the end. Then very simply the pastor of the church introduced Jeremy, not giving his history nor a list of his great achievements in the war. His decorations could tell that tale to those who understood.

Jerry stepped forward quietly and began to talk:

"I asked the fellows to sing that song for me," he said, "because it was a verse of that song that came to help me when I started out on my first bombing mission. Up to then I hadn't been greatly stirred by the things I had been through. I had rather enjoyed it all while in training, and I hadn't been in any serious fighting. I knew my duty, and it hadn't seemed to me anything very difficult to do as I had been trained. The element of fear hadn't been in it yet for me. Not until I was in my seat ready to go out on my first serious mission did I realize that I was going into possible death.

"Of course when I enlisted, I saw by the expressions on the faces of my family that there was dread and fear ahead for them. But I laughed at them and went on my way, enjoying every hard thing that came my way. My mother was brave and courageous. She never voiced her fears. She did not try to dissuade me. 'We are putting you in God's hands, son,' she said with that sweet, patient look in her eyes. That was Mother. I expected cooperation from Dad and Mother.

"Oh, there had been prayers for me every

night and morning in the few days before I left, and I listened to them as if they had been unnecessary farewell presents to bear me on my way. My family had always prayed for me, and I would be sure they would now as I was going off to war. We always had family worship, morning and evening in my home, and sometimes as a little kid it had rather bored me, but that last morning, it seemed the right and fitting thing. My father always read a passage of scripture and prayed, and sometimes, when we had more time, we sang a hymn. That morning I went away we sang that song the boys just sang.

"I remember when we reached the second verse that somehow those words seemed written for my mother, and I felt she was singing them to herself, although all our voices were joining in.

"Be still, my soul; thy God doth undertake
  To guide the future as He has the past.

"Those words stuck in my memory, and for an instant I had a brief vision of the night my older brother went away to war, and I had a passing sympathy for what Mother must have suffered during the months he had been away. Now she was having to take it again! But she was brave, and she would stand up and trust, with that wonderful faith of hers. A gallant little mother. And a father with a strength and a faith like a rock.

"So I went out.

"I didn't have any fear then. I think I must have supposed that when *I* got into the war, that would end everything. But it didn't take me long to find out my mistake. Nevertheless, I went through the preliminaries, thrilled with the enormity of the undertaking to save the world for peace and prosperity. And it was not until I was seated in my bomber, awaiting the word for me to start out on my first solo mission, that I began to realize what it all might mean. Oh, I had been out with others, I had watched some battles, I had seen some of my comrades fall, but as yet I had no fear that it could come to me. Death? Why, I was young and strong. I was *trained.* I had courage to go right among the enemy and down them. Of course I didn't exactly say that to myself when I started.

"Now I couldn't understand this feeling of fear that had come over me. It was like the time when I began to play football and I saw the other side rounding up against me. Suddenly I found that I hadn't experience in meeting just such a setup as was coming, and I began to quake. How I despised myself. Then I was just a sissy after all. Afraid to go out and fight. Me! Jerry Graeme!

"Then strangely there seemed to come to me a strain of a song. But it was very far away, like all my old courage that I had always been so proud of. And then at that instant came the signal to start, and I *had* to go. I must not be an instant behind.

"I started. My hands did the things that they had been trained for; my brain out of habit directed my actions, but I was going out all alone with nothing but the strain of a hymn to give me heart:

"Be still, my soul: thy God doth undertake!

"But it was so far away, as if it scarcely belonged to me, as if it were a song out of some other fellow's memories. But my mind grasped out for it, to make it mine. 'Thy God doth undertake.' Would God undertake for me? I had always supposed of course that God was on my side. But now I wasn't so sure. I began to go over my life, swiftly. There wasn't much time to take stock of one's self then, but I had heard that when a person faces sudden death his whole life in every little detail comes over him in a flash, and it was so with me. I thought I had been fairly good, no sin, except the original sin I had been born with and taught about. Or was that true, no sin? Well, suddenly I wasn't so sure. I had lived a clean, moral life. Yes, but was that enough to help me meet God if I had to go at once into His presence?

"It was almost as if I were talking the matter over with God, presenting my claims to enter His presence.

" 'I've always gone to church? Why, I *like* to go to church. Of course I'm a *member* of the church!' But still that did not seem to make things any better or give me any comfort. Well, I wasn't a liar or a thief. I had never killed anyone, no, nor hated anyone enough to *want* to kill them. I began to count over the cardinal sins, and my estimate of self began to bulk up before me, but none of those things seemed to count, and then I remember that my mother used to teach me that the one great sin that included all others was unbelief. But even that was not my sin — *was* it? I had grown up knowing the Bible, believing in God, that is, in God with my mind. I believed what God had done, I believed that Jesus Christ had lived and then died for me. I had accepted all that a sort of a formula of doc-

166

trine. I believed He was the Son of God and that He not only died but had risen from the dead. I knew and believed that when Christ died He took my sins upon Himself as if they had been His own, He who never sinned Himself, and that He bore the sins, as well as the penalty for my sins. I could remember that when I united with the church they had asked me if I would accept what He had done and take Him for my personal Savior, and I had assented. Quite casually it must have been, or so it seemed to me as I rode along in God's air, about to come into His actual presence, perhaps, and I didn't feel ready. I just didn't *know* the Lord. Oh, I had prayed and read my Bible, but now it began to seem to me that it had all been almost nothing but a mere form, done because it was the thing a Christian was supposed to do. And my heart quaked within me.

"I began to see planes ahead of me. I would soon be at the scene of my first great activity, and I was so engaged with thinking that I didn't know God and might be going right into His presence that I couldn't seem to keep my mind to the duties that were before me.

"And then, suddenly, as the critical situation approached, I felt I was not alone. A

Presence was there beside me. There was glory in the air. And then I realized it was the Lord. He had come to me in my need! And I felt a sudden strength, and the fright that had made me weak before went away. I looked into His face and I was not afraid anymore. 'Don't be afraid, I will go with you,' He said, and His voice was clear, in my heart. And I wondered why I had never taken such joy and strength from Him before. Then I realized that I had never really looked into His face. I had not seen Him before. I had not *known* Him. But now I knew Him *Himself,* and I could do *any-*thing. That is, anything He wanted me to do. I could accomplish my mission. I could crush the enemy. And if it meant I was to meet my death, too, it would not matter, for I would be with Him, either in life or death, with Him forevermore!

"The enemy was all but upon me then, the sky was full of the sound of battle, but I was not afraid because God was with me, and He was undertaking. One swift resolve I made, and that was that if I went through this war and ever got home, I would go to all the fellows who were going over pretty soon and would tell them that they must get acquainted with God before they went. It made no difference how much they were trained or how skillful they were in the use of the implements of war, if they didn't know God, their preparation was not complete, for only in the strength of the Lord Jesus Christ could they be fully prepared to do the best that a serviceman could do. And that is the message I am bringing to you tonight. If there is only one fellow here tonight who is pretty soon going out to the great fight, my message is to you. Get acquainted with the Lord Jesus Christ, *now* while there is time. Get to know Him so well that there will be no fear in your heart no matter what situation you may be called upon to go into. But there is one thing about it, once you have seen Him with the eyes of your believing heart — and you cannot help but believe in Him when you have *met* Him — once you have seen Him you can never be afraid anymore of anything that your enemy the devil in the form of evil men and arms can do to you."

From that thrilling moment Jeremy went on to tell of the battle into which he presently went, making it so vivid that the audience felt that they were looking into reality. They could even see the smoke and the fire, hear the bursting of the bombs. And for an hour and a half Jerry held that audience, yes, even the gang in the gallery, listening with tense attention, clenched hands, eyes blurring with tears at times. And yet Jeremy was only telling in simple, vivid terms just what had happened, and how through it all there was that majestic Figure by his side, that glory in the air that did not come from fire of battle, the glory of the Lord in the face of Jesus Christ, protecting Jeremy as he went on in the way his duty ordered.

The story of the young man's work in the service was not being told for Jerry's glory; it was openly apparent that every word was spoken for the glory of the Lord Christ, whose he was and whom he served. He kept the Lord ever present as he spoke and never once lost sight of the Central Figure.

As he sat down and dropped his face behind his hand as if in prayer, the minister came to the front. His voice was husky with tenderness as he spoke. "I do not feel that I have fitting words to thank our brother for his wonderful message, or that any words should be added. I am going to ask our speaker's brother, Lieutenant Commander Rodney Graeme to close this meeting with prayer."

And then from that front row tall Rodney Graeme arose and, lifting his face, began to pray. "Our gracious God who hast made Thyself known to us through Thy Son, let

Thy Spirit work in all our hearts tonight to humble us before Thee. Show each of us our sin and guilt. May every one of us receive in the blood abundance of that life which Thou alone canst give, and may we be so yielded that Thy life may be lived through us, to the glory of our Lord Jesus Christ. Amen."

CHAPTER 10

There was something in the timbre of Rodney's voice that stirred old memories in Jessica's mind, and suddenly she sat forward and looked down. She saw his face uplifted; she caught the strong, sweet expression as he prayed.

He was standing so that the full light of the great chandelier was flung upon him, and it brought out a face that was both strong and engaging. In school days he used to lift his head and look up at her and smile, and the strength and courage he had gained amid the terrible surroundings of war had in no way diminished the stunning charm of him. And he *used* to belong to her! And would yet if she hadn't of her own accord given him up for what she had *thought* to be wealth and fame and a great position. What a fool she had been! Would it be worth her while to win him back again? Divorce her elderly husband, whose charm had already vanished for her?

Then suddenly that vibrant voice caught her attention, and she began to listen to the prayer, till it seemed to her that he was praying just for her. Yet of course he didn't know she was in the audience. She never used to be eager to go to church or attend any sort of a meeting. He couldn't suppose that she would be there. Yet, because the old charm of his voice stirred her, she listened to every word and wondered. Why, Rodney never used to pray in meeting. She was sure of that. Oh, his family was religious of course, had family prayers, and went to all the services of their church and all that, but Rodney had never talked about such things.

So Jessica sat in startled wonder and stretched her neck to look down and make sure that it was really Rodney who was praying, although of course his voice was unmistakable.

She listened to that prayer that seemed to be directed at herself. Talking of *sin,* that horrid antiquated word, in which nobody now believed anymore. The prayer was a direct charge of sin, coming straight at her shivering heart. The words stung frightened tears to her eyes. They flowed down her face like rain, and a great anger arose within her. How dare he pray like that? *Sin! She* had committed no sin in returning his ring and marrying another man, and if he was daring to take a chance of her being present and say those things to make her ashamed, he would find himself greatly mistaken. She was no sinner, and he had no right to think of her as such! She would get out of this awful place before the prayer was over, before people could see she was crying.

She arose precipitately and stepped across the people in the pew, making her way silently and swiftly to the aisle. She climbed like a quick-moving shadow to the top of the aisle, dashed down the stairs and out the open front door into the darkness of the street. She fairly ran to the next corner, hailed a taxi, and was borne away out of sight before the notes of the organ proclaimed the service was over.

And when Louella Chatterton looked up with an interested smile, Jessica was not there! She tried in vain to find her among her other friends. She had simply vanished.

Louella bustled down the aisle to the other girls who were standing there talking together, pointing out different acquaintances down on the main floor. They were mostly watching Jeremy and Rodney and the girls of their party, wondering, speculating as to how they came to arrive together. Trying to decide whether they would go down and give old friends greeting and congratulations. "Yes, let's go," whispered Louella. "Tell him what a perfectly beautiful prayer that was!"

"Yes, wasn't it sweet?" exclaimed Bonny Stewart. "I just adore men who can pray like that."

"But where is Jessica?" asked Alida Hopkins. "Did she go down alone to speak to the boys?"

"I don't see her down there anywhere," said Isabelle, leaning over the edge of the gallery to look.

"Oh, she's probably just going down the stairs," said Garetha Sloan. "Come on girls, let's go down. We don't want to get left out of the affair." Garetha started up the aisle followed by the others, and Louella, bringing up the rear breathlessly, said to herself what selfish things young girls were anyway. Never waiting for an old friend, even though she was the one who had brought the news of the meeting to their attention. But she puffed excitedly along after them, stretching her neck to try to find Jessica.

But Jessica was not in sight anywhere.

And now Louella could see the top of Rodney's head towering above the crowd, and she rushed the harder. Jessica of course must have gone straight to him, and she wanted to be in at the meeting herself.

But unfortunately for her plans, it happened that Jeremy, who was just coming down the steps from the platform, caught sight of the pestiferous cousin. Casting a quick glance behind her he saw several of Jessica's girlfriends also coming on and took instant alarm. Quickly he reached his brother's side and said in a low, penetrating whisper, "Watch out, Rod! Louella and her gang are coming."

Rodney cast a hasty glance up the aisle, wondering if that meant Jessica was there also, but he could not see her.

"There's a picture of your friend Carl Browning back in the Sunday school room, they tell me," went on Jeremy in a low tone. "If you need an out, that might be an excuse."

"Thanks, Jerry," said Rodney with a swift, grateful smile, and he went on shaking hands with the old friends who were still swarming up to greet the brothers.

It was several minutes, however, even with all her talent for getting ahead, before Louella and company managed to penetrate the outer edge of the crowd. And there they won from the brothers only a friendly handshake. Even Louella's voluble tongue failed to carry on much of a conversation over the heads of the crowd.

Just as Louella thought the crowd was thinning and they might have a chance to monopolize the heroes, suddenly Rodney leaned over and spoke to the girl from New York who had come in with him. Then without warning the Sanderson crowd followed him out the little door at the side of the platform, into the Sunday school room, closing the door behind them, and not even Jeremy was left where they had all been standing but an instant before.

"Well, upon my word!" said Cousin Louella, indignation and dismay in her voice. "What do you think of that?"

"Well, if you ask me, I'd say that Sanderson crowd doesn't intend to let other people have a chance at them," said Isabelle. "Perhaps we'd better just go to the house. I'm sure the Graemes were *here.* I saw them once, and they've probably gone home and prepared some refreshments. We'll just go and get in on it."

"Well, if you ask *me,* " said Bonny Steward, "I'd say they've all gone to the Sandersons' house. They brought Beryl Sanderson and her friend. They would naturally have to take them home."

They looked at each other dismayed.

"Well," said Cousin Louella, brightening up, "then I think we better go at once to the Graemes' house. We'll be there when they get home. They won't stay at Sandersons' long tonight, with a wounded serviceman in their company, and if we're there when they arrive they'll have to let us speak to them for at least a few minutes."

So they went back to Riverton and drove to the Graeme farm.

The house was all dark. "The family hasn't come home yet, or perhaps Father and Mother Graeme arrived first and retired," suggested Louella. "But that's all right. We can sit in the car till the others arrive."

But where was Jessica? they began to question.

"You don't suppose she's gone with them to Sandersons', do you?" asked Isabelle.

"Mercy no," said Marcella Ashby. "Not to Sandersons'. Don't you remember there was always a feud between Beryl Sanderson and Jessica? At least, I don't know how Beryl felt, but Jessica always despised Beryl because she was rich and everybody admired her."

So they sat in the car under the tall old trees and yawned and waited and discussed what could have become of Jessica.

Finally Isabelle said, "Well, what are we waiting for anyway? It's after midnight, and they won't want to see us when they do come. They'll be tired and want to get to bed. And if it's Jessica we're waiting for, I don't see waiting any longer. She went off and left us without telling us where she was going, and now if she went with them let some of them bring her home, or let her get home the best way she can. I don't see sitting around for her any longer. We've got lives of our own to live without hanging on to the fringes of Jessica's performances. Drive on, Marcella. We'll take Louella to her hotel and then we'll go home. I'm fed up with this act, and if you don't start now I'm getting out and walking."

So they drove away and went disappointedly to bed and to sleep, dreaming over the strange, unexpected meeting on which they had been in attendance. Somehow there was nothing to gloat over in the whole time, and deep in their hearts there remained an uneasy feeling that perhaps there *was* a God and a heaven, and sometime they, too, might get into a situation where they would need both and couldn't find the way. It certainly had been strange to hear merry-hearted Jeremy Graeme talk as if he knew God personally, had met *Him* out there in that awful sky with terrible death menacing below and little hope of ever getting through alive.

And what had become of Jessica? Could it be that she had gone with the rest to the Sandersons'? Could it be that she would even descend to putting on a religious act to subjugate Rodney Graeme again, now after she had married a rich old man?

The clock in the old-fashioned tower of the town hall was striking a solemn one o'clock as the Graemes turned into their driveway. Their voices sounded sweetly happy, full of a quiet joy, as they got out of the car and went into the house. They had all been to the Sandersons' and got well acquainted, old folks and young alike.

Mother Graeme had a moment's talk with Rodney at the foot of the stairs before he went up to bed.

"Son, I cannot tell you how happy I am that you have learned to know God well enough to pray as you did. That prayer of yours was the answer to all my prayers for you while you were away fighting, and tonight has been a blessed time for me. I can truly say I am thankful that the Lord sent you to war, since it has resulted in bringing you to know Him."

Rodney took his mother's soft hands

gently in his and stooped to give her a tender kiss. "Thanks, Mother dear," he said. "I've been wanting to let you know how it is with me, heavenward, but somehow there hasn't been much time yet."

"Dear son!" she breathed. And then in a minute, "And I'm glad that you have found such nice Christian people for friends. I like the Sandersons so very much. And that girl from New York, that one they call Diana. She's so very sweet and dear. It somehow struck me that that was the kind of a girl for a young lad to come home to, after he's been off in peril and death. I wish you had known her years ago."

"Yes, she seems to be a grand girl," said Rodney simply. And then after a minute he added, "You never did quite like Jessica, did you, Moms dear?"

Mother Graeme lifted honest eyes to her son's face. "Well, no, Roddie dear. Not for *you*!"

"And yet you never said a word against it, Moms! You're a brave little woman. Why didn't you?"

"No," said Mother Graeme. "I figured it wasn't for me to decide your life. It was your life and I'd done my best to give you right ideals, and if you couldn't figure out what you wanted to do with your life I didn't think I ought to interfere. So I just prayed and trusted that the Lord would show you what He wanted you to do."

Rodney looked deep into her eyes with a great adoring tenderness.

"He *did*!" said Rodney solemnly. Then added, "Dear Mom, you're wonderful!"

CHAPTER 11

Dumped in front of her hotel by the unfeeling girls who had brought her home from the meeting, Louella unlocked her door and went to her telephone, calling up Jessica.

She was answered after some delay by a very cross voice that sounded strongly of recent tears.

"Oh, my dear! Is that really you?" said Louella excitedly. "I've been so worried. I nearly went wild about you. Whatever became of you? I looked everywhere, and you weren't in sight. What happened to you?"

"Happened to me? Why nothing happened to me. That was the trouble. I was bored to death. I couldn't see staying there any longer and listening to that religious twaddle. They certainly have got it bad!"

"Then you didn't go with the rest to the Sandersons'?"

There was just a fraction of hesitancy

before the answer. "*Sander*sons'? Did they *all* go to the Sandersons'? Heavens, no! I wouldn't be seen drunk with those people. I despise them. *Did* they all go to Sandersons'?"

"Apparently," said Louella in a mortified tone. "That is, they suddenly all disappeared together, out through the back of the church somewhere. I heard them say they were going to see a picture of one of Rodney's buddies in the war, but they went, definitely, and didn't return. Then the janitor began to put out the lights, so we came out and drove over to the Graemes' and waited till now, and yet they hadn't come home."

"So they went to Sandersons', did they? Hm, well! I suppose that means something. But if I couldn't compete with that little washed-out Diana, I definitely would give up. But since I've heard that religious twaddle, I don't know as I'm interested anymore, anyway. I feel that this has been an utterly wasted evening. I really do. I don't know why I ever got the idea of coming back to Riverton. It is always disappointing, don't you think, to go back to the little primitive country hometowns? The things and the people that used to interest you seem very tame after you've been in a city and got used to city ways."

"Well, yes, I suppose they do," said Louella. "Still, you've only been in Chicago, and that's almost a little West, don't you think?" said Louella. "While Riverton is decidedly East, you know. Not too far from New York to run up a little while very often."

"Yes, New York, of course! But it's not what it used to be, I understand."

"Oh, my dear child! Who've you been listening to? You're all wrong, you know. New York is definitely the tops, of course."

"Well, if you want to pose as belonging to the East of course. But say, what did you find out this afternoon? You thought you were going to have something worthwhile to listen to. Did you find out what the boys are going to do as soon as they are out of the service?"

"Well, I found out that they are not going out of the service. That was stated as a fact."

"You don't mean they're going back overseas, Louella?"

"Well, no, not that, but they are to have some very responsible position here at home, I believe, and still be in uniform."

"You don't say!" said Jessica, all interest. "Well, that's quite exciting, isn't it? It might be really worth my while to play up to Rod and get to find out a lot of information I could write up for my editor. I'll have to look into that. You don't know what branch of the service they are to be in?"

"Well, no, they seemed very reluctant to say. Perhaps Margaret Graeme didn't know, but she's not so dumb. She probably was just keeping her mouth shut about it. You know so many of those things are being kept secret these days. It seems ridiculous."

"Why, that sounds really exciting," said Jessica. "I was thinking of seeing if I could get reservations for tomorrow night, but in that case, maybe I'll stay a day or two more and see if I can find out where he is and what he is doing. It might help me in my writing. You know, if I could get into something really new and thrilling I would just be on easy street."

"Well, why don't you stay awhile, and I'll do my best to find out what it's all about."

"All right, Louella, maybe I will. I'll think it over. But make it snappy, won't you? I'll have to be sure there's something worthwhile in all this, for I mustn't waste my time."

"All right, Jessica. I'll do my best and call you up and let you know as soon as I find out anything," said Louella.

Louella cast a quick eye at the clock, wondering if she should venture to telephone Margaret Graeme tonight, make up some plausible excuse for disturbing her, but she decided against it. She would begin the first thing in the morning. That would be better and not get everybody in the family up-in-arms against her, as so often happened. It really wasn't good policy, for one could never find out facts from people who were angry and disturbed at you.

So very early in the morning Louella began. "Is that you, Margaret? Oh, so you did get home at last, didn't you? I was really worried last night. We drove over to congratulate Jerry, and we waited until after midnight, thinking you would surely be home pretty soon, and then after I got home I got to worrying about you lest you might have had an accident on the way home from the meeting and been taken to the hospital. Are you all right?"

"All right? Why certainly! Why shouldn't I be all right, Louella?" said Margaret Graeme with a touch of asperity in her tone.

"Well, you were so late getting home last night, I was really afraid something had happened to you, an accident or something."

"Oh, no! Nothing happened. We were with friends for a while."

"Friends?" said Louella in a tone that asked a question, pointedly if ever a simple word did.

"Yes, Louella. We do have a few friends, you know."

"Oh," said Louella and waited for an explanation, but none came.

"It was kind of you to call, Louella," said Margaret Graeme as the pause grew irksomely extended. "By the way, are you going to the Red Cross meeting this morning? If so, I'll meet you there. It's almost time to start, and I have two or three things to do before I leave."

"Oh, *well,*" said Louella offendedly, "if you haven't time to talk to me, of course I'll get off the line. Good-bye!" And Louella hung up sharply.

It was just about that time that Beryl Sanderson and her guest, Diana Winters, got up from a late breakfast and went slowly into the sunny sitting room, settling down with businesslike knitting bags, and took out their knitting, socks and sweaters for servicemen.

"Now," said Beryl, settling herself comfortably and pulling out her work, "let's have a real old talkfest. We haven't had a minute for one since you came. And first let's begin with yourself. Are you really engaged to that splendid-looking officer I saw when I was at your house? I had a letter from Rose Alters, and she said that it seemed to be a settled thing, although you hadn't announced it yet. Is that so? *Are* you engaged?"

Diana's lovely face flushed a little, and a troubled frown rumpled her delicate brow. She didn't answer at once but spent time straightening out her yarn, which had tangled itself around her needles. Then she said slowly, almost hesitantly, "Well, no, not definitely."

Beryl laughed. "Will you tell me how you would manage to be *in*definitely engaged?"

"Well," Diana said, laughing amusedly, "that is a funny way to put it, isn't it? But the fact is, Bates Hibberd has been hanging around a lot, insisting on an answer, insisting on being at least engaged, and I didn't seem to be ready with an answer yet. In fact, he wanted to be married right away before he has to go overseas, but I just couldn't see that. I don't really know him well enough to be sure I want to spend the rest of my life with him. I told him I had to have more time to decide, and I ran away to you here to think it over. I knew if there was any place in the world where quiet and sanity reigned and one would have a chance to really think, it would be here."

"Thanks, Diana," said Beryl. "I consider that a great compliment. And does that mean that you would rather not be questioned about this matter while you are thinking it over?"

"Oh, no," said Diana. "I shall need your help to make a sane decision."

"Say, that's a pretty big order. I don't know that I'm equal to advise on a subject like that. I know so little about the man."

"Oh, I can easily tell you. He's rich, handsome, has personal charm, he's well educated, and he comes of a good family, one of the best. Several signers of the Declaration are in his family, several noted writers, scientists, a poet, an essayist, even two millionaires and one preacher among his forebears. He's bright and smart, a man full of good ideas and fine morals and manners, a leader in society, and popular everywhere. Before the war he had some thought of going in for politics. But I don't know what he'll do when the war is over. Well, I guess that's about the picture. What do you think I ought to do about it?"

"What's the matter with him?" asked Beryl matter-of-factly.

"Matter with him?" questioned Diana perplexedly. "Why, there is nothing the matter with him. That's it. That's why I can't decide what to do. There is *nothing* whatever the matter with him!"

"Well, then, why don't you marry him?"

"Well, I don't quite understand it, but I'm not just sure I *want* to marry him. Isn't that silly?"

Beryl looked at the other girl keenly. "Do you mean you don't love him?"

There was a long pause before Diana answered. Then she said slowly as if she were considering each word as momentous, "*Love* him? I don't know. No, I don't suppose I really *love* him. But nice people don't really *love* one another before they are married, do they? I mean that emotional, demonstrative kind of love."

"Why, *Diana,* where did you get such an idea as that? Of course nice people love one another. If they do not, why should they ever marry? And if they are not *sure,* beyond a shadow of a doubt, that they love each other with all their hearts, how *could* they ever bear to live intimately with one another? How perfectly terrible to be tied for life to a man you did not love and honor and respect with all your heart!"

"Oh, I could honor and respect him, of course," said Diana. "But I doubt if I could *love* anybody that wasn't really a saint, a real angel of a person, you know."

"But, my dear, doesn't he seem that way to you?"

"No," said Diana thoughtfully, "he doesn't, and I'm sure I *don't* love him, not now. But I supposed I'd grow into loving him if I lived with him."

"You *never would,*" said Beryl out of her deeper teaching from a mother who knew how to instruct her daughter in the intimate things of life. "Don't marry him, dear, not unless the time comes when you feel as if you would die if you could not be with him always. Do you feel that way about him?"

"Mercy no," said Diana. "Sometimes I'm really bored with him, and I wish I could get away."

"Then don't marry him, Diana! That's not love. You'll never be happy with a man who bores you. Say, tell me something: Is there anybody else you love, or ever did love?"

"No, not anyone."

"Are you *sure*?"

"Yes, positive. Oh, there was an ugly little boy in school when I was in the third grade. He was always getting into trouble with the teacher and getting a whipping, and I used to feel sorry for him, and wished I could comfort him. It went on for several years till he left school and moved away somewhere, and I never saw him again. But that wasn't real love, I suppose. Anyway, I was only a child. And the last I ever heard of him was that he died in the war. I haven't thought of him in years, except when I heard of his death. And then there was another boy in high school. I thought I adored him till I heard he had run away with the worst little rat of a girl who lived down in the slums. Oh, Beryl! How can you ever tell about *any*body?"

Beryl looked at her pityingly. "You *can* tell," she said positively. "That is," she added, "if you turn down the man you *aren't* sure you love and just wait till the man God has planned for your life comes along."

"Do you think God does that? *Plan* somebody for your life?"

"Yes," said Beryl with her eyes cast down and her cheeks a little more rosy than usual.

"Well, but suppose you don't like the man God picks out."

"Oh, but you would, I'm sure you would, Diana. God would understand and send the right one."

The visitor gazed at her perplexedly. "Beryl, how long have you thought God cared what became of us?" she asked. "You never used to talk this way."

"Well, perhaps not. But Diana, I was very early taught that God cared about us in every little detail. Perhaps I never paid much attention to it when I was a child, but

I think in the back of my mind I have always *believed* it. But anyway, Diana, I'm quite sure you ought *not* to marry that man whom you do *not* love. Don't tie your life up with someone before God has shown you what you might have."

"Well, perhaps you're right. I don't know, Beryl, but somehow you have impressed me. But tell me, Beryl, are you in love with anyone?"

Beryl looked at her friend with a startled glance, her cheeks grown rosy. "Why, no, Diana, not in love. There is someone I admire very much, but I'm not sure he's ever looked at me. We are just good friends, that's all, but it's very pleasant to have even a good friend that you really like and feel at home with, even for just a few minutes' talk."

"Yes," said Diana thoughtfully. "Do you know, it's odd, but I felt that way, just a little, last night when I was talking to that nice Rodney Graeme. I had a feeling that I would like to know him better and that I could really enjoy his company. But of course he's a perfect stranger and is probably very much engaged to someone else."

"Oh, yes — Rodney. He's nice, isn't he? Those brothers are both nice. They couldn't belong to that family and not be, of course.

But no, I don't think Rod is engaged now. It seems to me I heard he was once engaged to some girl he had known since childhood. But I thought I heard that was all off and she is married to someone else. But now, *there's* a man that a girl could trust. *He* would never bore you."

"But Beryl, I'm afraid a man like that would be too far above me," said Diana. "A man who could pray like that! I shall never forget that prayer. It was like a creed, so brief and yet so very clear and comprehensive."

"Yes, wasn't it?" said Beryl. "My dear, if war does that to all the boys who have been over, what will the world be like when they all get home? We shall have to look to ourselves, or we won't be good enough to company with them even now and then. Do you know I was thinking that while Jeremy was talking. He has grown up so wonderfully. Although he was always a wonderful boy, even in his school days."

"How well did you know him?" asked Diana.

"Not so very well," said Beryl thoughtfully. "I thought he was wonderful in school, but we never saw each other outside of classrooms. I used to often wish I knew him better, but he was not at any social affairs, and neither was I. I don't know how it happened. Of course we lived in separate townships. My father picked out that high school over in Riverdale because it had several quite superior teachers. He had to pay to get me in there, and I had to be driven over every day, which was another separating fact. But I never forgot Jeremy, and I was so delighted when I met him a few days ago and had an opportunity to greet him."

"Well," said the other girl, "if you would ask me some of the questions I've been asking you, I think I could unequivocally answer yes, by all means, let your interest center around that lad. I liked him a lot, too, and what a wonderful message he had. He almost made me believe a lot of things I never was sure about before. Do you know his brother? Is he as nice? I certainly enjoyed him last night, even just sitting by him in a meeting. He made me feel as if I had known him a long time."

"No, I never met him at all until a couple days ago. He was off at college when Jeremy and I were in high school, and then he went right overseas. He enlisted, you know, and he's been a long time away. They tell me he has done a lot of marvelous things in the war and won a lot of honors. You saw the ribbons he was wearing."

"Yes, but you mustn't interest me too much in him," sighed Diana, "for it isn't thinkable that he isn't already taken. I simply must not complicate my life any more than it is already, with any more *impossibles.*" Diana laughed rather bitterly. "Perhaps I don't know what love is about. And anyway, I wouldn't be up to a notable Christian man like that one." Diana sighed almost enviously.

Then they heard Mrs. Sanderson calling them to come upstairs and see some photographs of Beryl's baby days she had promised to show them, and they sped up to answer her call.

"We'll talk again," whispered Diana, and Beryl, with a sweet smile, caught her fingers in her own and squeezed them lovingly.

CHAPTER 12

A couple of days later, Jeremy Graeme called up Beryl Sanderson.

"Hello there! Are you busy today, you and Diana? Because Rod and I have to take quite a drive on some business errands for Dad, and we thought you girls might like to go along. It's business so it's legitimate to use the gas. My sister can't go because she has to be at the hospital all day, but Rod thought it would be great if you girls should want to go. We're packing a lunch, coffee and sandwiches, enough for a regiment, and we thought we'd start right away if it was all right with you two. How about it? Like to go?"

"Oh, wonderful! Wait a minute till I ask Diana."

She was back in less than a minute with a voice full of eagerness. "Yes, Diana thinks it will be wonderful, too. We'll be ready by the time you get here."

The two excited girls hurried up to make ready and to explain to Beryl's mother, who seemed well pleased when she heard who they were going with.

"Take that box of candy your father brought home last night," she said, smiling. "That will help out with the lunch."

And so in a few minutes they were off.

It was a glorious day. One of those perfect days in the opening of spring, and the sunshine had that yellow quality that is so alluring after a long, dreary winter of cold and fog and gloom.

"It almost seems as if the war was over!" said Beryl with a relieved sigh as she settled back in the car. "Here we have real sunshine and flowers and birds and two of the best fighters home from the war."

"Thanks awfully!" said Jeremy with a grin. "Hear that, Rod? Better salute after that." So Rodney stood up and gravely lifted his cap. "It's something fine to have won that title," he said.

That was the beginning of a wonderful day. Not even an April shower to mar its loveliness.

Occasionally Beryl cast a glance over her shoulder at the backseat of the car where Diana and Rodney were sitting, deep in talk, and she couldn't forget the last thing

199

Diana had said to her before they left the house. "Oh, I'm just scared to death," she had breathed as they hurried downstairs.

"Scared?" said Beryl looking surprised. "Why in the world should you be scared?"

"Why, I'm scared to talk to that wonderful man. A man who can pray as he can must be a very holy man indeed, and I'm sure he thinks I'm a little heathen. I won't know what in the world to say to him."

"Nonsense!" Beryl said, laughing. "He's not like that at all. Don't worry. You'll get by all right."

And there sat Diana in the backseat laughing and talking vivaciously. She seemed to be enjoying herself immensely. What's more, the navy man looked very pleased himself. So Beryl cast off her anxieties and gave herself up to the enjoyment of the day and the company of Jeremy, whom she admired greatly.

It was a long, delightful drive to the three towns that were their destination, and every minute of the time was filled with joy for all concerned. Even the three stops were interesting. The first was at an office, where they could see Jerry through the window, spreading out papers on the desk, pointing out certain items to be noticed, waiting courteously for the signature, and then talking genially with the man they had come to see. He was evidently being asked questions concerning his war service overseas, for the stranger pointed to his decorations, and Jerry was laughingly explaining then perhaps telling a few words of what he had been through.

The next stop was a small grocery where the proprietor came out to meet them, arguing about some matters in the papers before he glumly took Jerry in and signed.

The third was a large old farmhouse where a very old man sat on the porch with a big old-fashioned gray shawl over his knees and a gray felt hat pulled down to shade his eyes. They could hear the conversation at this stop, a learned discussion of roads and why this protest was necessary.

Jerry got away at last with only a brief sketch of his experiences in service and climbed back to his seat in the car with a sigh of relief.

"There, that's that!" he said. "Now we can start to have fun."

"But it's all been fun," said Beryl.

"It certainly has," said Diana with shining eyes, and Beryl settled back, content that her guest was enjoying herself.

"Now," said Jeremy, "how about lunch? I'm hungry as three bears. What about the rest of you?"

"There couldn't be a better suggestion," said Rodney. "I'm always hungry now."

"That sounds wonderful!" said the girls in chorus.

So Jeremy turned down a dirt road leading into the woods, and presently they were winding among hemlocks and pines and maples, with bird songs overhead and chattering squirrels skittering from limb to limb on the trees.

The lunch was ample with many surprises in the shape of delightful sandwiches and little frosted cakes, and berries, olives, and pickles, and cheese and jellies. There just seemed nothing that could have been thought of that had been forgotten, including plenty of hot coffee in the Thermos bottles. They ate it in a leisurely way, with many a joke and a laugh. Beryl twinkled her eyes at Diana as if to remind her of her fear that these young men would be too grave for her light-minded self.

It was after they had finished, washed the dishes in a convenient little brook, and packed away all that was left in the basket that Rodney suggested a walk.

They locked the car, left it in a nest of trees, and started off for a stroll.

"There are some pretty spots around these

woods," said Rodney as he and Diana went along. "Some of my old haunts of bygone years, if they haven't been destroyed during my absence. If you'd like to see them, this way," and he parted the branches and showed her a hidden path that a stranger would scarcely discern.

Diana stepped into the opening he made for her, and Rodney turned his head before he followed her, and called back to the others, "So long! Be back in an hour or two!" and grinned as the answer came back, "Okay! See you subsea."

It seemed to Diana as they penetrated into the green depths of that lovely woods that she had never seen such beautiful, quiet remoteness.

Rodney made a delightful escort. He found pleasant walking for her feet, and when they came to rest for a while, he arranged a seat from hemlock branches. When they were seated in the beautiful stillness he finally said, looking into the greenness above him, where little glimpses of sunlit blue sky were visible, "Isn't this great? It seems as if this must be one of the places in which God delights, doesn't it? It seems as if He were here with us. Or don't you feel that way?"

Diana looked up fearsomely and half shuddered. "Oh," she said in a little frightened tone, "I don't know much about God. But you" — she paused and gave a shy look toward the young man — "you seem to know Him so intimately." Her tone was almost envious.

Rodney looked down and smiled. "Yes, I do," he said pleasantly, as if he were owning to an earthly friendship, "but no better than you may know Him, too, if you want to. I was brought up to know all *about* God when I was a child, but I didn't get to *know* God until I met Him out in the air over enemy fire."

"Oh!" said Diana. "Tell me about it, please, if you don't mind."

Rodney smiled.

"No, I don't mind. I love to talk about my Lord. Since I've met Him and know Him so well, it gives me great delight to talk about my Lord."

And so he began to tell the thrilling story of how he started out in his own strength to fight the enemy and began to realize that death was waiting just ahead for him, and perhaps the end of things down here. And then as he drew nearer and nearer to his doom, he heard the Lord calling to him through all the thunder of shells and planes. And the words He called were the same words he could remember his father reading at family worship, those mornings away back home when he was wishing the morning prayers would be over and he might be free to go to his work or his play. They were words that God spoke: "Fear thou not; for I am with thee: be not dismayed; for I am thy God: I will strengthen thee; yea, I will help thee; yea I will uphold thee with the right hand of my righteousness."

"It reminded me," went on Rodney, "of the time when I was a little kid and my dad sent me out in the dark to get something I had left out there, and I was afraid. I was just a little kid, you know, and Dad came and took my hand, and said, 'Don't be afraid, Roddie. I'll go with you. I'll help you.' It was just like that. It was as if I heard Him call me. 'Rod! I'm here. I'm here to go with you!'

"And over and over again when I grew fearful, there was my Lord beside me. Sometimes going before me, right into battle, and the fire whistling all around me, but none of it touched me. I was safe because He was there!

"It happened again and again and always when I had to go on some fearful mission, He was there with me. It was almost as if I could look up to the clouds above me, and say, 'Come, Lord, are You going with me this time? I'm not afraid if You'll stay by!' And that's how I came through. Do you wonder that I feel I know Him, that I can talk with Him as if a man were talking with his friend? He's my friend!"

There were tears on Diana's cheeks as he was telling this. "Oh, that is wonderful!" she said. "But does one have to go through death to know Him?"

"No, oh no! Not if you will take Him without having to be shown *that* way."

"But you were taught when you were little. You sort of grew up knowing Him, didn't you?" There was almost a hunger in Diana's tone.

"Yes, I knew *about* Him. I knew His history, the story of His life and death, and that it was for me, but I never took it to my heart until death drew near, and I had to fly for refuge. Many times at home when I was young I might have got to know Him and didn't. I just couldn't take time. I knew it was all true, but I'd never looked into His face before. Not until He took me up there in the sky alone with Himself, and menacing death was just below and all around. Then I looked up, and I saw Him. But that is something that cannot be described. You have to see Him yourself to understand. You have to know Him."

"Oh!" said the girl disappointedly. "Then I'm afraid there is little likelihood that I could ever understand. I can't go overseas and get into combat."

Rodney looked at her quickly. "No, you're wrong," he said. "You don't have to go overseas to see Him. I had every chance to know Him before I went into death, but I was just too much interested in my own affairs and in the world and worldly people to look up. I just wouldn't look at Him. But you, you would like to see Him? If you long to find Him, He will come to you. The only condition is that you believe. That is, believe that He took your sin and took your place and suffered your death penalty. Take Him for your personal Savior, that is. Are you willing to do that?"

"Why, yes. I could believe because I have seen the faith in your face. I have heard it in your words and in your wonderful prayer. Is that the right kind of belief? Because I don't really know much about Him, only the set stories that churches talk about, and I never paid much attention to them before. But I'd like to know Him now."

"That's great!" said Rodney with a joyful ring in his voice. "Shall we tell Him so?"

They were sitting on a smooth bank of lovely moss, under a great tree. The young man bowed his head, and Diana, awed at what might be coming, almost frightened again, bowed hers.

"Lord Jesus," said Rodney in his quiet conversational tone, "I'm bringing this little girl to You because she wants to know You and says she will take You for her Savior. Please show her how You love her, how she needs You, and help her to understand what You have done for her. May she now be born again, and will You let her see You as You are and get to really know You and love to serve You in her daily life?

"And now will You listen to her while she tells You what is in her heart? Thank You, my Father."

There was a long pause in the still greenness of the woods, while a thrush trilled out some high sweet notes of praise, and then Diana's little frightened voice trembled on the air. "Dear God, I want to be saved. I want to know You, as Rodney does. Won't You please show me how? I do believe, as far as I understand."

Into the silence that followed this brief prayer came Rodney's ringing "Amen!" And after a moment of silence, he reached over and took her hand in a strong, firm clasp.

"Welcome into the family, little sister!" he said tenderly. She looked up into his eyes, and her own were filled with tears of joy, and there was a smile on her lips.

They lingered for some time in the quiet retreat, talking over what the Christian life meant, what it was going to mean to her, and to him now that he had come back to his own country and had to live with a world that hadn't been to war and hadn't met Christ in the clouds above death.

Then suddenly Rodney looked at his watch. "Say, our two hours are more than up! What do you know about that? How fast time can go in a place like this, the two of us alone with God."

Diana looked up at him, her eyes full of gratitude. "I shall never forget it," she said. "It's been the most wonderful two hours of my life."

Rodney smiled down at her. "I'm glad," he said. "And I'm greatly glad that you know my Lord. For now, you see, we have much in common. I had begun to think there were no Christian girls except my sister in the world. I'm awfully delighted that I know you."

"And if I hadn't met you," said Diana fervently in a soft little voice, "I probably never would have been saved."

"I don't know about that," said Rodney with a smiling acknowledgment of her words as he caught her hand and pressed it gently. "I'm glad to have had the privilege of leading you to know my Savior, but, you know, the Lord isn't dependent on my services for bringing souls to know Him. He has other servants who know and love Him as well as I do."

"Yes? But I'm glad He sent you."

"Yes, so am I," he said, and this time he caught her hand again and drew it within his arm, helping her over the rough ground as they slowly made their way back toward the rendezvous.

And at that, they got back to the car before the other two wanderers had come yet and, climbing into it, resumed their talk.

"How much longer are you going to be in this vicinity?" asked Diana suddenly. "I do so wish it would be long enough for me to ask a lot of questions that I know will come to me when I get by myself and try to read the Bible alone. You're supposed to read the Bible, aren't you, when you are a saved person?"

"It's the best way," Rodney answered with a smile. "Prayer and Bible reading are the great helps to knowing God and living as He would like to have you live."

"Yes, well, I never could make anything out of the Bible. I tried several times to read it by myself, and it didn't mean a thing. Then someone told me it was only tradition and wasn't meant to be read literally. Is that so?"

Rodney grinned. "That's what unbelievers tell you, and many college professors, when they even mention it at all. But there are wonderful Bible schools, of course, in almost every region. I certainly would enjoy introducing you to Bible study if it might be my privilege. I'm not a Bible teacher, and only know my Bible as my mother taught me long ago when I wasn't paying much attention, and as the Lord has taught me to live it since I met Him. I'll be pleased to tell you what I know while we are together, but there is a better teacher than I am, one whom it is every Christian's privilege to study under, the Holy Spirit. Christ promised He would come and 'guide you into all truth.' Reading your Bible with the help of the Holy Spirit makes all the difference in the world. Even with no earthly teacher, men have found the way to understand. But to answer your question, I'm not sure just how long I can stay here. I may get orders to report in Washington soon, or at the hospital for examination."

"Oh, will you have to go back overseas?"

"That isn't settled definitely yet. Perhaps

211

not, and then again, perhaps yes. I ought to know in a short time. In any case, I'm glad I found you. I shall always feel glad. And I wonder if I may have the privilege of getting you a Bible? Or have you one already that is precious to you?"

"Oh, no," laughed Diana. "Not precious. I have a tiny red leather one with gold lettering on the back and very fine print, which I won in the primary class in Sunday school when I was five years old for the perfect attendance for one year. But I have never even tried to read it. Only its red cover ever appealed to me. But I shall treasure a Bible that you gave me, because you are the one who helped me get acquainted with Jesus Christ."

"Thank you," he said. "I am proud to have you feel that way. And I shall always remember this day, even if orders come to move on at once. I should never forget the sweet converse we have had today. But there! Look ahead! Isn't that my dallying brother and your friend, Beryl? I guess our talk is at an end for the time. But, I'm going to be praying for you. Do you mind?"

"Oh, *will* you? That will be wonderful! And I'll pray for you, too," Diana said shyly, "though I don't suppose my prayers will do you much good, I'm so new at it."

"Thank you. Yes, they will. The Lord is ready to answer even the newest of His children." The look he gave her seemed afterward as she remembered it to be almost like a caress, or maybe a better word would be *blessing,* she decided as she thought it over.

CHAPTER 13

That was the beginning of ten days of delightful fellowship between the four young people, with sometimes the addition of Kathie and her special army chaplain, John Brooks. They all fit together beautifully and had many grand rides and walks and picnics and meetings together. And then there was the day that they planned to run down to the shore for a few hours for a dip in salt water. They were to go down on the train, and they had taken special pains to keep Cousin Louella from knowing their plans, lest she might want to go along.

For Jessica was still in town, hobnobbing with Louella constantly and very subtle in her methods. They thought they had been very clever in their plans, but when they were waiting for their train at the station, Jessica and Louella came walking down the platform together. They were obviously not planning to take the train, for they were wearing house dresses and no hats. It was of course quite early in the morning, and Jessica had come out to hunt up Louella and ask if there was any news of what the young naval officers were going to do. They had walked together down to the station to mail an important letter Jessica had just written her husband — demanding money — on the early train, and there they were waiting for the train to come in.

"Can you beat that?" said Jeremy under his breath as the two came in sight. "Such luck! Come on around the other end of the station, over in the edge of the meadow, as if we were picking violets."

Rodney seized Diana's arm and propelled her swiftly out of sight behind a lilac bush. And the two conspirators walked on slowly down the platform, without seeing them, while the travelers scuttled down to the other end of the station and bore up against the wall, with a kindly shrub sheltering them.

"Isn't this too ridiculous!" Kathie said with a giggle. "I hate to be always on the sly."

"How could you help it with a cousin such as we possess?" Jeremy said, grinning. "She's got eyes like a gimlet that would go through a steel helmet, and a tongue that

215

can talk faster telling gossip than an electric fan. I hate to say it about anyone who is somewhat related to my revered father, even if only by marriage, but it is the truth. And as for that other person, we certainly want no part with her. She's deadly."

"Yes," said Beryl sympathetically, "I always did dread it when she came around. But wasn't she once pretty intimate with your brother?"

"Oh yes, she tried to be when Rod was a mere kid, but that's all off. She's married now. Married some rich old guy and took herself out of the picture for a while, though it looks as though she's trying to get in the spotlight again, but I guess she won't make it. Rod is pretty fed up with her. She isn't exactly his kind, you know. Listen! There comes the train now. Skim across behind the shrubbery to the last car. The enemy is up front mailing a letter."

When they were safely seated in the train, Jeremy returned to the subject.

"I wondered," said Beryl, "I never could feel quite comfortable in her company. She always managed to say something catty. Well, that's not the way to talk about a former classmate, is it? And it certainly isn't the kind of thing your Christian principles advocate."

"No," said Jeremy with a wry grin, "it isn't. But it always makes me furious to see that girl barge into the scene, just to annoy my brother! Well, maybe there's some reason why he needed this, so I guess we better take it smiling, keep our eyes on the Lord, and let Him work it out. It's curious sometimes, to watch how He does that, and remember that He is both omniscient and omnipotent. He knows all and has power to do anything that needs doing."

"I guess you're right, Jeremy. But you didn't always feel this way about Christian things, did you? I remember thinking you were a keen scholar, but I did not know you were interested in religious things. Oh I knew you were upright and all that, but nobody ever told me you went to church much or cared for things like that."

Jeremy answered her soberly, after a moment's pause. "Well, I always went to church. It was the rule of our house. And I always believed the main things about the Bible that I was taught, but I didn't waste much time over doctrines and things like that till I really knew the Lord. It was probably my mother's prayers that followed me and kept me, laid me open to meet the Lord when I got frightened and didn't know where to turn."

"Oh," said Beryl, "I suppose any of us might feel that way if we were suddenly confronted by death. But isn't it odd we feel so easy about things like that when we all know everybody has to die, and it may come suddenly to any of us."

"Yes," said Jeremy, "it is. And there's another strange thing, and that is how much we miss while living an indifferent life like that. You know I've never been so happy in my life as I have been since I found the Lord and was sure that I knew Him forever!"

She looked at him wistfully. "You know, Jeremy, you're rather wonderful."

"Oh, no," said Jerry, shaking a decided head. "I'm not wonderful at all. I've just got my eyes open suddenly. Do you know I found myself described wonderfully in the Bible the other day when I was reading about that fool guy Balaam, the fellow who had the wonderful privilege of being God's prophet and didn't know any better than to use his great gift of divination for his own glory and personal aggrandizement. And then after he had missed a lot of chances to make good in God's sight, God had to send a poor old donkey and an angel to teach him. He knew what God wanted, but he wanted to serve himself. He hedged and hedged trying to get God to give in, until the Lord finally got his eyes open, and then he saw. And after that he called himself the man 'whose eyes are open.' That's me, now, I hope. I'm the man whose eyes are open, opened by the Lord, and I pray that no more I shall go around equivocating, and viewing questions from this mountain peak and that one, trying to get God to agree with me. I pray that I may always be the man 'whose eyes are open' to what God wants me to do."

"Oh, Jeremy! Is that what the story about Balaam and the ass means? I always wondered why that was put in the Bible."

Just then two seats in front of them were vacated, and the young people moved together. Then they had a jolly time and almost forgot for a while that there was a war on the other side of the world and the servicemen might have to return to it. The day was bright and the water just right. By the end of the day all felt rested and had got to know one another wonderfully well.

Back at Riverton there was gloom.

"Whatever becomes of those two navy men?" asked Jessica impatiently. "They never seem to be anywhere, and I really can't waste my time hanging around for them. I've got an order for some writing, but I simply must have a few facts, and I'm dead sure I can get better ones if I could just once get Rod talking. I always used to be able to do that in the old days, and if I had a good chance at him all by himself I'm sure I could again. You promised to make this possible, you know, Louella. And you haven't even found out yet what service those boys are likely to be called into when their leave is up. By the way, isn't it almost up?"

"Why, yes, I'm sure it is," said Louella. "Their mother was sighing the other day that she might soon have to be saying good-bye to them again, for they were sure to be going away somewhere."

"Well, Louella, I've promised my husband to get some really authentic news from my old friends who have been all sorts of places and will be able to tell me lots of stories about the enemy and their plans."

Then Louella, interestedly said, "Why that sounds wonderful, Jessica. It sounds like your old self, and I'm sure you are on your way to fame. But don't get impatient, dear. I'm doing my best for you. I'm almost sure I'm on the right track. I was over at the house yesterday morning, and I happened to mention a phrase or two I had heard, and I was sure Margaret Graeme pricked up her ears and gave a swift look toward

Kathie. I didn't say anything more about it just then, because I didn't want them to know I was getting on to any of their secrets, for then I know from past experience that they would shut right up. But I'll be mentioning it again, and then I expect to have a more enlightening report to give you."

"What were the phrases you mentioned, Louella? You haven't forgotten them already, have you?"

"Why of course not. Did you ever hear of a place in the city called Bankers' Security, Jessica? I think it's a whole building somewhere. But I wasn't quite sure what it had to do with the other phrase."

"How aggravating you are, Louella! What was the other phrase? How can I make head or tail out of the things you say if you can't be a little bit more explicit in telling me?"

"Now, Jessica, that's very rude of you. I don't know at all why I take all this bother for you when you are so cross and unpleasant about it."

"Oh, well, Louella, you're very trying. But what was the other phrase?"

"Well, the other phrase was Naval Intelligence. Does that mean anything at all to you? And I'm quite sure it's something very secret, for the way they guard their looks shows that they are really afraid I'll find out something."

"Well, yes, Naval Intelligence might be a branch that would interest me very much if I could really get at any of their vital matters. Find out if that is the branch they are really going to be in, won't you, and how soon they start? Gracious! I wonder how they got into that, if they really did. Well, get a hustle on and see what you can find out."

Therefore, Louella took her way to the Graeme house the next morning. She arrived not more than ten minutes after the young people had left for the day, and Margaret Graeme gave thanks silently that she had not come sooner.

"Well," said Louella, settling down in the most comfortable chair and getting out her crocheting, a delicate little nothing of pastel shades of silk, or near-silk, designed eventually to hold sachet powder and figure as an asset to handkerchiefs, "what's new, Margaret? Don't tell me the boys aren't up yet. They'll be getting lazy, and that won't be a help when they get back into service. And of course you are keeping their breakfast hot for them. You always did spoil your children terribly, Margaret, and I'm sure you'll be sorry for it yet. You can't get by without such things catching up with you."

"Yes?" said Margaret Graeme lifting a smile to her unpleasant cousin. "And what do you think is going to catch up with me, Louella?"

"Why, your pampering of your children. It will surely bring sorrow to you in some way. You'll see."

Margaret Graeme laughed lightly. "And how am I pampering my children now?"

"Why, letting them lie in bed a lovely peppy morning like this and then cooking them a separate breakfast when they choose to get up."

"Oh," said Margaret Graeme, "but my boys are not lying in bed. They were up an hour ago and had their breakfast and milked the cows and curried the horse, and now they are off on their own business."

"Oh, *really,* Margaret? How did you manage that? Why, that's wonderful! But where have they gone? Then it's true, isn't it, what I heard last night? They are in the Naval Intelligence Service, aren't they? I was so hoping it would be that, for that would keep them at home, wouldn't it? And I know it would so break your heart to have them go back overseas again and go on any more of these terrible 'missions' as they call them, out to bomb human beings. It seems a terrible misnomer to call them by the name of missions. I supposed missions were for Christianizing heathen, not killing them."

Suddenly Margaret Graeme was overcome by merriment, and she burst into a bubble of laughter.

But Louella, who had never quite understood her cousin-in-law's laughter, turned an offended eye to look at her. "Well, really, Margaret, is that a new way you have acquired to escape answering my question? Laughter?"

Margaret Graeme sobered down till only her sweet eyes bore the merry amusement. "Question, Louella? Did you ask a question?"

"I certainly did. I asked you if it was true that your sons are being assigned to the Naval Intelligence Service. I was told so last night by someone who certainly *ought* to know the truth." Louella reconciled this statement with the truth and her conscience by her emphasis on the word *ought.*

"Oh, is that so?" said Margaret Graeme gravely. "Well, I wouldn't know about that," she said pleasantly. "You see, no one has told me anything about that. If it is so, I suppose it will come to light in due time. If the boys have heard any such thing they may have kept it to themselves that I might not be disturbed. They have always been thoughtful of me that way. But I doubt if any order of any sort has come through for them yet. I am sure I should have known it if there were anything important soon. Of course ultimately, there will be something. We are expecting that. But we do not know what form it will take, yet. And now, Louella, tell me about your plans. You told me a week ago that you were obliged to hurry right home because an important deal was likely to come. Did it come through all right?"

"Oh," said Louella, with a confused look. "Why, no — yes — that is, not yet. There was an unexpected holdup. The people who were thinking of buying my house felt that they first had to sell the one they were occupying, and I thought it best to wait here for their decision."

"Yes? Well I should think that might be very wise. A bird in the hand is worth two in the bush, of course." Margaret Graeme's voice was steady and her lips did not twitch, but there were little lights twinkling in her eyes. She was used to Louella's boasting and knew pretty well that Louella's property in the West was a mere mirage that had faded long ago into a hopeless mortgage foreclosure, but why let Louella suspect that she knew it? There were unpleasant points

of difference without adding an unnecessary one. Margaret Graeme was used to
looking upon these sessions with Louella as
a sort of game in which the winner was the
one who could keep the question going back
and forth over the net without answering it
out and out. Thus she made it interesting
rather than a bore, and always kept her
temper. Though Louella, not having a keen
sense of humor, kept dropping stitches in
hers.

Then Margaret Graeme took pity on her.
"How would you like to go out on the
porch, Louella? It's a glorious morning, the
sun so bright and the perfume of the flowers beginning to scent the air. I just love
these early spring mornings."

"Oh, yes, they're well enough, if it's not
too chilly. I never like to get a cold in the
spring. It's so apt to linger all summer and
keep one's nose looking red and one's eyes
full of tears. But perhaps if you can lend me
a shawl or a sweater . . ."

"Why, of course, I have shawls and sweaters, but if you are afraid, perhaps we'd better stay right here. Just move your chair over
by the window and get a little more light on
your work. How pretty that is, what you are
making. Is it to be a handkerchief?"

"No, a sachet for a dear old lady at the

hotel. She does admire my work so much."

"How sweet of you!" said Margaret. "I often wish I had leisure to do nice things like that for people, but somehow the days are not half long enough for all I have to do."

"Well, I say you do too much! You ought not to pamper your daughter. You make all her clothes, don't you? And she's always dressed like a doll. You would have plenty of time for anything you want to do if Kathie made her own clothes. When a girl gets to her age, she ought to understand the art of sewing thoroughly."

"Oh, she does," said Kathie's mother with a loving smile. "She's made all her own clothes since she was in high school and often has made some of mine. She seems to be very gifted in that way."

"Oh, really? You don't mean *all* her own clothes, do you? I'm sure she never could have managed that lovely suit she was wearing last Sunday night. It fit too perfectly to be homemade."

"Yes, she made that last spring. It does fit nicely, doesn't it? And she takes such good care of her clothes that it's always well worth her while to get good material. After all, it does make a lot of difference if you have good material to work with."

"Well, I suppose it does, but, after all, if you encourage a young girl to spend a lot on her clothes what kind of wife will she make for some of these poor soldiers when they come home?"

"I trust that Kathie will have good sense about spending her money. But, after all, she is making a very fair wage in her hospital work, and I think she will know how to spend what she has worked for."

"Well, you always think your children are perfection, Margaret, don't you? But if she works so hard and makes her clothes besides, how will she ever get out to know any young men? You know she might not get married at all. Then what would you say?"

"Well, I think I could bear even that, Louella, for then I should have my girl with me a little longer," Kathie's mother said with a smile.

"Margaret! You wouldn't want your only daughter to be an old maid, surely!"

"Why not, Louella? There are worse fates. But unfortunately for your theory, Kathie isn't likely to be unmarried. She is already engaged to a delightful young man whom we all honor and love."

"Margaret! You don't mean it? When did this happen? And why wasn't I told?"

"Well, it happened in the winter sometime.

The last time he had a leave of absence before he went overseas. He is a chaplain in the army, under some special orders. He was just back again last week for three days, and he's likely to be back again next week for three days before he goes again."

"Oh, Margaret, isn't that too delicious? Somehow I thought that would never happen to Kathie, she's so quiet and unworldly."

"Oh, do you think all men prefer noisy, worldly women?"

"Well, no, I suppose not. Not if they know they are good cooks."

"Mercy!" said Margaret Graeme with an amused laugh. "What an unpleasant idea of marriage you must have!"

"Why no, I haven't really, Margaret, only naturally a man would take some account of what he was getting into when he set out to get married, and if a girl wasn't stunningly pretty or a smart dresser or a good cook and housekeeper, why naturally he wouldn't let himself get crazy about her. Oh of course, Kathie is fairly good-looking, not stunningly pretty as Jessica was, you know —"

"There are differences of opinion, you know, about looks. I certainly never felt that

Jessica was even pretty, certainly not beautiful."

"How funny, Margaret. You certainly are strange. I always thought Jessica was a raving beauty, but your ideas and mine never did jibe. However, as I was saying, I never did think Kathie had enough initiative to go out and get herself a man."

"I should hope not!" said Margaret fervently. "Of all disgusting things, the worst I think is a girl who lowers herself enough to let it be seen that she is out to try to *catch* a man. That isn't a girl's place, Louella, to go out after a man. If the man wants her, it is his place to seek her."

"Oh, Margaret Graeme, you are so far behind the times you don't understand that no man in these days would ever go out after *any* girl unless she first courted him. Certainly not one as quiet as Kathie. I used to think it was hopeless for Kathie ever to expect to get married."

Margaret Graeme only smiled. "Well, I'm glad my daughter isn't the type to go out after a man. Better a thousand times that she go unmarried than that she would demean herself by setting out after a man. What kind of a marriage would that make? There would be no happiness at all where the girl had lowered herself that way."

"Oh, Margaret! You certainly are old-fashioned! But that isn't the way the world looks at that question today. The girls all understand that they must do all they can to get them a man before somebody else gets him, and I'm sure Kathie is to be congratulated on getting one that you think is so fine, but remember, after she's got him she must keep him, and she'll never do it by being such a demure little thing as you've brought her up to be. She simply can't compete with the girls of today."

"I'm afraid I wouldn't want her to do that, Louella. A happy marriage is not built along such lines, and there is nothing worse than an unhappy marriage."

"Oh no, you're mistaken, Margaret, not in these days. There is always divorce now, and it is so common today one is not outlawed by it. In fact, divorcées are very attractive to men. They really have the advantage of young girls in many cases."

"Well, Louella, divorce is something we do not consider in our family. In fact, I don't think many Christians do. We just don't believe in it, you know."

"Oh! *Christ*ians!" said Louella with a shrug and a sneer. "Of course, I forgot how narrow-minded you are. By the way, Margaret, who is that coming up your front

231

walk? Isn't that a telegraph boy? He's on a bicycle. Yes, I'm sure it is. He has brass buttons on his cap. Would you like me to go to the door for you? Then you won't have to disturb your knitting."

"No, thank you, Louella," said Margaret Graeme gently. "I don't disturb so easily."

"Well, I'm sure I only offered to help you," said Louella offendedly.

Quietly, without replying, Margaret Graeme laid her knitting down and went to the front door. She came back immediately with the telegram in her hand and stepped into the kitchen to give an order to Hetty, and then came back, standing the telegram up on the mantel by the clock, where Louella tried in vain to read the name it bore.

"Well," said Louella at last, impatiently, "what was it?"

"A telegram. You were right, Louella, it was the telegraph boy."

"But what was the telegram? How really trying you are, Margaret! I've just been quivering to know what has happened. Was it from Washington? I'm dying to know what the boys' orders are."

"Oh! Why, Louella, the telegram was not for me, so of course I do not know what it was about."

"But is was for some member of your family, wasn't it? Didn't you open it? Aren't you *going* to open it and find out?"

"Certainly not, Louella. I don't open other people's telegrams. What do you think I am? It is a private message, and I would not think of opening it."

"But — your own family, Margaret. How ridiculous! If it's for some of your children, or even your husband, surely you have a right to find out about it. It might be something quite important that ought to be attended to at once."

"No," said the mother. "It would not be my business to open it, unless I had been told to open it and find out and send them word."

"How perfectly silly you are. I'm sure I wouldn't like to live with your conscience. Well, then suppose *I* open it for you, and if anybody finds fault you can blame it on me."

"No!" said Margaret with finality. "The telegram is not ours, and you will *not* open it."

"Well, I'm sure I never heard of anything so silly! Suppose we dampen it and pry it open and find out if it is anything important and then seal it up again. I used to be quite expert at that sort of thing when I was a girl."

"No," said Margaret firmly, "we do not do underhanded things like that in this house. Let's forget the telegram, Louella, and suppose you show me how to make that crochet stitch you told me about the other day. Here is some pink wool. Is this the kind of needle you use, or would you rather a larger one?"

And so for the time being the subject was changed, but Louella kept turning wistful eyes toward the mantel shelf where the yellow envelope stood. Twice she tried strategy, inventing reasons for her hostess to go into the kitchen and see who was at the back door, after she had heard Hetty go upstairs, so she would have an opportunity to get nearer to the address on that envelope. She was consumed with a desire to know whose name it bore. But Margaret Graeme was canny and could explain every noise at the back door and did not leave her trying guest alone with that letter. At last Louella got discouraged and decided that it was high time for her to get home and telephone Jessica if she expected to catch her before she went out for the afternoon. But she felt that she had at least *some* progress to report. And then of course she was never at a loss for filling in from her prolific imagination what facts did not give her. And there was that mysterious telegram on the mantel for a start.

And so at last Louella departed. Making excuse, however, to return to search the floor and her chair for a possible dropped handkerchief she was sure she had with her when she came. And during her careful search she had opportunity to see that the telegram was still on the mantel, and Margaret Graeme had been as good as her word and had not taken opportunity to open the envelope as soon as she had left. That was what she had hoped to catch her doing, and then surely she might be able to discover to whom it had been sent.

But Margaret was sitting there serenely where she had left her, still thoughtfully, almost wearily, knitting. Louella always did make her very weary. Her mind had to be so keenly on the alert to avert disasters of one sort and another, especially the leaking out of private family matters that Louella ached to discover and broadcast.

So at last Louella was gone, and Margaret might draw a free breath. She walked to the window to see her going down the hill toward her hotel — just to make sure she would not be returning within the minute.

Rodney came in a little while later and read his telegram. "Has Chatty been here yet today, Mom?" he asked as he cast his eye about the room and noted Louella's favorite chair brought in from the other room and placed to good advantage for conversation.

"Chatty" was the nickname given the unloved cousin in derision. The mother smiled. "Why yes, how did you know?"

"Isn't that her ball of yarn under the chair and a handkerchief with red cherries around the border? They could belong to none other than our garrulous relative." He grinned, and the mother smiled sympathetically back again.

"Well, Mom, that telegram is my bid to come down to Washington next week and broadcast, but don't tell her, in case she comes back to find out what it was."

"Oh no, of course not," said the mother with a twinkle. "I've already had my troubles to keep her from opening the envelope and discovering for herself what it was."

"Brave woman. I'll pin a medal on you for that," said the boy, stopping over and planting a kiss on his mother's smiling lips.

Jeremy stood at one side grinning and watching them. "What do you suppose she wants to know for?" he asked. "Is she just curious, or did she have some ulterior motive?"

"I'm sure it would have been ulterior, whatever the reason," said Rodney with a wry grin.

"Well, if you ask me, Rod," said Jeremy, "*I* think she was gathering fodder to feed to your old flame, Jessica."

"*What?*" said Rodney, looking at his brother sharply. "What makes you say that? Have you got some information you haven't told me about?"

"Not definitely, but I know the habit of the woman — or perhaps I should say *women.* What do you suppose your former fiancée is hanging around here all this time for, anyway? I understood she was only here for a day or two, didn't you?"

"I didn't understand anything about it," grouched Rodney. "I wasn't interested."

Afterward, upstairs in their room together, Jeremy said loftily, "Well, if I might advise, I should say it might be to your advantage to find out what's going on, brother. You know that baby isn't one who ever does anything without reason, and it's just as well to find out and take the sting out of it before she gets in any of her deadly work."

"Hm!" said Rodney thoughtfully. "Perhaps you're right. I'll look into it. But you understand, Jerry, I don't want to be connected with Jessica in *any* way. I'll look into it, but it will have to be through you or somebody else. I simply *will not* have anything more to do with that double-crossing, slippery little sneak. She is not to be trusted for an instant, and I want nothing more to do with her. Not even to stop her connivances. However, I'll take some means to let her understand that it is of no use to try anything more with me, and I feel it in my soul she's plotting something of that sort and is trying her best to make that silly cousin of ours help her get it across."

"Well," said Jerry, "I'm glad you see that much. I certainly am. I was afraid there one time you were going to feel sorry for the poor little brat, the way you used to do sometimes when you caught her in one of her flirtations in high school, and then she turned weepy on you and you made up with her."

"Yes, I know," said Rodney with his brow in a heavy frown. "I was a fool then, but I've found it out now. I didn't spend all those days and nights up in the sky with nobody but God and the enemy around for nothing. I found out a lot of things about myself, even besides my sins. But Jerry, you were only a little kid in those high school days, just in the freshman class. How did you know anything about all that?"

"What do you think I was? Dumb? I reckon I saw a whole lot that you didn't even know. I saw, and I heard, and I watched, and I grew up watching. And maybe I did worry a lot about my big brother. For I didn't trust that sleek hypocrite of a girl, not one little bit. I saw and heard a lot more than you thought I would, and I'm not meaning mebbe."

Rodney studied his brother's face searchingly for a minute, and then he said, "I'll bet you did, kid, and the more fool I was that I didn't see it, too. Yes, with the kind of mother I've got, I ought to have seen it myself, first off the bat. Thanks, awfully, kid, for having seen it and stuck by me and kept your mouth shut. But now I hope I can get by without any more contacts."

"Well, it may be so," mumbled Jeremy, half whistling as he talked, "but knowing that gal as I've watched her, I think not. I think she means to get it back on you yet, unless you're mighty cautious, lad."

"I guess you've forgotten something, haven't you, buddy? I've got a Lord now, and He's keeping guard over me. 'He'll not let my soul be lost,' you know, 'He will hold me fast.' "

"That's right, brother, I forgot you had that now. The enemy may be strong, but he can't get by that defense. I say, Rod, it's something great, isn't it, to be at home again and to live this new life together, with a Savior like ours? Able to keep, and to present us faultless! Sometimes I just revel in that thought, 'able to keep' and to present us *'faultless.'* " And then in the dimness of the hall as they started downstairs for lunch, the two brothers felt for each other's hands in a strong happy clasp of rejoicing.

CHAPTER 14

But the next day there were letters and phone calls, some of which sought to change the bright future and good times the young people had planned.

The letters were for Diana. One from her mother, saying she was so glad that her daughter was having a delightful visit with her old college mate, but wasn't she almost ready to come home? Didn't she realize how many lovely affairs she was missing, how many old friends were home on furloughs, who would be going back again overseas, perhaps for a longer stay? And they were being given parties. There were even a few weddings, unexpectedly soon, weddings in which of course Diana must participate. There was Rush Horrmann's and Lannie Freeman's wedding. She mustn't miss that, and Lannie had just called to say she wanted Diana for her maid of honor. And there was a simply huge affair for the Red

Cross Drive. She mustn't miss that on any account. She owed that to her mother who was president, even if she were not interested on her own account.

"And then my dear," went on the mother, coming gently to the crux of the matter in her last few sentences, "do you realize at all how you are treating poor dear Bates Hibberd? Does that seem quite fair to him that you should go flying off after an old college mate, just at the time when Bates was coming home with new honors? And he has always been so devoted to you. Why, he confided to me only yesterday that he had hoped to get you to name the day while he is home this trip and was planning to coax you to get married right away. And just think, my dear, how much you'll be missing of pomp and ceremony if you should happen to wait so long that the war would be over and you couldn't have a real military wedding. Uniforms do make a wedding so picturesque, you know, and it would be simply calamitous if you were to miss that. I could never forgive you. I was looking at Bates yesterday while he was talking with me, and he did look so handsome in his new officer's uniform. It is just gorgeous. And so, my dear, I wish you would bid goodbye to your fascinating new friends and come home not later than Monday, but really I suggest that you come Saturday. Say to your friends there that it is *imperative.* After all, you've certainly outstayed your invitation, I am sure, and we all are getting quite hungry to see you again. The house seems terribly empty without you."

The other letter was from Bates Hibberd, perfect of diction, impeccable of stationery, demanding of tone, as if he had a perfect right to demand and didn't understand why she hadn't come home of her own desire days ago.

Dear Diana,

I cannot understand your absence. After all, since we are engaged, it seems high time that it should be announced.

How long do you intend to keep me waiting? I told you that I was coming home especially to talk over a very important matter with you, and I simply cannot understand why you are treating me this way.

I wish you would come home AT ONCE, taking the first train after you receive this. I am making plans for a delightful surprise for you, and it is necessary that you be here before I fix the date.

There was more in this general line, in a most possessive tone, indicating that the young officer felt that she was virtually his to order around and that his usually reasonable temper was roused beyond further endurance.

Diana sat pondering this letter for a few moments with a frown of worry on her lovely face, and then she went to her room and wrote an answer to that letter.

Dear Bates,

I am sorry that you feel that I have not treated you fairly, but it was just your very insistence that made it necessary for me to run away for a little while and do some thinking.

You know, my friend, I have never agreed to your desire that we should be engaged. I have told you more than once that I do not want to marry anyone at present nor to be engaged. We are not engaged, Bates, and it has been made very plain to me during my absence that I do not want to be engaged to you at all. You are my good friend, and that is all, and I wish you would accept that statement as final. I do not care for you as one should care for the man one is to marry, and I mean that definitely.

I am sorry if I am hurting you by saying this, for you have always been my good friend from childhood, but this is truly the way I feel, and I would have no right not to make it plain to you.

But I do hope you will understand and that someday soon you will find someone else for whom you can truly care, who will make you very happy.

Please forgive me for not having told you this sooner. I did not realize the situation fully before. But someday I hope you will be glad that I have written you this letter.

Your true friend,
Diana Winters

The answer to her mother's letter was not so easy to write, because she knew her mother would be terribly disappointed at her decision.

Dear Mother,

I'm sorry not to be able to come right home as you request, but Beryl has planned several lovely affairs for the next few days, in which I figure, of course, as her guest, and it would be quite disappointing both to her and to me if I could not be here. So, I feel, after the Sandersons have gone to a good deal of trouble to show me a good time, that it would not be courteous for me to leave so abruptly. I cannot possibly see my way clear to leave before the middle or end of next week. One of the expeditions planned is a trip to Washington with a few friends, and they have secured us some rare privileges. Some returned officers from overseas are to broadcast, and it will be an interesting experience to be a part of the group.

And now, Mother, you speak of Bates Hibberd, but you know I have told you several times that we are not engaged, and he has no right to attempt to order my comings and goings. He is only an old friend, and I have just written him quite definitely that I do not want to be engaged to him, and that this is *final.* I wish you would understand that I mean this, Mother.

I'll be home in time for your Red Cross Drive, if possible. And I'll wire Lannie about her wedding. But meantime, I'm having a delightful time here, and I wish you wouldn't worry about me.

Your loving
Diana

These letters were dispatched special delivery, air mail, and Diana drew a long breath and took courage. She felt that she had taken a very decided step in her new life and that she was being honest with her own heart for the first time since Bates Hibberd had begun to pester her to marry him. In the light of the new life she had, she was surprised to find how such questions fell into place and were clear and plain before her. For one thing, Bates Hibberd wouldn't be in sympathy with her living a Christian life, that she knew definitely. He did not go to church and hated religious things. But clearest of all came the knowledge to her that she did not love him and that she could not enter into a close relation like marriage with one whom she did not love. Yes, he was handsome and rich and influential and could give her a fine social position, but those things did not count now. She had found a Savior, a Redeemer, a Guide, and she had found a joy that no royal social position could give her. She was content.

So Diana had one night of restful, happy sleep, and then very early the next morning, the telephone rang, and her mother's angry voice called her, demanding that she come back into the world from which she had fled.

"I'm sorry, Mother —" she began, but the

sharp voice at the other end of the wire interrupted her.

"No, there is no use for you to begin making excuses," said the angry voice of her mother. "I'm not going to have any more of this. You are my child, and I know what is right and fitting for one of our family. I'm not going to have you playing fast and loose with a man as fine and distinguished and definitely wonderful as Bates Hibberd. It just can't be done, and I *demand* that you come home at once, starting this morning! That is an order from your mother!"

There was a distinct moment of silence, and then Diana, trying to keep her voice from trembling, said firmly, "Listen, Mother! Have you forgotten that I am of age and have a right to control my own movements?"

"Indeed!" said the icy voice of the parent.

"I don't like to talk like that to you, Mother dear, but this is something that I have to decide for myself. I am *not* going to marry a man because he is fine and distinguished and wonderful. That isn't what you married my father for, I know, for you've often told me how you cared about him, and I certainly do not care for Bates in that way. I think marriage would be awful without love!"

"Nonsense!" said the mother. "You don't know what love is! You're too young to know!"

"Then I'm too young to get married," said Diana firmly.

"That's ridiculous! If you are as young as that you'd better realize that your mother knows what's best for you, better than you do. You'll love him all right when you are married to him. Besides he's likely going away to war again very soon, and you'll have plenty of time to get used to the idea after he's left for overseas. It would really be best for you to marry him at once and get the question settled. It isn't fair to him to keep him uncertain."

"He need not be uncertain, Mother. I have written him very fully, and I'm sure he could not misunderstand. I told him I hoped he would soon find someone else to make him happy and that we would of course always be friends."

"Yes, I know that you have written. Bates brought your letter over to me to read the first thing this morning, and I consider it was a most insulting letter for a daughter of mine to write to a good respectable young man, one who belongs to a fine old family and has always been most kind and attentive to you. A man who has offered you his love and his name —"

"I beg your pardon, Mother, I don't think he ever did. He just ordered me to be engaged to him and told me we were going to be married, in spite of the fact that I told him I wasn't *ready* to marry *anyone* at present; and that isn't my idea of love. I said no every time he talked about the subject, and that is the reason that I ran away from home when he came back. I wanted to think this thing all out and know exactly how I felt. And now I know, Mother, and I am *not* going to marry Bates. I'm not even going to be engaged to him *tentatively* or anything like that. And I *mean* what I say! I've grown up, Mother, and I know what I *don't* want. And I'm not coming home just now. I'm sorry to disappoint you, but I've made certain engagements to do things and go places here, and I'm going to keep them. I'll run up to New York for a day or so for your drive, just to go on record, but I'm coming right back here until you've put aside all idea of this Bates Hibberd proposition and I can come home and be myself without danger of running into an argument."

"Diana, I *insist* that you come home at once!"

"No, Mother, not now."

"Diana, you don't know what you are doing to your life!"

"Yes, Mother, I definitely do, and it's what I want to do."

"You'll be sorry!"

"No, I won't be sorry!"

"Diana, you never talked to your mother this way before."

"No, Mother, and I wish I didn't have to do it now, but if I had done it before, perhaps I wouldn't have to be doing it now. I mean if I had told you long ago how I felt about Bates and the way he took me for granted as if I belonged to him, ordered me around and everything, I think you would have understood that I would *never* care for him."

"Diana, I can't listen to any more of this silly twaddle over the telephone. You simply must come home at once! If you think you are grown up, then act it. This isn't the way a refined, well-bred woman acts toward her mother. I want you to come home now and get this straightened out at once. It breaks my heart to have any differences come between us. You must come without delay. I am sure I'm on the verge of a nervous breakdown over this, and you must come today if you want to prevent any such result."

"Well, Mother, I'm sorry I can't come for an appeal like that, but it just happens that I have promised to go with Beryl this morning, and she really needs me. There is quite a good deal involved in this. We're going down to the canteen to teach the servicemen to sing a chorus for an hour on the radio that we're preparing them for, and I have to play for the singing, because we have only one copy of the music and I'm the only one who knows it."

"How silly! Let them choose another song then."

"It's too late, Mother. Beryl has already gone, and I wouldn't know how to reach her. She had to go early to get the chairs arranged. And besides, it's almost time for their last rehearsal, and they come on at two o'clock, so you see I've got to rush, even now."

"Well, then, come on the three o'clock train."

"But Mother, we're due at a dinner right after that. We've barely time to get dressed after we get back from the broadcast. And Mother, it's just as I told you. Every minute is arranged for up to the last of next week. I really couldn't change things. It would be awfully rude after Mr. Sanderson has spent so much time and money arranging to get us tickets and reservations for all the activities we've planned."

"But Diana, I don't know you. You never acted like this before when I asked you as a favor to me to do something."

"Mother, you were always reasonable, all my life. You never wanted me to do rude things, simply for a whim. I am quite sure anything you want to say about this matter of Bates can wait until I come. And I'm sure if I came now you would get no other answer from me than the one I have given. I am not engaged to Bates, and I never will be, no matter how desirable you may think he is. It would be I who would have to live with him afterward, and that I *never will* do."

"Oh, Diana. How you are grieving me! I am sure when you think this over you will be ashamed, and I shall be waiting to see you arrive on a later train this evening."

"No, Mother, I can't do that. Good-bye now, I must go." And Diana, in response to a call from downstairs, hung up the receiver, snatched her hat and gloves, and hurried down the stairs and out the door. She was almost sure she heard the phone ringing again as she went down the street, but the bus was almost to the corner and she had to run to catch it.

Diana, as she settled down in the only

vacant seat, was not very happy in her heart. Somehow it came to her that this did not seem to be a very good way to begin a Christian life, being almost rude to her beloved mother, refusing to grant her request. But what else could she have done? If there had been any real need of her at home, if her mother had really been ill, of course she would have gone at once, no matter how many engagements had to be broken. But she knew her mother's ways, and she was well aware that if she had been quite free to go it would only mean a long session of arguments, with Bates dragged into them, until she was wearied of her life. She could not yield this time and get into the toils of those two again. Too many times she had been argued with until she scarcely knew how to answer, and this was what she had come off here for, to get away from that demand to marry Bates, or at least to let her mother give her an announcement party and be in the public eye in such a way that she could not get away from it without seeming to be dishonorable, or what would be worse in her mother's eyes, without making it appear that Bates had let her down. How her soul shrank from such dishonorable actions!

All the way into the canteen hall where

they were to practice, Diana sat with closed eyes and quietly prayed in her heart, *Dear Lord, show me what to do. Help me somehow to keep my obligations and yet not to hurt my dear mother.*

Now, she said in her heart as she got out of the bus at her destination, *please help me to forget this and do my duty till it is over, and then show me what is right.*

The rehearsal went well. Diana roused from her distractions and played with abandon and interest, and the sailors sang well. The radio man came in as they were singing the final song, and he applauded. "That's great!" he said genially. "If you do that well this afternoon, you'll bring the house down."

The rest of the day was so full that Diana had no time to think anymore of her own perplexing problems. She had cast them off on her new Burden-Bearer, and she was just resting on that.

But when they got back to the Sanderson home just at dinnertime, there was the telephone ringing, and Diana looked up alertly as the maid said, "Miss Winters, that phone is for you. Your mother has been try-ing to get you all the afternoon." Then the great burden of worry dropped down upon her young shoulders again like a heavy

255

weight. As she went toward the telephone, her hands trembling almost too much to take down the receiver, she was praying in her heart, *Oh my heavenly Father, please help me. Show me what to say, make me understand what I ought to do.*

Then came her mother's voice, no longer sharp and implacable. Just hurried, almost apologetic.

"Diana, is that you? Have you come at last? Well, I've been trying to get you for the last two hours. I'm glad you've come, for I have to leave almost at once. Your father is preparing to go to California for a couple of weeks and he wants me to go with him, so you better delay your return till I get back. I have just been talking with Bates, and he has received unexpected orders to report back at camp as soon as he can get there. He will be back again later, and all these matters can be settled then. So now you can keep your promises to your friend and turn over in your mind this question about your engagement, and see if you don't want to change your mind. So I hope you will be satisfied. But meantime, I forgive you for your rudeness, and I hope you will be able to see things sensibly by the time I get back. I will write you on the way and give you our address later so you can write me. Meantime, have a good time, darling, and get ready in your mind for a grand big announcement party when we get back. Now good-bye, dearest. I must go. Your father is calling."

As Diana hung up the receiver and turned to go, her face was alight.

"What's the matter, dear?" asked Beryl. "You look as if you had received a reprieve."

"I have," said Diana smiling. "I was afraid I was going to have to go home at once and miss all your nice times, but now the plans have changed and I can stay till we get back from Washington."

"How grand!" said Beryl. "But somehow the look on your face was more than just being glad over a good time."

"Well, it was," said Diana. "I was wondering if God always helps fix troublesome things for you when you cry to Him for help?"

Beryl's face grew suddenly grave. "Oh, I wouldn't know," she said. "I don't think I ever tried it, but I shouldn't be surprised if He *did.* You ask the boys. They'll know."

"I will," said Diana with a sweet look in her eyes. "But oh, I'm so glad God worked this out for me, for I was terribly afraid I was going to have to go home and have a very hard time, with my mother arrayed against me and an old playmate determined to marry me right away — and I didn't *want* to."

"My dear!" said Beryl. "I'm so glad for you. I knew you didn't love that man you talked about yesterday. Well, now we can have a nice time going to Washington, can't we?"

"Yes," said Diana with a happy smile. "And I'm so glad that my mother isn't angry with me. She has always been very domineering and insisted I should go her way, but I do love her, and I hate to have her out of harmony with me."

"Of course you do, dear. I understand."

"Beryl, you are the most understanding friend I have. Except perhaps my father. He always seems to know what I mean and to feel just as I do about things. He's a wonderful daddy!"

"So is mine," said Beryl. "But my mother usually understands, too."

"Yes, you have a wonderful mother!"

"Yes, I have," said Beryl, "except perhaps sometimes she's a little bit afraid of things I want to do."

"But that's because she loves you so and wants to put a hedge around you to protect you."

"Yes," said Beryl, "and perhaps if you

would study the subject carefully, you might find that the things your mother wants for you are things she *thinks* would protect you."

Diana studied her friend's face seriously. "Perhaps you're right," she admitted slowly. "She probably thinks Bates' riches and power and influence will be a wall around me to make me safe everywhere, and she doesn't realize at all what it would be to marry someone I do not love. She is so thoroughly sold on Bates herself, having always admired him from the time he was a child, that she cannot take it in that I am not. She thinks I haven't grown up yet and don't know my own mind, but that it would be all right if I found myself married to such a wonderful young man. This, I suppose, is because I was so undecided myself when I came away from home. I was trying to please everybody except myself, and yet not yield to my own uneasy feelings. Thank you for giving me that thought. I must treat my mother much more tenderly in the future. I can see I have not always done that, especially yesterday on the telephone. But I am thankful that she was in such a hurry getting ready to go with Father that I think for the time being she had forgotten it. I must write her a sweet letter and help her to keep forgetting."

And then there came a call from the Graemes, proposing a tennis match for the morning, dinner in town, and a meeting in the evening at which a wonderful Bible teacher was to speak, and the conversation ended with joy on their faces. Still there was something about it that could not be forgotten, and its essence returned to Diana's newly awakened conscience again and again.

CHAPTER 15

The next two days were quiet ones, little excursions planned on the spur of the moment. It was taken for granted that all the group would go everywhere together. No more apologies for keeping up this constant friendly fellowship. It was as if they were a lot of children, brought up together, glad that they belonged together. Yet behind it all was the constant realization that this could not last forever. It would soon be over when the boys were sent somewhere. There would be lonely days after this delightful companionship.

They were taking every day as if it were something precious, dealt out to them hour by hour, knowing that when it was gone there might be no return of the joy they were spending so lavishly. Not that they thought it out in these phrases. They would none of them perhaps have reached the place where they would be willing to admit how much it all meant to them, but at night, when each was by himself, they would think the day over almost breathlessly and plan that the next day should be savored even more happily.

They were doing all their planning toward their trip to Washington for the broadcast, as if it were a kind of climax of their happiness. When they returned, well, there would doubtless be something soon to separate them, at least for a time. For one thing, Diana was likely to be called home by an irate and demanding mother, and she had hinted more than once that there would be problems for her to solve, problems that would not only affect her new Christian life but might even make trouble for her at home. Rodney had thought a great deal about the few words she had dropped along these lines and had been praying for her, not only that her anticipated trials might not be as great as she feared, but that she might be able to bear them, even if they were worse than feared.

She had noticed that a great gentleness had come upon him of late, and when they walked together his words would be low and quiet, and now and again his strong comforting hand would be laid over hers as it rested on his arm. And once, when they were walking so, quietly, on the shady side of a moonlit street, it suddenly came to her to wonder what it would be if this were Bates walking so with her, and she knew that she would shrink from such contact with his hand. Bates' immaculately cared-for hands! And yet their touch would not be welcome to her, would not be so comforting, would be almost revolting to her. Then suddenly she knew beyond the shadow of a doubt that she did not love Bates Hibberd.

Oh, she had been saying so for several days, to her mother over the telephone, to Beryl, tentatively to herself, reassuring herself, just to be sure she hadn't made the mistake that her mother and Bates would keep telling her she had made. For she had been dreading the time when she would have to go home, very soon, and meet all this again. *How* she had been dreading it! But now, she was not afraid anymore, for something new had come to take the place in her heart that had been so uncertain. What was this something new? Was it just that she had a new friend who had taught her to love the Lord? Was that a little thing? It seemed so great, so wonderful. And it was something apart from the friendly relations of earth. Something that almost seemed like a holy relationship, one that had nothing to do with world-ideas or jealousies. A relationship that had its center in Jesus Christ, that did not base its being on good looks, although there was plenty of that if one were counting it, or on wealth or even on possession. It was something bigger than worldly relationships.

Of course it would be a wonderful thing if a man like this one loved her and wanted to marry her. She would not have to wait and ponder over a question like that. She would feel that just to walk with a young man like Rodney through her life on earth would be the greatest blessing heaven could bestow. But she had not a thing like that to consider. He had not asked her, and it was not a thing that was likely to come to her. She was not good enough for him. And she had not been thinking of love with reference to him. But she could see that God had sent him her way that she might know and understand what a man whose life was hid with Christ in God could be, and how she must on no account link her life with a man who did not know Christ. And while this was no time for her to be considering any new idea of marriage, it certainly was a time to decide whom she should *not* marry.

And suddenly with that thought, a great burden rolled away from her. She did not have to consider marriage anymore. Not unless God sometime sent her a companion of His own choosing. She might be just happy now and have a good time, learning to know God and to follow her new Guide.

But while Diana was thinking these thoughts, Jessica was on her way to a consultation with the husband she had married so hastily, called to him by an insistent telegram, peremptorily ordering her attendance at once.

Jessica was very much annoyed about it because Louella had particularly promised to have some more news for her this very morning, news that would have reference to the immediate movements of the Graeme brothers, and she had not had time to get Louella on the telephone before she took the train designated in her husband's orders. She had already learned by the hardest way that it did not do to disobey orders. No one else in the world but Carver De Groot had ever been able to make Jessica do anything unless she wanted to do it, and she certainly did not want to drop her present pursuit of her former beau and go traveling away off out in what she called "the sticks" after a mere husband, from whom the glamour had long since worn off. But Carver De Groot had ways of his own, severe ways that did not waste time in coaxing. He gave the word of command and expected it to be obeyed, and one disobedience needed but the one penalty to bring about a future obedience. Jessica had learned her lesson the hard way, but she had learned. And perhaps her almost penniless condition made her the more easily adaptable.

For Carver De Groot had a deep purse, though he held the purse strings exceedingly tight. Still, there was a great wealth behind those purse strings. When they were loosened to an obedient one, there was a generous sum and sometimes a jewel now and again. So it behooved Jessica to go when he called and to cast about her a cloak of unaccustomed humility.

So it was with haste and a meek spirit that she walked into the old De Groot homestead, set away back from the highway amid shrubbery well hidden from curious eyes, and maintaining a shabby outward show, to further camouflage its inner glories. This quality of staid ancient shabbiness was by no means an asset to Jessica, and she had wasted many precious tears and angry words to try to change this feature but found she could not change a jot or tittle of the place. At last she began dimly to understand that behind it all there was some fixed and unchangeable reason, something that had to do with the war mysteriously, and because it frightened her to think of it, she calmly put it out of her mind. It wasn't her problem. And when she protested that he had promised her good times — how could she have good times so far away from everything and everybody at all interesting? She was told that she need not stay there for her good times. There would be plenty of opportunities to go out and away, and she would be hindered in nothing she wanted to do except at certain times when he would demand her attendance and help, often in matters of great importance to his business. But she need not ask about that business. When the time came he would tell her all she needed to know to help him, and nothing more, so she would be in no danger of giving out forbidden information. He had impressed it upon her that he was working for the government — what one? — and she certainly knew there were many matters that for the time of war must be kept secret. So there would be no use of her asking questions just to satisfy her curiosity. In fact, she had considered this matter before marrying and decided that she would be a girl most discreet, able to keep her mouth shut and do as she was told.

So she walked hastily up the steps of the old shabby house, down the luxuriously furnished hall, to the door of her husband's office, otherwise designated as the library.

She tapped lightly with the tip of her well-cared-for fingers a kind of a code that she had been carefully taught.

There were sounds of voices inside the door, which ceased with her knock, and a cold voice bade her come in.

Chin up, she walked arrogantly into the room and faced the hard, cold eyes of her elderly husband. The man with the cruel mouth and the sharp, sharp eyes that always saw too much and searched back into any past in which he cared to interest himself.

The cold eyes were searching her face now, and the cold voice said, "Well, so you decided to come back at last!"

"I came as soon as I got your message," drawled the girl indifferently. "I understood you ordered me to stay there until I heard from you."

"Hm! I didn't notice that it was a very great trial to you to go to the town your former fiancé was soon to come to."

"I understood that was the reason you sent me there," said Jessica. "You distinctly asked me to look him up at once when he arrived and get in touch with him."

"Did you do it?"

"I certainly did my best."

"Just what did you do? I haven't had any report yet."

"There wasn't anything to report," said Jessica in a calm tone. "I wasn't able yet to get in touch with him."

"Just what did you do? Why couldn't you get in touch with him? He arrived at his home, didn't he?"

"Yes, he arrived, and I went at once to the house and entered just as I used to, going right out to the dining room where they were all sitting down at the table, but by the time I got there Rod wasn't there, and nobody seemed to know where he was."

"Well? What then?"

"He didn't come back. And nobody would tell just where he was. If it had been in the old days, of course I would have gone through the house hunting for him, but they didn't give me any chance to do that."

"I thought you were a clever girl."

"Yes, I thought so, too."

"Why didn't you go to some of his family?"

"I did. I did everything I knew how, but apparently they are all in league with him. I chased him everywhere I heard of his being, but there was always somebody with him. I even went to an old religious meeting to try and see him, and he just walked out on me before I could get near him. I got close to a stupid old gossip of a cousin of his and she tried to work things for me, and she's getting news about his movements for me now, but so far I haven't got any definite news. If you hadn't sent such an imperative order for me to come back, I should have stayed, for today was going to be a critical time. The stupid cousin seemed to think she was right on the verge of a discovery. She thinks it's going to be Naval Intelligence. Does that mean anything to you?"

"It certainly does," said the man with a glint of fire in his stony eyes. "It's most important. I had begun to think you were a flat tire, but if you can manage to get into an office where that matter is carried on, especially if you can manage an intimate meeting where you would have opportunity to ask a lot of questions, perhaps overlook some papers with important writing, get familiar with the office, arrange to meet him at his place of work. Of course it will likely be well guarded, but you would have to plan a way to get in there. You would probably know how best to get around your man, having known him for years. Then when you get that far there will be a way to get hold of some important papers we want, and you will have to keep your eyes open. I'll write a list of words and phrases you are to look for. And there is a paper we very much need for evidence that must be destroyed."

"Destroyed? How could I destroy anything?" asked Jessica with a startled look. "You promised me there would be no danger connected with what I had to do."

"No, no danger. There are ways, you know. Little time bombs that can be left around near a safe or close to a file of records or wherever you discover they are keeping the kind of papers we need. That, of course, is the most important part of your mission. And the danger will be scarcely appreciable. Of course when you have arranged your blast — it is just a little thing like a pencil, scarcely noticeable — you will have to arrange to get out quickly and get downstairs out of danger, but I'm sure by that time you will be familiar enough with the place to have that all fixed up beforehand."

"But there must be danger connected with a thing like that!"

"Look here, Jessica. Did you ever see a stone like this?"

Jessica turned frightened eyes toward the velvet case the stern husband was holding out to her. It was white velvet, and in the center shone a great blue diamond, its wonderful lights stabbing her in the face, stirring her heart with envy and longing.

"Oh, that's wonderful!" said Jessica. "It's a blue diamond, isn't it? Yes, I saw one once in New York in an exhibit of stones, but I never saw such a lovely one. Oh, Carver, where did you get it? Is it yours?"

The sinister eyes were gloating over the look in the girl's eager face. Then he pronounced the words for which he had demanded her presence. "It is yours, if you carry out my orders!"

"Oh, Carver! I'd do *any*thing to own that!"

"Even if there were danger connected with its possession?"

The frightened look came back and peered out through the eager light, but it was as if with an impulsive movement of her hands she brushed the fear aside and made her quick decision.

"Yes," she said. "Yes, no matter what the danger. I should worry. I want that stone at all costs."

"Very well!" said the cold voice, now full of calm satisfaction. "Just do your part and the stone will be yours! Now, you better get back to the job and don't let any opportuni-

272

ties pass you by. Get intimate with that old-time boyfriend, and I don't mean maybe."

There followed instructions, some in code that she had already learned, some given orally.

When Jessica started back to Riverton, she carried in her mind's eye the gleaming stone of which she had just been given another gorgeous glimpse. She had even been allowed to hold it against her white hand and note the rainbow tints that shot through it, her face full of gloating eagerness. To have that jewel for her own! What more could any girl desire?

All through her return journey, Jessica was thinking about that jewel, though occasionally her conscience, or whatever it was she used for a conscience, told her that she really ought to be planning how she was going to recover her old hold on Rodney Graeme.

But it was the thought of the jewel and how it would look on her slender hand. That sustained her. She could go in triumph back to Riverton. She would show it to Rodney and let him see how she had gained by giving up his little white diamond. Oh, of course his wasn't really little. It was wonderfully large for a boy in college to be able to get with his own savings, and she had been proud of it then, but of course it was silly to try to stick to it when she had a chance at bigger things, and she was glad she had had the courage to send that ring back. Perhaps she had been foolish. She might have kept it and strung him along. Then she would have had another ring in her collection. Of course there was the emerald she got from the French diplomat that winter she spent in Washington, and the star sapphire the young Russian officer had given her at the beginning of the war, and the ruby from that silly man she met at the mountains that last summer before she was married. Why hadn't she kept Rodney's diamond? Just because she hated to tell him she had let him down. She had sent that ring back to break it to him gently. Just because the Graeme family were so frightfully conscientious and would think she was so awful to keep a diamond ring for nothing.

Wild thoughts like these kept flashing through her mind, and then an idea came to her. After all, it was what she was supposed to be doing on this journey back to Riverton, thinking up some way to get back into Rodney's good graces, and wasn't that ring a key to it? That was it. A legitimate reason for getting into touch with him. She would ask to have the ring back!

How could she manage it? Well, there would be a way. And that nice little diamond would make a good guard for this lovely big blue jewel!

So visions of diamonds with big blue lights danced through her empty head as she settled down in the Pullman coach and went to sleep. What would Louella say when she told her about the blue diamond? Or should she tell her? No, probably not. Part of the agreement was that she could keep her mouth shut.

CHAPTER 16

As the trip to Washington drew nearer, the little company of young people who met almost daily, at either the Graemes' or Sandersons', grew more tense and almost excited. It wasn't the young man who was to speak on the radio who was tense or excited. For Rodney had been too long in the service to count a little testimony over the radio as anything much. Rodney was excited for entirely another reason. For he knew the time of their companionship was drawing nearer and nearer to a close, and he knew that in a very few short days not his own fate was to be decided, whether he would have to go back overseas or serve in some way in this country, as had been hinted to him more than once by subtle questions.

And it wasn't that he was so deeply concerned about where he was to be located, on his own account, except that he wanted to be near home if possible. But it had come to him more and more every day that this companionship with the lovely Diana might be almost over. For Kathie had hinted to Jeremy, who had promptly conveyed the news to Rodney, that Diana was more than half committed to a rich handsome officer in the army whom she had known since childhood, one of a noble family, and greatly favored by Diana's people. So not only Rodney but equally his brother and sister were deeply disturbed over the possibilities of the future.

Now was the time, of course, when Rodney had opportunity to make sure about this, to offer his own love, and hope to win the girl who had come to mean so much to him. But Rodney did not feel that he had a right to commit himself to any girl until he knew what his immediate prospects were to be. He was just as old-fashioned as that. If he only could have asked her out plainly if she were engaged, it would have been so much easier for him. But there was something innately fine about him that forbade him to rush her into a relationship with one whom she scarcely knew yet. And she was too fine herself to show more than lovely comradeship in her association with him. So it was only through their great expressive eyes, by a stray smile now and then, that any preference had been actually shown by either of them. Yet the eyes and a smile now and again can often start the heart beating, and so it was that these two were occupied with thoughts of one another, pleasant dealings with the outer edges of one another's lives, hovering around great questions each would like to ask, yet dreaded to broach lest the present joy of their fellowship should be in any way spoiled by bald facts.

And the other four young people were equally engaged in watching them. Kathie and her young chaplain were as much interested as Jeremy and Beryl. For little by little, Beryl had spoken of Bates Hibberd, and, with an occasional question now and again, Jeremy was pretty well acquainted with the complications and dreaded lest his beloved brother had another disappointment in store for him. Oh, no, not *that,* dear Lord, not for Rodney!

As the day of the Washington trip drew near, Jeremy came in the night before looking troubled.

"Say, Rod, that young hysteric of a Jessica didn't stay away after all. You know I told you I saw her taking the westbound train the other day. Well, she's back. Yes, I saw her this morning, and I'm almost certain she'll try to horn in our trip if she finds out and we don't do something about it."

"Hm!" said Rodney with perplexed brows. "What would you suggest we do? The railroad trains are free, we can't stop her, and we can't likely get gas enough to *drive* down. Besides, Dad needs the car."

"No, I don't need the car today," said the smiling father, walking in just in time to hear the talk. "Take it and welcome. If that brazen girl once gets the idea that you are going somewhere, she'll manage somehow to go, too. She's like a leech when she once gets hold. As for gas, Rod's broadcasting for the government, isn't he? He'll have no trouble getting what gas he needs."

"Sorry!" said Rodney, looking exceedingly troubled. "Dad, I know you do need your car. It's all my fault, of course. I should have had better sense than ever to have thought she was worth anything. Somebody ought to teach little kids that a pretty face isn't everything. But there, probably my mother did, only I didn't take it. I'm the sinner. I ought to pay the penalty. I might take the midnight train and go down by myself."

"No you won't, Rod. I don't intend to use the car today anyway," said the father again.

"Okay," said Jerry. "We'll start an hour earlier than we had planned and go in the opposite direction. Get Mom to send a jar of honey to Aunt Polly over in Andersonville, and go around by Prattsville. It can't be more than two or three miles out of the way, and we can get into the highway easily from there. And then when 'Chatty' comes over to Mom to find out what has become of us, she can tell her we took some honey to our old cook. See?"

"Good scheme, brother. That ought to relieve the situation," said Rodney. "I don't know what I'd do in my little old life without you, Jerry."

"Okay! Let's get to work. I'll call up the girls and tell them to be ready an hour sooner."

The next morning was bright and clear, and the young people were ready even earlier than necessary.

"Say, this is grand!" said Diana, smiling at Jerry. "When did you think of this?"

"It's just a scheme to get away without having uninvited guests," said Jerry, grinning.

"Uninvited guests?" said Diana with a puzzled frown. "Would anybody try that?"

Jerry gave another wry grin.

"There are that would," he said with a

280

comical wink. "Ever meet Jessica De Groot? Ever know our cousin Louella?"

"Oh! Would *they*? *Both* of them?"

"They work in pairs just now. Besides, they know the car holds seven passengers. One too many more or less means nothing to either of them in their young lives."

"What impossible people!" said Diana. "Of course I don't know them. I think I was introduced, perhaps at that meeting we attended when you spoke, but I didn't talk with them even, and I've only seen either of them in the distance since."

"They're best seen from a distance," said Jerry grimly. "Avoid them if you can!" And with another grin, Jerry swung himself into his seat behind the wheel, and they were soon on their way.

There was perhaps more joy in that little carload of six young people on their way to Washington than in any place in that land. Oh, there were still possibilities of separations and dread in the future of course, but for that day at least they had sunshine and a blue sky, they had each other, and no jealousies, no bitterness, no animosity in that whole company. Just gladness that God had made them and brought them together and let them have this day with each other. They had escaped from a possible enemy of discord and were having a nice time.

But back in Riverton, the two allied enemies were holding a conference and getting ready to go to work in earnest. For now Jessica had something real to do, and she knew what she wanted to find out. She had spent some of the hours in the train, when she ought to have been sleeping, planning out just how Louella could best help her. She had planned also just how she would open her campaign in order to lead her elderly ally to see what was expected of her and would not be startled into drawing back or hesitating. For at present, Louella was Jessica's only possible connection with the source of her needed information, and Louella was not only proud but flattered to be her emissary on so important an errand.

They held their conference in the morning, and after a heartening lunch, Jessica went back to her room to take a restful nap, feeling that her morning had been well spent. Louella put herself in battle array and betook herself to the Graeme house to begin her first engagement of the new campaign.

She arrived at the Graemes' house just as Margaret Graeme had retired to her room to get a much-needed nap while her household moved on smoothly without her. The children would not be at home to dinner that night. They would probably all stay over in Washington, to drive home by moonlight if the weather continued favorable. So this was a good time to rest. She and her husband were going to be on hand to listen to the radio, of course, when Rodney was speaking, and then they were going to take the bus over to a friend's house to dinner. It was almost an unheard-of thing for them to be able to get away together this way, and it made a real holiday for them both. So Margaret had gone to rest with a real feeling of luxury upon her.

Father Graeme was out about the farm, looking over his fences to see if there were any places that needed mending and getting things ready for the evening milking so that he would not be late in starting to the dinner party.

Hetty had gone on her semi-annual visit to a cousin in the country, so there was nobody at home to go to the door when Louella rang persistently, over and over again, and Margaret Graeme slept calmly on, not aware of its ringing nor of the feeble, angry pounding of Louella's fist on the door. Just for once, perhaps because she was unusually wary, or because she was so fully relieved of the constant pressure from the daily routine, she slept on.

Louella at last was furious. She stepped out into the driveway and looked up at the windows, where the muslin curtains were blowing pleasantly in the afternoon breeze.

"Margaret! Oh Margaret!" she called insistently. "Where on earth are you?"

After several more calls, she gave up and sat down on the steps to consider what she should do next. Then she heard the ring of a scythe against a stone, and listening sharply, she located the sound over behind the barn. She got up immediately and marched around the house till she could look out over the meadow, and there she saw Donald Graeme. Climbing fearsomely up the rails of the fence she called in her refined, angry little voice, "Donald! *Oh,* Donald: Donald *Graeme!*"

Most emphatically the words rang out over the meadow, chiming in with the occasional ring of the steady scythe, going on with its rhythmic swinging.

Growing more and more indignant, Louella at last climbed the fence, at great risk to her treasured stockings and, incidentally, starting a run in one of them. Then, after stopping to express a few anathemas at the splinters on the fence rails, she arrived on the ground, struggled to her feet, and went storming over a strip of plowed ground that lay between her and the field where Donald was mowing.

He saw her plunging among his carefully planted furrows of corn and finally laid down his scythe and came to her rescue.

"Why, Louella!" he said sternly. "What is the matter? Has something happened?"

"Happened!" said Louella almost in tears. "I should say there has. I can't get into your house. I've rung and rung at that old bell of yours, and I've knocked till I've got the skin all off one knuckle, and then I went out and called and *called* up to your wife's window, but I could not get a response. I should like to know where that lazy Hetty is, and why doesn't she answer the bell? I wouldn't put it past her to have looked out the window and seen who it was and refused to answer the bell just because she saw it was me. I declare, Donald, I must have my key back again. I can't get on this way. It is too inconvenient. Here I've put a run in my new expensive stockings getting over that fence to reach you. I ought to charge those stockings up to you, Donald."

Donald grinned, looking very much like his son Jeremy. "On what ground, Louella?" he asked.

"On the ground that you took away my key."

"But it wasn't your key, Louella, it was mine. And besides, if we are going to pay for things in that way, how much do you think I'm going to charge you for tramping and wallowing all over my nicely planted cornfield?"

"Corn?" said Louella, looking wildly around. "I don't see any corn."

"No," said Donald. "But it's there. I just got it planted yesterday, and now you've stepped everywhere over it."

"Well, how was I to know? There's no sign of any corn. It's all smooth. I don't think you should leave corn lying around loose that way if it's so valuable. But anyway, I came over here to find out where everybody is. I'm sorry if I've spoiled your cornfield, but I guess it'll come up just the same even if it is all messed up. Now, Donald, tell me where everybody is."

"Well," he said pleasantly as he guided her carefully over to the grassy edge of the field where she could do no more harm, "I think this is Hetty's day out. I saw her go down the lane a little while ago with her best bonnet on, and I don't think she's coming back before tomorrow morning."

"The very idea! Giving her all that time.

No wonder she's so horribly spoiled. I shouldn't think you'd allow Margaret to spoil her that way."

"What was it you came over for, Louella? Why did you want to see Margaret?"

"Oh, I just wanted to ask her a few questions."

"Well, suppose you ask me," smiled Donald genially. "You see, I don't want to waken Margaret up just now. She got very tired yesterday, and I've made it my business to keep it quiet for her till she wakens of her own accord."

"Is Margaret sick?" asked Louella sharply. "I'm afraid you spoil her just the way she is spoiling Hetty."

"Well, that's the way I like to have it," said Donald Graeme pleasantly. "That's the reason I married her. I loved her and wanted to take care of her always, and I'm doing it, Louella, to the best of my ability. So, now, what was it you wanted to ask?"

Louella was annoyed. She hadn't exactly formulated her questions to meet Donald's clear comprehension and sharp eyes. He wouldn't just smile and pass it off the way Margaret was apt to do, nevertheless letting out a glint of information now and then so that she could enlarge upon it for her own purposes.

"Well," she said, fabricating a story in her mind rapidly as was her habit when she got in a corner, "I was thinking of having a little tea at the hotel for a few of my friends, and I wanted the boys to meet them. They are crazy to know them, and I thought Margaret would tell me just when she thought it would be convenient for them."

"Well, I'm sorry about that. I wouldn't be able to tell you about the boys' engagements. They change every day, you know. But I can tell you that they are not keen for any teas or anything of that sort. I warn you, they'll get out of anything of that sort if you let them know about it beforehand. I haven't seen a single returning soldier or sailor who wants to be shown around and exhibited and asked what they did over there, so if you take my advice, Louella, you'll forget it. If you happen to meet them on the street or somewhere and have any of your curious friends along with you, well, snap up your chance and introduce them if you can catch them long enough to accomplish it, but otherwise I'm sure you'll miss out. And don't ask me or Margaret when and where they'll be, for we really don't know. The boys have been so long under discipline that all they want now is freedom to do as they please. So we're determined to help them get it as long as they are with us. Of course we don't know how long it will be before they are ordered off again. And of course we don't know, but they may be sent off to the Pacific. After all, they are trained men and will perhaps be needed."

"Oh, you don't really think that, Donald. You are expecting the boys to stay over here, you know you do. Why, somebody told me the other day that they were almost positive those boys would both be retained over here for very important positions."

"That being the case, we have not yet been informed, and I think it not advisable to say any more about it. If it were so, we should probably not be allowed to say anything about it, so we'll just change the subject, shall we? Suppose we go over to the spring-house, shall we? I could get you a glass of ginger ale or some grape juice. The boys took a lot of bottles down and left them in the springhouse last night. It's handy to have some cold there when we're working in the field, you know. And there are two or three glasses there. Come on. It's just as easy for you to get to the highway back to your hotel as to go back the way you came. I don't think you're much of a fence climber. Come on."

So Louella was definitely cajoled across

the rough ground to the springhouse where she was served with delightful cold drinks, apple juice first and then a mixture of ginger ale and grape juice, which proved a pleasant change from the ordinary drinks Louella was used to. Of course she wouldn't have minded if there had been a dash of something a little stronger in it, but for an afternoon refreshment at her dull, overconscientious cousin-in-law's house, especially when no one but this tiresome cousin seemed to be obtainable, it was better than nothing. And at last baffled in spite of herself, Louella went back to her apartment and took to the telephone, calling up the sleeping Jessica and complaining to her of her inability to get any information for her.

But Jessica was all filled with her new ideas of how she was going to get back her hold on Rodney, and she had a lot of questions to ask. What had been going on during the few days she had been away? Had those Sanderson people been around any? Had that Diana gone home to New York yet?

Of course Louella was in no position to answer these questions. In fact, she hadn't been around much even with the Graemes during Jessica's absence. But always what Louella didn't know she could easily make up, and she managed a fitting little story that hovered near the truth while allaying the fears of Jessica.

"I'm satisfied I shall be able to answer all those questions after I have seen Margaret Graeme for a few minutes. I am expecting to have a long talk with her tomorrow, in the morning, I hope. And don't you worry, for I am sure from what my cousin Donald said today that the boys have not received their orders yet and that nothing at all is settled. Donald even spoke as if there might be a possibility that the boys were to be ordered to the Pacific, but he said it in such a satisfied tone as if he were not worried that I'm sure that is not it."

"Well, I've got to have more definite information than that immediately," said Jessica with frustration. "I thought you promised to have it for me by the time I got back."

"Well, I didn't exactly promise," drawled Louella. "I said I'd do my best. If you think you can do any better, why don't you go over there and try? I shouldn't think it would be so impossible for you to talk to some of the family."

"Well, if you can't do any better than you have, I may do just that. I can't simply fool around and wait much longer. I have a job to do, and the people I work for are getting impatient."

"Well, I'm doing my best," said Louella offendedly. "After all, I'm simply doing this for you because I like you, you know, and if I do not please you, perhaps I better go home. I'm simply staying around here because you asked me to."

"Suit yourself," said Jessica. "Don't let me hinder you. If you can't find out a thing for me, I'm sure I don't know why you should stay. Unless of course you could find out something else for me."

"Such as what?" said Louella's cold voice.

"Well, I should like to know whether that Diana girl is still hanging around Rod, or whether she's gone home to New York."

"Oh! Why didn't you say something about that before? This is the first I've heard of that. I would have had plenty of chances to find out if I had known it was important."

"Well, go work on it then and see how far you can get with that."

"I'm not sure there will be any way to find out. Especially if she's gone back to New York."

"You might call up on the phone and ask for her," suggested Jessica.

"Hm! You might try that yourself, you know."

"Yes, but I don't think I care to. I might run on that disagreeable Beryl. I can't abide her."

"Oh, well, I'll think it over and see if there's anything I can do about it before I go home. I really ought to hurry away. There's a possibility that somebody wants to buy my house, and I really need to sell it. I need the money."

"I see! Oh, well, see what you can do and let me know. I really have some letters to write. But, by the way, if you find out where she is, you might get some further information about her. I heard the other day that she is as good as engaged to some big guy over in New York. If I knew all about that, I might even get somewhere with Rod. He might not have heard it, you know."

"Yes, that's quite true," said Louella thoughtfully. "It seems to me that I heard something about that, too, but I'm not sure. Well, I'll see what I can do. Will you be home this evening?"

"I'm not sure," drawled Jessica. "I had thought of going out for a while, but I may not go."

"Well, if you do, suppose you drop in here on your way. I may have something more to tell you. I have more than one source of information, you know."

Louella waited until she was sure Jessica would not be likely to call her back, and then she called up Isabelle Graham and asked quite casually if she knew Diana, the girl from New York who was visiting Beryl Sanderson.

Isabelle did. She was fairly gushing with news. She had a friend in New York who had just written her the latest about her. She was engaged to some rich guy in the army who was coming home soon, and they were going to be married at once, and she'd been down at Riverton killing time until the wedding was over. She had her trousseau all bought and everything ready to be married. Weren't some people lucky?

Louella finally hung up after she had extracted every bit of information she could possibly get and sat back to digest it and turn it over, with bits of her own devising, and then she called Jessica again.

But Jessica's line was busy. To tell the truth she was actually calling up the Sanderson number and about to ask for Diana, but there was no one at home to answer that call, so Jessica, after trying for some time, hung up and so was ready for Louella's next call.

CHAPTER 17

It was later that same evening that one of the girls called up and asked Jessica if she heard Rodney broadcasting that afternoon, and, "Wasn't he great?"

Jessica paused long enough not to show her astonishment and vexation that she had missed it, by not knowing about it, and resolved to blast Louella for that, and then she said with a characteristic drawl, "Oh, well enough, but I can't say I care for that line he has now. I thought he'd get over that religious twaddle, didn't you, when he went to war? He seems to have sort of stolen his little brother's theme, doesn't he?"

"Well, no, I don't think he has," said Alida, who happened to be the girl who had called her. "I thought it was so entirely different, and yet just as interesting and just as convincing. The war seems to have affected a good many of our boys that way."

"Oh, I hope not! What a bore that would

be," said Jessica. "I hate boys to turn old before their time. Just think what it would be to go dancing with a fellow who talked religion all the time."

"But the Graeme boys never did go dancing, did they?" asked Alida.

"Well, no, I suppose not. They were too much mamma's little boys to do a wicked thing like that. But I did suppose that they would get over such silly, old-fashioned notions when they got away from mamma's apron strings."

"Well, they haven't," said Alida sharply. "If anything, they are more markedly old-fashioned than ever, and do you know, I *like* it. They sound like real men."

"Oh, merciful heavens, *you, too*? Have they converted *you,* Alida? This is too much. And you used to be such a good sport."

"Well, I can't help it. I think they are fine. I never heard young men talk like that before. If everybody felt that way, there wouldn't be so many wars and bad things in the world. There wouldn't be so many divorces and drunkards and gangsters."

"Oh, heavens, Alida! Cut it out. Tell me something — do you know how and when they went down to Washington? Was it just Rodney all alone? Didn't he have anybody with him?"

"Why, sure he did. They drove down. My brother met them early this morning going over toward Prattsville. They had their big car, and there were six of them. Jeremy and Beryl, Rod and Diana, Kathie and her young chaplain."

"Rod and Diana!" said Jessica in disgust. "Do you mean that unspeakable girl is sticking around yet? I declare she is disgusting, and she's supposed to be engaged to some big rich guy in New York and getting ready to be married when he comes home on furlough."

"You don't mean it! Where did you hear that? I don't believe that. Diana is not that kind of a girl. She's sweet and quiet and lovely."

"Oh yeah? Who told *you* that? I heard very differently. That sweet, quiet character she is putting on is just an act to deceive poor blind Rod. You know, really he's awfully easily deceived. Anybody can make him think he's talking to an angel."

"Yes, I remember when *you* did that little act yourself, back in our happy school days. But remember that Rod is grown up now and has been to war and done great things. You'll find he's as sharp as a needle and can see through anybody. Remember he's been through an experience with you and has learned quite a little. There was a time when he simply adored the ground you walked on, but not anymore. You have thoroughly disillusioned him, and you did your work all too thoroughly. You couldn't deceive him now, and I don't mean mebbe."

"Oh yes? Well, I'll wager I *could.* Just watch me and see."

"For sweet pity's sake, Jessica, you're married! Lay off that stuff and act like a decent woman, or we'll be ashamed we ever knew you."

"Ashamed? *You?* Well, I like that! I could rake up a few things you've done in your time, if I cared to take the time to try."

"Jessica, you're quite impossible," said Alida harshly. "I'm sorry I called you up. Yet I suppose it is rather hard to watch your discarded beau take so kindly to a rich, cultured girl, and find her so entirely willing."

"Yes?" said Jessica hatefully. "Well, I could fix that, too, if I wanted to. There isn't much you can't do with a nice little sweet mamma's child like Diana if you go about it in the right way. So long, Alida. I'm going out this evening so you'll have to excuse me from further talk. Good night."

But Jessica made no further attempt to go out that evening. Instead she sat in deep thought, into the small hours of the night, making plans.

The next day Diana had gone down to the city on an errand for Mrs. Sanderson, while Beryl was addressing some of the Red Cross notes for which her mother was responsible and had promised to get into the mail that day. Diana had finished her errand and was walking briskly through the store on her way back to the house when Jessica saw her, gave her a quick sharp look, and then quickened her own steps and caught up with her.

"Aren't you Diana Winters of New York?" she asked.

Diana turned with a quick look at the other girl and smiled.

"Why, yes," she said sweetly. "Are you somebody I ought to know? I seem to have seen your face somewhere, but I just can't remember your name. I'm sorry."

Diana's manner was altogether disarming, but Jessica was in no mood to be disarmed. She had come out to fight, and she meant to do it.

"I'm Jessica De Groot," said Jessica. "I think we were introduced at that meeting where Jeremy spoke, but it was such a mob I don't wonder you can't remember my name. However, that makes no difference. I thought it was high time you and I had a little talk. There are some things I think you ought to know. Shall we go somewhere where we can talk without being interrupted? Right up these few stairs to the half gallery there is always a place to sit."

Diana, a bit perplexed, glanced down at her watch.

"Why, I think I can spare a few minutes, if it won't take long," she said, and allowed herself to be led up the stairs and seated on a long bench overlooking the many counters below.

"Now," said Jessica, "I have seen you going around with Rod Graeme a lot, and I thought it was high time you understood that he's not for you. He really belongs to me, you see. We were engaged long before he went to war, and he just isn't for you, that's all. And I decided to tell you to lay off him. I won't stand for anybody else taking him over. He's mine, see?"

Diana sat there in amazement staring at Jessica, and for the moment saying nothing, so Jessica went on. "Besides, I've been finding out a lot about you, too. Things I suppose Rod doesn't know or he never would be going around with you. He's so religious that he would drop you like a hotcake if he knew. And if you don't let up on this, I'll good and well see that he does know. See? You see, I have friends in New York, and they tell me you are engaged and going to be married right away to a swell guy who thinks you're all right, and naturally *he* doesn't know what *you* are doing in Riverton. But if you keep this thing up, I'll see that he *does* know all about it. I often go to New York, and I can hunt him up and tell him *everything* that goes on here, see?"

Diana looked at the girl as if she were crazy, and in her heart she was saying, *Oh, Lord, what is this? What shall I do? Help me, please.*

She was smiling faintly when this tirade began, and the startling things this girl said had, for the instant, driven away her usual calm from her expression, leaving only that faint smile set there like something that might fade quickly.

Then, as if some unseen strength had come to her she began to speak in a steady voice, "Are you quite through? Is that all you wanted to say? Then if you'll excuse me I think I must go, for someone is waiting for this package," and with all her old, sweet self-possession, the result of years of cultured training, she arose, walked quickly across the gallery, down the steps, and out through the crowded store, head up, shoulders back, and an undisturbed expression upon her face.

And Jessica sat in amazement and watched her go. Her hateful words had not even fazed the girl. What kind of a girl was she anyway? And somehow Jessica almost envied Diana, to be able to take it that way. That was what it meant, probably, to be "to the manner born," while *she* was only born to the wrong side of the tracks and couldn't seem to get away from it no matter how hard she tried, nor how hateful she was to other people. She simply could not understand it. What did it mean? Wasn't it true about her being engaged? Well, why didn't she say so then? Or was there nothing much between her and Rod? Or what? Had she only put herself in worse with Rod by attacking the girl he had been going with? Well, it was done, and now what? She must follow this up somehow. She would have to go to Rod, get to him somehow, even if he didn't want to see her, and tell him what kind of a double-crosser his latest girl was. With all his religion he couldn't stand a girl doing that. She would get in touch with Rod tomorrow, in spite of all his scruples. In spite of the Graemes. In spite of Louella. She would beat them all and get it back on everybody. Get it back on Rod and perhaps get him just where she wanted him, and then she would ask him to give that ring back and have it to show to other people. She would do that little thing tomorrow morning. She certainly knew how to make plenty of trouble for a lot of people when she really set about it.

So, dressed in her most innocent morning frock of delicate-wash material, fragilely trimmed with simply expensive lace and a wide hat with a wreath of wild roses, the kind of thing Rod used to admire, and delicate white sandals, she took her way slowly up the old familiar drive. She went to the side door where she always used to go, knock, and walk in without ceremony or waiting for anyone now, so she stayed a little on ceremony and stood with her wide hat in her hand, sweetly smiling. And Jessica knew how to smile, sweetly, *almost* innocently.

"Are you here, Mamma Graeme?" she called in a pleasant voice. "I've come to see you. I hope you're home, and not busy."

Margaret Graeme came out a little anxiously, not knowing just what to anticipate, and she looked at the smart girlish figure and was thankful in her heart that this girl was not for her boy. She had never felt her to be the right girl for either of her children, though there had never been a danger from her for Jerry, for he had openly despised her, raging to his mother now and again on Rodney's account.

"Why, no, not too busy. That is not for a while. I believe I have to go to a committee meeting at eleven. Sit down, won't you?"

So Jessica spread her filmy orchid-sprigged skirt out engagingly in the rocking chair that was offered and settled herself for a good home talk, with a nice air of pleasant anticipation.

She spoke of the lovely weather they had been having, rattled on a little about her brief trip west, with a unique fabrication of a story to explain her going. She told enlarged stories of her husband's estate, described the wonderful old house and its fine, costly antique furniture. She told of a wondrous blue diamond her husband was getting for her that was to be set in a new fancy way, and at last she looked at her little trick of a watch and remarked nonchalantly, "I hope I haven't come too early to catch the boys when they come down. I know they like to sleep late these furlough mornings. Dare I stay till they come down?"

"Come down?" said Margaret Graeme, lifting amused eyebrows. "Why, bless you child, they aren't even here. They left late last night."

"Do you mean they've been sent back overseas?"

"Oh, no, not that, that is, not yet."

"But where have they gone? I'm always asking that question about Rod and never getting an answer. Is this intentional?"

Margaret Graeme smiled. "Well, it has been rather hard to place them. They've so many things to see and do, and they have felt that perhaps they had so little time in which to do it."

"Well, then, suppose you give me an answer now, Mamma Graeme. Where have they gone?"

Mrs. Graeme laughed merrily. "Well, I'll have to give you the same answer," she said. "They didn't tell me. They simply said they were called to headquarters."

"Do you mean they've been called back to Washington?"

"It might be, of course, but I'm not sure. It depends on what headquarters it is, I suppose. I really don't know much about these things. I haven't had much chance to talk over their affairs with the boys yet. It seems there are several headquarters, I think, depending on whether you are talking in terms of military orders or personnel or home efficiency. I'm not even sure I'm using the right terms. I'm afraid I'm rather a dummy about such matters, and it hasn't seemed too important to take time to understand. But undoubtedly we'll learn in time and be able to give them their true standing in the eyes of the world, that is, as far as the world is going to be allowed to know. If it is, yet."

"But don't you really know pretty well where they are going? Surely you could tell me that much. Remember, Mamma Graeme, how near I came to being a member of the family, and then I would have had to know."

Margaret Graeme laughed. "I'm afraid not," she said amusedly. "We don't know yet, and may not be told everything even when the boys get their orders, for the government has found that there are some things that *must* be kept absolutely secret, even from the nearest and dearest."

"But I think that's perfectly horrid. That's unreasonable. No families would stand for that."

"Oh, yes, they would. They have to, you know. Why, there were months and months when the boys were overseas that we had no definite idea at all where they were. It was understood that we wouldn't. It was the only safe way to win the war."

"Nonsense!" said Jessica. "I think that's ridiculous! As if all those thousands of soldiers would stand for that! They wouldn't stay there and fight if they were treated like that."

"Oh yes they would. They understood why such orders were given, why such precautions were necessary. No, we got rather used to not asking too many questions. We knew that if we asked one that shouldn't be answered they would just laugh and give an evasive reply. So we just waited till the boys got ready to tell us. If they didn't, we knew it was because they were forbidden."

"Well, I certainly wouldn't stand for that."

"I would rather stand for that and help the war along than just to satisfy my own curiosity and persist in demanding to know everything. You know, you want your dear ones to be true soldiers and to submit to laws and ordinances."

Jessica was vexed and showed it. At last she got up and started toward the door. "Well, it seems I came on a fool's errand," she said.

"Oh, I wouldn't call it that, child," said Mother Graeme. "We've had a nice talk, haven't we?"

"We didn't get anywhere, and I wanted to talk to Rodney. There is something important I want to ask him about. When do you definitely expect him back?"

"I'm afraid it will have to be the same old answer. I just don't know. It might be a day or two or more, or even a week or a month. Depends on what changes are going to be made in their work."

Margaret Graeme was getting to be a master of evasion indeed. Of course she did not know definitely what was to be done with her sons in the immediate future, though she could guess perhaps and not fall far short of the truth. But she had been adjured not to tell *any*thing, not even what she *knew* to be true, so she told nothing. And at last Jessica, much vexed in spirit, took herself away, went and hunted up Louella, and complained to her.

"Well, Jessica," said Louella sympathetically, "that's exactly the way Margaret Graeme always treats me. You wonder why I can't get any of the information you want. Well, now you see, I simply can't get anything out of her no matter how hard I try. I'm glad you've seen it yourself, and then you won't be so hard on me."

"Well, at least now we know they've gone somewhere, and it ought to be definitely settled soon where they are to be permanently. I wonder if we could get anything out of the postman?"

"I'm afraid not," said Louella. "I tried him awhile ago, asked for the address of somebody overseas, and do you know he wouldn't give me the address, not without an order from the person. He said he would mail my letter, but he had no right to give me the address. It seems to me that government affairs take too much on themselves, refusing to give out the address of your best friends or next-door neighbors, perhaps."

"Well, there must be some way," said Jessica. "I'm not one to give up so easily. I'm going to find out where they are as soon as they are located definitely, and believe me, I'm going to visit Rodney in his office, too, government or no government. They can't simply turn a lady out of an office."

"Well, I don't know about that," said Louella doubtfully. "You know, the government is very severe. Army and navy regulations are simply unreasonable, *I* say. And I wouldn't hesitate to step over some of their old regulations myself. Nobody would certainly put *me* out of anywhere, office or whatever. But maybe *you* ought not to try. You are a young woman, you know. And perhaps your husband wouldn't like it if you did. You might get your name in the papers or something and be misunderstood."

"Well, anyhow, I'm going to talk to Rodney Graeme. I've got things to tell him that he ought to know, and I intend he shall know them. Remember I used to be very close to him, and if I know something to his advantage I think *I'm* the one to tell him, don't you?"

"Well, of course, Jessica, if you put it that way. But you must remember there are always consequences to things like that, rash actions, especially when you're dealing with government regulations. I'd be careful what I did, Jessica."

"Oh, I'm not afraid. Just wait till I find out where that office or plant or whatever it is, is located, and I'm going straight in and track Rod to his office. Then believe me, nobody, not even a mother, is going to put up any bars to keep me out. I'm going to his office, and I'm going to stay there till I've told him plenty about that little white-faced Diana that he's trotting around with, and when I get done you won't see him out riding with her anymore, I'll guarantee. One thing that Rodney Graeme is mortally afraid of is to do anything that will make narrow-minded people talk about him. He seems to think God is just waiting around the corner, watching, to see if he goes wrong some way, or if anybody can find anything to accuse

310

him of. I'll show him that that girl is no mate of his. A girl that would be all ready to be married and then go off and visit and run around with other men when she's got a perfectly swell guy of her own who is expecting to marry her. I know he'll draw the line at that."

"But, after all, Jessica," said Louella, "isn't that something like what you did, sending Rodney's nice pretty ring back to him and marrying another man?"

"Well, I sent it back, didn't I? I didn't keep it, though I wish I had. I may go and ask him for it. I wonder if he has it in the bank. See if you can find that out for me, Louella."

CHAPTER 18

Diana walked all the way home instead of taking the bus as she usually did after shopping. Somehow she wanted to be alone to think and not be herded in a bus with a lot of other people to distract her thoughts. She felt as if she had been struck sharply or had a shocking fall and didn't want even to think for a few minutes, till some of the pain was past.

She was thankful that the way she had chosen had very little traffic and few pedestrians. She walked rapidly, as it seemed easier that way, but when she came to the park that was across the road and only a block below the Sanderson home, she turned sharply into it and sought out the bench where she had often gone to read when Beryl was busy or away at the Red Cross for her mother.

There was no one there now, and the sunshine was shimmering through the lacy hemlock boughs that were planted behind it. She sat down under the shadow at the end of the bench and drew a relieved breath, feeling as if she had reached a real refuge. For an instant she just sat and looked out over the lovely scene and tried to realize that she was no longer under the fire of that awful girl's eyes, her look of contempt and challenge. Then the memory of it all rolled over her like a great wave of trouble and fairly took her breath away.

She dropped her face into her lifted hands, her head bowed over, and if she hadn't been still so conscious of the great world outside that might at any moment step into the picture, she certainly would have groaned. The whole matter seemed so utterly sordid and humiliating. To think any girl would dare to talk to another as that girl had done. Real trouble she was in, and she had no one to go to. She would be ashamed to tell Beryl or her mother, and as for her own mother, even if she were home and she might go to her at once, her mother would only be very angry and annoyed with her. She had stayed away against her advice and laid herself open to gossip and criticism.

Somehow the only one she wanted to go to with her trouble was Rodney Graeme, and of course she couldn't do that. She wouldn't for the world have Rodney know a thing like this. It seemed to put a great blight upon her soul, a great insult to her life, which she had always hoped was sweet and clean. She felt as if she had suddenly fallen into pitch and did not know how to get rid of its stains. If only there were somebody to whom she dared talk! But the only one who came to her mind as possible was Rodney, and that was impossible. Perhaps she never could talk to him again. And there would be his sweet mother, too, but of course she wouldn't have her know for anything in the world that a girl like that would dare to talk to her the way Jessica had talked.

Then suddenly there came to her, like a voice speaking quietly behind her: *"Fear thou not; for I am with thee . . . I will help thee."* Where did that come from? Out of her childhood past, or out of the meeting where Jeremy had spoken, or had she heard Rodney repeat it lately? Why, surely that was the verse Rodney had used among others when he was telling her about the Lord, and it reminded her at once that she need not cast about for someone to comfort and help her. She had a new Helper, a Lord who cared, and who had promised to be with her everywhere. She had no need to go to earthly friends, to men and women, or even her girlfriend. There was One closer to her now. Who would understand fully. Before whom she need never feel humiliated, even though He and she both knew she was a sinner. But He had taken that sin upon Himself, for her sake.

Then she remembered how she had once before cried unto the Lord in trouble and He had helped her, smoothed her troubles all out without any effort on her part. Would He do it again?

So she prayed, "Oh, my dear new Lord, I am in trouble again, and no one to help but You. I can't do anything about it myself. Won't You please take over? I don't understand why this thing has come upon me. Was it something I did wrong? But somehow I'm sure You can make it right. And if there is something I should do, please show me what it is, and give me guidance now, and strength. And now, please help me to go back to the house and the hours that are ahead and not act frightened. I will trust You all the way and listen for Your guidance. Thank You. Amen."

She remained with bowed head for a moment, and it seemed to her she felt a hand upon her head, laid there in blessing and a promise. And again came that voice from far away, back down the ages, and yet, as if the words were just spoken. *"Fear . . . not . . . I will help thee."*

A moment more and then Diana lifted her head, and the trouble and burden seemed to be gone. God was there, and what *she* could not, He would do for her.

She brushed her hair back from her hot face, straightened her hat, and got up, gave one glance around the quiet park, and then started briskly back to the house. It did not matter now what that girl had said, what she had threatened to do. God would take care of that for her. What a wonderful thing was this that Rodney had done for her, whether she ever saw him again or not! Whether his steps ever crossed her path again, that was in God's hands, too, but at least she would always be glad that she had known him and that he had introduced her to God. Perhaps in heaven they could talk it over, but maybe by that time all this would be as if it had not been. Just like that trouble with her mother and Bates Hibberd. It might go away. Of course there might be more of that coming to her again when she got back to New York, but God had helped her once. He could and would surely help her whenever the time came that she needed help.

So she went smiling into the house with a real glad light in her eyes, not any artificial smile either, but a smile of resting and trusting.

But over in her own room, not many miles away, Jessica was fretting and fuming.

For three long days she waited for her chance to get it back on this little indifferent New Yorker whom she hadn't been able to down with the most bitter and unpleasant words she could find. She had gone each morning early to the Graeme house, telling Mother Graeme that she simply *must* see Rodney at once, and gotten the same answer, that he had not yet returned. And she knew no more of what was to be his orders now than she had known when Jessica was there before.

"Well, then, you'll have to give me his address, Mamma Graeme. I've simply got to ask him some questions. I've got an order to write an article, and I told my editor that I had a friend just returned from service, and I would get some local coloring for him, and I've only a few more days to get this article in, so please give me his address."

"But I don't know what it is, Jessica," said Margaret Graeme, glad in her heart that

317

she didn't know. "You see, the boys know that I understand I mustn't worry if I don't hear. I've been through months and months of that, you know, and so have they, and they would be sure I would wait and know that they would write as soon as they had anything definite that they had a right to tell."

"But they are not overseas now, you know."

"No, I wouldn't know that for sure. You know, the war needs are peculiar and changeable. They might have been sent right off to the Pacific, without a chance to either telephone or write. They would feel that I would understand. But then again they may be returning tonight or tomorrow or even sometime today. They'll come when they come," and she smiled quietly with a faith that was used to trusting her very life to God.

But that utter trust only made Jessica angry. "You're the most unfeeling mother I ever saw," she snapped, "or else you're holding out on me for some reason."

"Why, no," said Margaret Graeme, "I'm not holding out on you. I just haven't the information you want, that's all."

But Jessica had slammed away and gone over to Louella's hotel to blame her. She was due to report to her husband either by letter or in person in three days, and as yet she hadn't got anywhere, except to blast Diana, which though it gave her personal satisfaction, had left a great uneasiness because she couldn't interpret aright her reaction. She had never seen a girl react to an insult as Diana had done, and with apparently no after-climax of retaliation, and she was constantly fearing what form it might take when it did come. For she was sure a girl with spirit enough to have such steady poise to walk out on an insult, head up, shoulders back, must have initiative enough to bring a real sting when she finally decided to act. So she watched and planned and tried to bully Louella into doing something drastic. She hadn't been even able to find out whether she had driven Diana back to New York yet, or if she was still at the Sandersons.

But at last the boys came home again, arriving on the late train Saturday night, to stay just over Sunday, they told their mother as they kissed her joyously. And from that embrace she gathered that their news was good, whatever it was. She could wait till they told her.

The news of their arrival got around the town by way of Bonny Stewart, whose brother spent much of his time hanging around the station, especially at the time of the arrival of the late trains, hoping to pick up an extra dollar or two conveying late passengers to their homes to build up his depleted bank account.

In due time the word got around to Jessica, by way of several of the other girls, and she lost no time in going to the Graeme house, but found them of course all gone to church.

"The very idea!" she said to Hetty, who had informed her. "I should have supposed they would have stayed at home together if the boys are going away again. A strange kind of a mother they have that she would let them go to church and go herself when they may be going away again, perhaps never to come back."

"Dat's mostly de case wif everyone," said Hetty wisely. "When you go out an' away you can't say if you'll ever come back again. But dat ain't sayin' you shouldn't go right on livin' de best you can. But dat's how it is. If you want's ta see dem boys, you'd best go ta church yourself."

Very angry at this, Jessica walked out but decided on the way to the gate that she would go to church and hold up Rodney, *make* him walk home with her, and show the town who had him now. So she went to church.

She entered noisily and took a back seat, and the first sight she saw was the Graeme family all sitting together in their usual pew. Later her eyes wandered to the other side of the church, and there sat the Sandersons, with that Diana in their midst! The effrontery of her. After all she had said to her to think she would dare come to a public place and appear with Rodney's friends. Well, she would settle that once and for all. She would get hold of Rodney before any of them and make him promise to walk home with her. He simply couldn't say no, or get out of it in public this way.

So while the last words of the benediction were still echoing in the air, and while the soft tones of the organ began to play for the close of service, Jessica was halfway up the aisle, marching straight to the Graeme pew and making everyone turn and stare wondering if someone had died or something strange had happened. Jessica had not been seen with the Graemes for several years, yet there she was leaning over Father Graeme and Mother Graeme, to speak most earnestly to Rodney. Well, that was something to look at and mistake!

"Rod," she said with her sweetest smile,

recalling with her tone the days when he would always spring to do her bidding, "will you please walk home with me? I have something very important to tell you, and it won't wait. And can you come at once, so I won't take too much of your precious time?"

She was waiting, still leaning over the Graemes, effectually blocking the way for them to get out into the aisle. Margaret Graeme's heart almost skipped a beat as she heard the request made of her boy. Just how would he handle this matter? Then the assurance came back to her eyes and she knew that God was managing this affair as well as the war, and she might relax and just trust.

But Father Graeme's face was stern and his jaw grim. Most of his fellow Christians could tell pretty well how he felt about the matter, for well they knew that expression and didn't care to get into any argument with him when he looked like that. Then they all looked quickly at Rodney, especially Jeremy, who was just beyond his brother at the other end of the seat, and his eyes were both stern and anxious.

But Rodney had a calmness about him that his brother knew was not his own. Jeremy felt he had just been praying.

Rodney gave Jessica one sharp, stern,

searching glace, and then he let his lips relax, and he answered in a pleasant voice that all around could hear, "That would be quite impossible, Mrs. De Groot. Someone is waiting for me with a car, and I have to leave at once. Mother, Dad, will you kindly let me pass? I promised not to be late," and though Jessica put on an act of trying to detain him — "But oh, Rod, this is most important! Then when *can* I see you? Sometime today?" — he brushed by her brusquely and went marching down the aisle, smiling at everybody but getting quite away.

And though she did her best to follow him up for just one other word, trying to think which ugly truth she could convey briefly to fling at him, she only arrived at the church steps in time to see Rodney assisting Diana into the backseat of the Sanderson car and sitting down beside her. So, that was the way it was, was it? That girl hadn't taken her warning, and now she was due to get her full punishment. Well, she, Jessica, would do her worst. She would go to the Sandersons' and ask to see him. He surely couldn't get away then. And she would tell him all she knew, and more that she had made up, about that girl Diana.

Jeremy watched her from afar, but she wasn't noticing Jeremy. The fire was in her eyes, and he knew she meant to do mischief. He had watched her too many years, to protect his brother, not to know what her expressions portended.

So as soon as he reached home he went to the telephone and called up the Sandersons'.

Rodney came to the phone.

"Hello, Rod! I just wanted to tell you that you left an enemy in the church aisle when you went away, and you better be prepared for almost anything. I think you're due to meet her shortly, so get in touch with your Guide. I don't know just what form this will take, but I didn't want it to get you unawares, and it will be plenty. Get on your armor. And oh, Rod, tell Beryl I'll be over in about an hour, and if you need any help call me also. See you subsea!"

So Rodney was warned, but not definitely. And certainly Mr. Sanderson was not warned, for it was he who opened the front door for Jessica when she arrived, just as dinner was being put on the table and the family were on the way to the dining room.

Mr. Sanderson bowed courteously and showed the caller into the small reception room nearer to the front door than the living room, where the more intimate guests were always taken. Then he stepped to the dining room door and called, "Rodney, here's a caller for you." Then under his breath he whispered as Rod went by him, "Got your pen ready? It's probably an autograph!"

So Rodney came to stand in the doorway and looked into the room.

Jessica had taken pains to sit in the most sheltered corner of the room where she would not be seen, or at least recognized at once by the person entering, and so Rodney came all the way into the room and looked around, and then seeing her he said "Oh!" in a tone that was anything but flattering.

Jessica put away a delicate handkerchief with which she was doing a preliminary plaintive weep, and rising came toward him. "Rodney," she said softly so that her voice would not reach to the other room — not *yet* — "I have something very important to tell you. Something that when you have heard you will be glad I told you. It is something I felt you ought to know, and for the sake of my old-time fondness for you I have put aside my natural timidity —"

"What?" said Rodney sharply. "What did you say? Your *natural timidity*? I don't remember that. But go on. Let's get it over

quick. You are holding up my host's dinner."

"That won't matter when you have heard what I have to say."

"Go ahead," said Rodney, flinging up his head impatiently.

"But Rodney, there is something else I want to ask first, for my own sake. I want you to do a personal favor for me."

"Yes?" said the young officer looking her straight in the eye with a wry grin on his lips. "I thought there would be some catch. Proceed!"

Jessica drew a quivering breath and swept a swift glance of reproach at the young man, but she hurried on, knowing that he was quite capable of terminating this meeting without notice, but she meant to get in her work this time.

"Well, then, Rod, I want my ring back again. I've suffered no end of trouble to think I ever gave it up, and I want it back again. Please, Rod. Be good to me. I'm so sorry I ever gave it up. Please give it back!"

"What do you want it for?" asked the young man with almost a sneer on his nice lips, because he didn't believe anything this girl was saying.

"I want it to remember you by!" she said with almost a sob, and a quiver between every word.

"Yes? Well, I wouldn't care to be remembered by you, even if I had the ring. And I haven't got it!"

"You haven't *got* it? What have you done with it? You haven't given it to that other girl *yet,* have you? Oh, *Rod!*" And Jessica's head drooped, and she bowed her face in her hands. "Oh, Rod! I didn't think you'd do that!"

"I certainly did not give it to any girl," said Rodney severely. "I wouldn't dishonor any other girl by giving her a ring that had been returned to me in scorn by a girl who had no honor herself."

There was a solemn pause while Jessica took in this implication, and then she cried out in a good simulation of despair, "Then what *have* you done with it?"

"I sold it to a dealer in China two years ago. I didn't want a thing like that cluttering around my life. I hated the sight of it and the thing it stood for. Thank God it is gone from my thoughts even, forever!"

"Oh, Rod! How *can* you be so cruel to me? You once used to love me!"

"The more fool I," said Rodney. "I only thought I did, but I am grateful that I was made to see what you really were before it was too late. And now, was that all you came to say? I could not get that ring back even if I wanted to, and I would not even if I could. So that is my answer to that. Now, what else?"

Then Jessica lifted her anguished head and looked him in the eyes with fire of anger in her own. "Yes, there is something else. And this is for *your* sake. I have found out that the girl you are going with now has a false heart. It is ironic that you should select two girls who are neither of them true to you. This girl you are courting here in Riverton is engaged to be married to a rich handsome fellow, of high birth, in New York, and she is to be married to him within a very short time. She has her trousseau bought, and her wedding dress is waiting for the time when he is expected home to claim her. I thought you ought to be told that before your affair here goes on any further. I had intended leaving Riverton myself a couple weeks ago, but I delayed till I could get opportunity to tell you this before it was too late. Now, I don't expect you to be grateful at once, but I'm sure when you find out that what I have said is true, you will write and thank me."

Rodney stood looking at her with almost fury in his eyes for a moment, and then he said with dignity and severity, "I am too angry to answer you as you ought to be answered. It would be better for you to go now. I don't care to talk with you anymore. Shall I open the door for you? Good afternoon. And don't try anything like this again."

Rodney's voice had been clear and decided, and the people in the other room could scarcely help hearing, though Mr. Sanderson did his best to create a diversion by dropping the brass tongs on the tiles of the hearth and tapping a spoon against a glass by his place. The family had not sat down, they had been sort of waiting for Rodney, but little by little they all perceived that Rodney was anything but pleased by his caller, and they all had more or less the feeling that he might presently need them to come in and say something that would make her leave. Mrs. Sanderson even ventured the thought to herself that if she went in and invited the girl to stay for dinner with them she would then take the hint and go, and she suggested this in a low tone to Beryl, but Beryl shook her head decidedly. "No, Mother, you don't know her. She would stay and put a crimp in the whole works." So the mother desisted, meditating whether or not it would be best for them to sit down and start dinner.

But just then to their great relief Jeremy breezed in and walked right into the dining room with his cheery greeting. This made the conversation so general that it could but be heard in the front reception room. The next sound they heard was the front door closing emphatically after the unwanted guest.

It did not take Jessica long to realize as she walked angrily down the pleasant street toward her bus that she had overstepped herself in this visit. If she had only stopped after the request for the ring and not gone on to tell about Diana, with all that horde where they could hear what she was saying, she might have had some effect. But now she saw that she had only made Rodney very angry by trying to run down Diana. Well, at least Diana had heard her and knew that she had made good her threat. She had attained that much. And she had made known the truth, or what she supposed was the truth, to Rodney. Though it really never made much difference to Jessica whether what she told was the truth or not, so it hit home on somebody and hurt, preferably the people she didn't like.

So Jessica went on back to Riverton and hunted out Louella to commiserate with her. Of course Louella told her she had been very, very brave, and she was sure something drastic would come of all this, but secretly she decided that she would stay away from the Graemes for a while till this blew over, or else she would be blamed with it all by Donald, who was rather plain-spoken and didn't mind hurting when he thought it would do some good.

But Jessica, weeping herself angrily to sleep, resolved that next she would go up to New York, hunt out that officer Diana was engaged to, and put trouble to brewing there for Diana when she got home to put on her wedding dress, which she felt pretty sure Diana would do, now that Rodney knew the truth about her. He hadn't said anything, still these closemouthed soldiers knew how to shut up, but they smoldered inside. She was sure she had seen fire for somebody in Rodney's eyes. He might blame her at first, but Diana would have to account for it all, and it wouldn't be so fine for him. She doubted if he would go to church tonight with her. Perhaps she would go herself just to find out.

Before Jessica fell asleep that night she decided it would be a good thing if she were to go up to New York the next morning and hunt out that bridegroom of Diana before Diana got home. For undoubtedly she would be leaving Riverton in the morning, after what she must have overheard today.

Then, after she had made that New York swell understand what had been going on, and put a crimp in Diana's plans, she had only one more thing to do. She had to find out just where Rod and Jerry were located, what work they were doing, and somehow get into their offices and hunt up those papers her husband wanted. Then she would have her blue diamond, and that was all she cared for in life. After she had that, maybe she'd get a divorce and hunt up some nice returning officer for herself, for she was done with Rod. The way he had looked at her when he put her out of the house had settled that for her definitely.

Then she went to sleep.

CHAPTER 19

It had been a bit embarrassing for Rodney when he came back to the dining room, to meet the family that he had come so to respect and love. He felt shamed and humiliated, until he suddenly realized that that was what Jessica had wanted, and that was why she had come there, just to humiliate him, in return for his avoiding her. He smiled to himself wryly.

"What's so funny, Rod?" asked his brother. "You certainly didn't sound like a comic opera in there. We could hear a lot of what was said. I suppose you realize that?"

"Yes," Rodney said, smiling. "I knew you couldn't help it, unless you all got up and shouted or went out in the kitchen and got spoons and pans and had a band parade. In fact, I *wanted* you to hear *some* of it. Though I certainly am ashamed, Mr. Sanderson, that I should have disgraced your home where you have so kindly made me welcome."

"Not at all, boy! Don't worry about it for a minute. We all knew of course that you couldn't be enjoying the session very much yourself."

"No," admitted Rodney, "I wasn't. It was just the dread of something like this happening sometime that made me almost not want to come home from war, but I knew that was foolish. It had to be got over with, and that was all. But I had hoped that fool girl had grown up since she got married and learned a little sense. But it seems I was wrong. Mr. Sanderson, I'd like you and your wife to know that at one time when I was a kid in high school, I thought that girl was the most beautiful creature on the face of the earth, and I fancied myself very much in love with her. I even got her a ring. And then when I'd been over in the war about a year she sent that ring back to me with attempts at proper apologies. She said she was going to marry a rich man, and she knew I would understand and forgive her. Well, I was pretty young then and the war was grim, and for a while I thought everything was gone. Death was everywhere. Nothing was genuine. But after a while I met the Lord, and then all was different. I was glad He had saved me from a girl like that.

"Forgive me, Mrs. Sanderson, for spreading my mistakes and troubles out before everybody, but since you had to hear some of it, I'd rather you would understand."

"Go on, Rodney," said the smiling mother. "Just act as if we were your own people and tell what you want us to know."

"Thank you, Mrs. Sanderson," said Rodney with gratitude in his voice. "I appreciate that. There isn't so much more to tell, but — do you know what that girl came here for today? She wanted me to *give her back* the ring she had returned!"

"I hope you didn't do it," said Mr. Sanderson amusedly. "Though I don't suppose you've carried it around in your vest pocket all these years."

There was a twinkle in his eyes that set everybody laughing merrily and relieved the tensity of the atmosphere somewhat.

"No, I didn't give it back," said Rodney fiercely. "I told her I had sold it to a dealer in China and that even if I *had* it I wouldn't give it to her. But there, I'm just ashamed that you had to meet up with my poor young mistakes. I hope I'm not that bad any*more,* but still one can never tell. I guess heaven may show up some more mighty big failures yet."

"Well, we won't worry about those now,

not with the God you have to forgive and cover them up with His own righteousness. Mother, I wonder if there are more hot mashed potatoes out in the kitchen? And more gravy, too? Jeremy and I both want some more, don't we, Jerry, my boy?"

And so the routine of the pleasant dinner table went on, and the incident of Jessica passed into the annals to be forgotten. After all, it had not troubled anybody but Rodney, and they all loved Rodney and wanted to comfort him.

The talk fell into more practical lines. The young men told as much as they could, as much as regulations allowed them to tell, of their own present prospects. The place where their work would be located at first, and the importance of what they were to do. There were shining eyes about that table as they all realized that immediate far separation was not to be their lot.

"Does Mom know yet?" asked Rodney anxiously, looking at his brother. "She's been rather worried, I know, though she hasn't said much. I hope you told her something, Jerry. We hadn't much time last night or this morning before church."

"Oh, I didn't tell her much, only that she needn't worry, we were not going far, not at present. That satisfied her for the time. You know, Mom has always been wonderfully understanding."

"Yes, I know," said Rodney. "She's about the best soldier in our family. Dad always wants to understand everything."

"Yes," said Beryl's father, "I'm like that, too. I run my family pretty well, and I sometimes think I could run the government, too, better than most other people. Well, couldn't I, Mamma?"

Such a pleasant, understanding family they all were, and so much like the Graemes, thought Diana, wistfully wishing her own family were like them.

Then suddenly she looked up and her eyes met Rodney's eyes, and there was something in them like a blessing. Her cheeks turned rosy, and somehow unexplained matters seemed all at once set right between them. Her heart grew gladly light, and she knew she was not going home to New York in the morning. Not *yet,* anyway.

After Jerry saw that look pass between them, he settled down to enjoy his third helping of mashed potatoes and gravy and spent the rest of the time looking at Beryl.

The afternoon came at last and Rodney could take a shy Diana out and have a talk with her.

"Well, Diana, are you off me for life since

you found out about my foolish past?" he asked after they had found a pleasant grassy place to sit among the trees.

Diana's eyes lighted happily.

"Everybody has a silly past," she said wisely enough. "Perhaps it isn't always their own fault entirely. It is sometimes the fault of older people who ought to know better. They fairly fling people at you and insist on making something of their companionship. That was my trouble. I was sort of paired off with a boy I had known all my life, and I couldn't seem to get away from it. He just ordered me around as if I belonged to him, and he got around my mother, till I finally ran away to visit Beryl and get away from it all, so I could think out what to do."

Rodney was watching her as she talked. "Then you hadn't got your trousseau and wedding dress all ready when you came away? And you haven't set the date for your wedding yet?" he asked, watching her meanwhile keenly.

"Mercy, no!" Diana said with a laugh. "I hadn't any idea of getting married." Then she turned to him suddenly and looked him sharply in the eyes. "Did *she* tell you that?"

He looked astonished. "Yes, Jessica told me. How did you know?"

"Because she threatened to tell you unless

I went home to New York at once."

"She *did*? The little rat!"

"And she threatened to go up to New York and find the young man she said she heard I was going to marry and tell him how I had been running around with all of you down here."

There was a kind of a frightened smile on her face as she said this, and Rodney knew it was troubling her. "Do you mind her doing that?" he asked, a tender note in his voice.

"No, only it may get to my father and mother if they come home soon, and it will trouble them. They have been awfully worried because I wouldn't come home and fix up an engagement right away."

"And you don't want that?"

"No, I certainly do *not,*" said Diana definitely.

Rodney looked at her earnestly another minute, and then he said firmly, "Well then, I guess we've got to do something about this right away. I wasn't going to rush things because I felt perhaps you didn't know me very well, and I was so uncertain about my future, but the immediate future is sort of settled for the present, anyway." He reached out and took both her hands in his. "You *dear*!" he said tenderly. "I love you, my sweet!"

Then he bent down and kissed her softly, and Diana looked up with a glad light in her face like a glory light. Their lips came together again in a long, sweet kiss, as he drew her closer.

"I love you, too," said she softly. "I think I've loved you ever since you prayed for me in the meeting that night when Jerry spoke."

He drew her closer and looked down into her face. "Yes, I was praying for you then," he said, wonderingly. "How did you know?"

"I just felt it in my heart," she whispered softly. "It frightened me a little and made me feel a sinner. I never had known I was a sinner before, although I joined the church when I was a child. But how did you now I needed praying for?"

He smiled. "I guess the Holy Spirit told me. I kept wondering and wondering if you knew the Lord, and tried to say you wouldn't have been in the meeting if you didn't, yet I knew that was no proof, and so I began to pray that you should know my Lord."

"Oh, my dear! This is wonderful! I never knew God could speak to people and guide them on this earth the way He is doing now. I am so glad I have found you. I didn't think there would ever be a man I could love. That is why I ran away down here."

"Then you didn't love the man they thought you were going to marry?"

"No, I didn't love him, and I didn't want to marry him. He is nice, you know, a really good moral fellow, but I didn't love him. Not even if he had been a Christian I wouldn't want to marry him. I couldn't *love* him."

"That's good," said Rodney. "That makes it all right with me. And Jessica can go around telling all the tales she wants to tell. It won't bother me any. But now, here's something else. Your mother and father. What will they say?"

"Well, of course they won't like it very much, not at first, anyway. At least Mother won't. She's very much sold on Bates Hibberd. And she doesn't know you. But she will. I'm satisfied she will. She'll like all those ribbons and decorations you're wearing on your uniform, too. Those things count a lot with her. Of course you're an officer, too, of some kind, aren't you?"

"Oh, yes, of a sort," Rodney said, laughing. "But will this mean we will have to wait a long time to get married? How old are you anyway?"

"Twenty-one last April," said Diana with

a glad smile. "I'm of age. I can do as I please, although of course I don't want to hurt my parents, but if they object I'll have to do what I think is right, even in spite of them. And I know my father won't object. He'll like you, too, I'm sure."

"But you said this other guy was rich, didn't you? And I'm as poor as that typical church mouse. Of course I've got a job with the government just now, but the war is almost over. There is no telling what will come afterward for me. I might have to be just a plain farmer. That's something I understand, at least."

"That's all right with me," said Diana, happily nestling closer to the strong arm that held her.

"Yes, but it might not be all right with your dad, my dear. And perhaps it's all right for him to feel that way, too. Parents don't like to hand their children over to penniless strangers."

"They won't object after they know you. Anyway, I love you."

"You dear!" he said, bending to touch her lips with his own again. "What a girl to come home to! And to think I was bitter when I returned because my girl had gone back on me, and I hated her for it. When all the time she wasn't my real girl at all. She was the girl I *thought* would be a right one and then found out that God had something better waiting and ready for me. What a girl to come home to! My dearest, the best in all the world! But now, see here, we've got to do something about this matter of your mother and father at once. If Jessica goes up to New York as she threatened, and gets in touch with that Bates Hibberd, he'll beat us to your parents, and that will not be so good. When do you say they are coming home?"

"Probably not till the end of the week," said Diana.

"Then we better go Saturday morning. I can get off then, I think. This isn't a thing that can wait. Do you think so?"

"Oh, yes, I'd like to get it over. I warn you it won't be easy. Mother is very much set on Bates. She'll probably call up when she gets home, and I dread that for she might insist on sending Bates down to accompany me home. That would just fit right in with her plans."

"Then don't say when you're coming. Say you'll try and arrange things here to get back soon. I believe perhaps we better just go ourselves early in the morning unannounced, and then there can't be anything like that sprung on us. You see, I've had

343

experience in this long-distance calling back and forth. There generally is some mix-up, especially when there is a difference of opinion. I'll be ready to go on that early train if you are. Are you sure you can get away?"

"Yes, I can go. Perhaps that is the best way, just take things in our own hands and announce what we are going to do, and say we've come for their blessing."

So they sat and made their lovely plans.

"Oh, it is going to be so wonderful to have somebody planning for me, somebody I can love and trust," said Diana. "It was awful to be ordered around by Bates. Oh, he was nice and pleasant, you understand, but I constantly resented his possessive manner."

"I'm glad of that," said Rodney fervently. "But maybe you'll find me developing a possessive manner, too. What will happen then?"

"Oh, but I *love* you! And that makes all the difference in the world."

"Darling!" said Rodney, gathering her close again and sealing the word with a kiss.

"It's odd, but Beryl said something like that to me the first day I came, and I didn't know just exactly what she meant. You see, I didn't know what love like this meant. I hadn't known you yet."

Time went very swiftly and happily out there under the sheltering trees, for those two. Occasionally they would pause in their gladness and make a plan or two about Saturday and then slip back again to merely exulting in the presence of each other.

"And it's so wonderful that you belong to the Lord. You seemed to understand and take Him into your heart right away. That set the seal right at first on my love," said Rodney thoughtfully. "I knew you were the right one by that very sign, for I had been knowing all the way home that I couldn't ever love anyone who did not give allegiance to my Lord."

"Oh," said Diana with wonder in her eyes. "And I told Beryl that I was afraid of you after hearing that prayer. You were so religious I was just afraid to talk to you lest I couldn't measure up to your heights. And just to think, you reached down to the level where I'd been living and lifted me up where I could see the light and glory in Jesus' face. I would have loved Him long ago if I had really ever seen Him. And oh, I'm so glad it was you that helped me find Him."

And out in another green place in the woods where there were no people, and only a sweet silence punctuated now and again by piercing sweet bird notes, Jeremy and Beryl were walking arm in arm, or sometimes hand in hand, according to the roughness of the going.

They had been talking about Jessica. In fact, it was almost impossible, after the scene that noon, not to talk about her. And Jerry had been telling Beryl of the early years when he was always anxious because that girl fairly possessed his brother and he couldn't do anything about it.

"For he was always such a wonderful chap!" said Jeremy soberly. "I just couldn't bear to see him get in her clutches. And then to come home and find her messing around in the way again. I just couldn't stand it."

"Yes, he is wonderful," said Beryl. "And he seems so very much like you in many ways."

Jeremy looked down at her with a quick appreciative smile.

"Thank you," he said. "You couldn't have said anything that would please me better. I always adored him."

It was then that Jerry reached down and took her hand, drawing it up within his arm and holding his own over it. It was the first time he had done it just this way. He had been almost shy with Beryl.

They walked along silently for a little, thrilling over the touch of their hands, the look in each other's eyes.

Then Jeremy, pressing the small hand he held, said with a relieved sigh, "Well, now, I've got my brother's worries off my hands, so let's talk about us. We've known each other a long time. Very far, for you always seemed unattainable to me. You were so beautiful, and so perfectly dressed, and so very gracious and full of lovely manners, that I felt like a gawky country boy, all hands and feet, whenever I came into your presence. But I think I've been loving you all these years. How about it? Could you stand me for the rest of your life?"

The shade of the woods was very dense just where they were walking, and Beryl turned and put her face against his arm. "Oh, Jerry!" she breathed softly. "I have always loved you. I was sometimes afraid you would see that shining in my eyes and written on my face."

And then Jerry folded her in his arms.

"Sweet! Sweet! Sweet!" sang a knowing little bird in a high tree above them, turning his bright little glance down at them, just as if he understood. And who knows, perhaps he did.

The shadows were low on the mossy way

as they went slowly back to the house much later.

"Now," said Jerry in a practical voice, "tomorrow morning, you and I are going to the city to buy you a ring. Not any seven-by-nine one, but a *real* ring that will match your dear self and all that you stand for in my life."

Chapter 20

Jessica had thought she was going up to New York that Monday morning to meet with the would-be bridegroom and show up her hated enemy, Diana. But there came a telegram before she was awake, ordering her to meet her husband out west on important business, and so she had to pack up and get off on another train, in another direction entirely.

She had only time to call Louella before she left, and order her to find out certain things for her definitely, before her return, which she hoped would be in the course of two or three days. And she promised to reward her well if she got all the answers to her questions ready for her return.

So Louella arose and set forth on her quest for answers. For, to tell the truth, she sorely needed the reward promised. She had lazed around too long running up hotel bills, which she hadn't paid and which would eventually fall to her relative to pay, as in the past.

She went first to the Graemes' of course, for that was her main first source of information, provided she could get *any.*

But the boys were both gone. Where?

"To the city, I think," said Margaret Graeme. "They said they had some shopping to do."

"Shopping?" said Louella curiously. "What kind of shopping? I didn't know servicemen ever did shopping when they got home."

"Now, Louella. You never can bear not to find out everything, can you?" laughed Margaret. "But won't you come in?"

"Oh, yes, just for a minute. There are some questions I want to ask you. What about the boys? Are they any better informed than they were?"

"Oh, yes," said the boys' mother. "They are not to leave the country for the present. They have a job here that is not far away. I wasn't given the exact location yet. It seems hard for us to get time to ask questions. It's so good to know they are not going back to combat, for the present anyway."

"Well, what are they to be doing? What is their title? They surely have some designation."

"Why, you see I didn't think to ask that.

350

They'll just be Rodney and Jeremy to me, just the same as they always were."

"Oh, Margaret, you're simply impossible," said Louella, and she finally took herself away, much to the relief of her relative.

But Jessica was by this time speeding away on an express train and trying to figure out just what she had to do in the near future, how soon she could hope to get that blue diamond.

The next day she was closeted with her husband and two other men in a bare little room in a dowdy boarding place, getting instructions.

One of the two strange men seemed a foreigner. He had a pompous, disagreeable air and talked with a strange accent, which she could not quite place. The other man was a sort of high-class secretary, perhaps, for he wrote everything down, including the papers she was given to guide her in the work she was to do. And strangely he seemed to be somebody who was over her husband in this work she was doing, which he said was for the government. She kept asking herself *what* government, and why he was telling Carver what to do. It was a new role to find her husband taking advice, or rather orders from anybody. It gave her food for thought and a sort of a frightening background for this work she had been ordered to do.

Carver, it developed from the talk between the men, was expecting to leave the country for a time, possibly soon. There seemed to be an uncertainty about it, maybe dependent upon her own success in the mission they were about to send her on. If he went, she would ask him to take her along. She was about fed up with this country, and it would be a relief to travel. Afterward, if she still was out of sorts with her husband, she could probably get a divorce over in Europe as well as in this country and could make her plans accordingly.

They suggested that the war might be over soon, and the possibility seemed fraught with peril for some of them. She tried to figure that out but couldn't quite make it. However, if anything unpleasant developed, she would just get away somewhere. It hadn't been hard to do so far, though she sensed that she had not been so clever as her husband had expected she would be when he married her. She really must exert herself and get this one across, for there was that blue diamond. She mustn't miss out on that.

The tiresome session was ended at last, and the men departed one by one, by devious unexpected ways, the foreigner going by way of a window and a fire escape. He was hurrying to catch a train he said, but when she looked out of the window he was walking away toward the woods as fast as he could go, with his hat pulled down over his face. It was all very odd and bewildering, and when she asked a puzzled question, her husband reminded her that she was to ask no questions whatever, and it was best to forget all that she had seen or thought she had seen. There seemed to be something crooked somewhere, though she couldn't quite make out what. Not that Jessica objected very seriously to crooked ways of doing things, but it didn't seem quite to fit with her well-dressed, immaculate, severe husband, and she did like to understand things. However, this wasn't the way to win blue diamonds.

So, reluctantly, she gave attention to the instructions that were being given her.

"This paper is the most important. You will put it in the small white bag and pin it inside your garments, right over the heart. Don't let anyone get possession of it. Guard it with your very life. Do you understand?"

Jessica blanched. "But you said there was to be no danger," she faltered.

"No danger if you do your work fearlessly.

No possibility of being suspected if you work calmly, fearlessly. It is safer that way."

Jessica caught her breath and kept on listening, and the stern old voice continued:

"Now, here are the papers that you will need in getting into the plant."

"Plant? What plant?" she asked with wide eyes. "Have I got to go and work in a plant?"

"Nonsense! Give better attention or you will never be equal to this. I would have sent someone else, but the one I had chosen was killed in an accident, and this matter is urgent. Listen carefully."

"Killed?" said Jessica in a frightened tone.

But the hard old voice went right on. "Yesterday your friends, those two officers you know so well, entered new positions in the service, and it is necessary that you make immediate contact with them and get to work. There are important papers that will be under their care, and you can better find them than someone your friends do not know. The elder of the two men, your former fiancé, will be your special object of interest. By nine o'clock tomorrow morning you should be entering his office. The office is located on the top floor of the building, and this paper contains the address. It is just outside your city and can be reached by bus or taxi. I should suggest taxi, unless you find the bus not too crowded. We don't want too many witnesses. You will have to use your discretion in some of these moves. Don't take any chances unless it is the only way. Remember I have told you. Don't blame me if you get into any trouble. You'll be all right if you just follow instructions."

Jessica flung a bitter look at her husband but said nothing.

"And when you get to the plant," he went on, "you will need identification papers. Here is your pass into the place, and your badge. I used an old snapshot of you to put on it. You won't have any trouble getting in, only remember you are Commander Graeme's private secretary, and if you should get there before he arrives in the morning so much the better. If possible, manage it so that you are alone in his office for a few minutes, even a short time might accomplish what you want. The main thing is to get this paper, the original of the one you have in the secreted bag. You will have to study it so that you will recognize it at once, even if you see only a part of it. We *must have* that paper before it has a chance to be sent to the government. If Mr. Graeme comes in while you are searching in the safe, as you may well have to do, you will know how to kid the gentleman along, even with endearments if necessary. Let him think you were hunting for a record you put in the safe Saturday. He won't know. He wasn't there then himself. Yes, I know definitely. I've had him watched for a week. Remember, the paper is the main thing, and it *must* be had!"

When Jessica came out from that meeting, she was trembling from head to foot, and greatly impressed with the importance of the errand on which she was about to embark.

She had just had a ravishing glimpse of the blue stone in the white velvet box, fed to her as a cat would tantalize a mouse. If it had not been for that stone, she would have taken the next train as far away from that frightening husband, and his kind, as it would be possible to get, but she simply must finish this engagement out and get that stone. Then she could stand anything. Just get away from Carver De Groot as fast as she could and never lay eyes on him again. She could dye her hair and change her makeup, and he might never know her, even if he hunted for her. Well, she had got to get through this somehow.

She went to sleep on the train and got a little rested, and then she began to study her papers and get into her memory what she had to do, for she had been ordered to commit all these notes to memory and then destroy all but that one paper that was so important and must be kept until the last minute.

Jessica found the way back to Riverton most tedious and tiresome. There were three changes, with long waits between trains, and nobody about the waiting places to look at or talk to, just little sheds with a platform and a bench and open country sizzling in a hot sun. She thought of the pleasant quiet sunny home of the Sandersons where she had been for a few minutes to fling her ugly words into Rodney's nice life, and a passing twinge of envy went through her. After all, what had she gained? She might have married Rodney if she had kept that ring and been a part of that nice respectable crowd at the Sandersons' or at the Graeme house where she had spent so many pleasant days in her childhood. Awful bores they all were, and Rodney was the worst bore of all of course, now that he had thoroughly adopted this religious phase, to which he seemed to have become heir. What a family! But better than her present lot, full of intrigue and peril and doing hazardous jobs of which she would have to take the blame if they went wrong.

She sighed heavily as she gathered up her bags from the hard bench and stood up to take the train as it crept along the rails to the shed where it was supposed to stop. Oh, she wished this whole thing was over. There was nothing pleasant to count on. Not even the small contact with Rodney was going to have any thrill about it, and to judge by the way he acted last Sunday, there was no telling what attitude he might take toward her. She was definitely frightened and wished she might run away and hide. She had entirely forgotten the scheme she had entertained of going to New York to find and inform that rich young officer about the defection of his supposed-to-be bride. Later it would come to her, and she would wonder if there were any chance for her to charm him away when she got rid of her old husband, but now she was entirely engrossed with the thought of what she had to do, and she did not like the idea. There would be guns around, perhaps, and she detested guns, and firing. She never had wanted to learn to shoot.

So now, while the people she had wanted to harm were having a happy time selecting rings, engagement and wedding rings, and making a memorable day of it, Jessica was beginning some of her punishment already.

CHAPTER 21

Jessica got back to her room in the Riverton Hotel very late Tuesday night and went right to bed. It was too late to call Louella, so she did not know what had been happening during her absence, but it likely didn't matter. She would call her in the morning, and besides she was too tired to care.

However, she awoke very early the next morning, suddenly aware of the unpleasant errand she had to do for her husband, and filled with excitement over it.

She should of course call Louella the first thing now and make sure that the Graemes really had that new job. She wondered what she should do if there had been some hitch and they were not there.

But when she called Louella, she was informed that Mrs. Chatterton had checked out early yesterday morning. She had received a telegram calling her west on important business and might or might not return later, depending on how the business came out.

This cut off Jessica from her only source of information about the Graemes, for she knew that her girlfriends were all gone to the shore for the week, and anyway they would not know much about the Graemes. Jessica suddenly felt very much alone, and quite frightened.

How she hated this town! How she wished she could get away from it at once. She dressed rapidly, resolving that as soon as this horrible business for her husband was finished she would pack up and vanish utterly from Riverton and all that could remind her of it. Just as soon as she had that blue diamond she would go away from everything. From Carver De Groot most of all. She shuddered as she thought of the look in his hard eyes when he threatened her. When he said, "Don't blame me if you get into trouble."

With that in mind, she began swiftly to fold up her garments and lay them in her trunk. She didn't want to be delayed a moment in getting away when she got her work done. She was also very nervous about that approaching mysterious errand she had to do. She had not expected to be afraid, but she was. Unaccountably she was wondering what might happen to her if she should get caught. Rather frantically she was considering what she should do in case she had to get away from this vicinity quickly. She wouldn't want to leave her clothes behind her. More and more as the moments went by she grew panic-stricken. She must prepare for any happening, and there wasn't so much time. If she could just get everything into her trunk and lock it, then if worse came to worst she could send for her baggage afterward, say her husband had been taken sick and she had to go to him at once, or something like that. Just in case she got very much frightened.

She glanced at her watch. There wasn't so much more time before she should start, and perhaps she should have something to eat before this trying expedition.

So she called up and ordered coffee, toast, and orange juice sent up to her room, and she continued with her packing. At least everything should be under lock and key if anybody tried to go through her belongings. She didn't know why they would want to do that, but at least she was taking no chances now. It made her feel more safely comfortable to know that her affairs were all out of sight and ready to meet the most inquisitive eye, even if she got into some kind of trouble through this doubtful escapade of her husband's.

She had thought out the different stages of this affair most carefully, so that no one around this part of the world would need to know where she was and what she had been doing today. She had arranged for the taxi to take her to the station for the early train to the city. Then she was planning, as soon as the taxi had gone, to walk swiftly away and get a bus going in the opposite direction, so that if afterward should there be anyone questioning her movements, there would be no link left unguarded to tell any tales. After that she would get another bus and then perhaps another taxi, whichever seemed to be most convenient, and by devious ways she would arrive at that plant in plenty of time to get in before the brothers came. Most of these movements had been planned by a sharp-sighted husband, but she had added a few of her own, instigated by fear, and some of her plans were clever indeed. That was what Carver De Groot had seen in her, that she was exceedingly clever.

So before Jessica left her room, she went carefully about, examining even the wastebasket to make sure there wasn't a scrap of precious notes or papers that could possibly tell any tales about what she was doing.

Her baggage was locked and her door was locked when she came down the stairs, for it was too early for the elevator boy to be on duty. She gave careful directions to the office man at the desk, explaining that she was going to see a member of her family who was very ill, and she was not sure how long she would be gone. If she found she was needed she might remain a few hours and return this evening. On the other hand, she might stay for several days or even for a week or two. In which case she would telephone for some of her baggage, but for the present she was retaining her room.

Then with high head, she went briskly out the door as if for a pleasant visit and got into the taxi, feeling, perhaps, much like the fliers about to start on their first bombing mission.

Jessica had started early, following minutely the careful directions she had been given by her husband, and she arrived at the plant early, even earlier than she had hoped, and some minutes before the brothers reached there. She had made her entrance carefully, showing the badge and card and identification papers as she had been directed, and she had no trouble in getting to the office where Rodney was soon to arrive. A pretty woman seldom had difficulty in getting by, she reflected with satisfaction. She was beginning to get back her self-confidence.

The officer in charge of the rooms on that floor had given Jessica a sharp looking over, wondering a little at the style of secretary the new man had selected, but he let her in and hovered near the door to explain, once Rodney arrived, that he had let in his secretary just a minute ago. "Was that all right? She had all her papers and badge," he said.

"Secretary?" said Rodney sharply, lifting his eyebrows, "Why — I — *haven't* — any — secretary." And then he stopped short and remembered that he was still a serviceman and there was no telling what the regulations here were to be. Perhaps they picked out his secretary for him! He didn't like that. But perhaps it was only temporary.

Then the door swung open and there was a woman, working away at the safe!

Jessica had been furnished with the safe combination and been drilled carefully on how to open the safe swiftly. Moreover, she had just found the paper she was ordered to take, and as she heard the doorknob turn, she dropped the paper inside her handbag and turned, smiling pleasantly, toward the stern face of Rodney, who at once recognized her.

"Good morning!" said Jessica sweetly.

But Rodney's face did not relax. He took one step to the desk that stood near the door, and whose accessories he had carefully studied before when he came to look things over. He slipped his hand across the top, down to the edge next to his chair where two small unobtrusive bells were located and touched them, one and then the other, twice. And instantly the door was stopped in its progress of closing and swung open again with the orderly standing there and the sound of tramping feet coming down the hall toward the door. Two burly officers came and stood saluting. "You called?" they said.

Rodney answered their salute.

"Take this person down to Major Haverly's office at once," he ordered. Gravely the officers advanced impersonally to the attractive, astonished, frightened young woman who stood before the safe with her hands full of papers.

"But — but — I'm Commander Graeme's secretary!" she said in a frightened voice.

But Rodney paid no heed to her. "See that she is thoroughly searched!" he ordered. "She has no right to be up here."

"But her papers seemed all right," said the alarmed orderly.

"They can't be all right," said Rodney. "Take her at once, and don't let her out of your sight. I'll call Major Haverly."

He went to the telephone. "Major Haverly," he said in a low voice when the door was closed again, after the frightened girl and her escort, "I have just sent a young woman down to you under guard. I found her in my office standing in front of the safe, taking out papers. Please see that she is thoroughly searched and pay no attention to any of her claims. She is *not* my secretary and never has been, and you cannot always believe what she says. This is important. I haven't had opportunity to see what is missing from the safe. I will check the list at once."

"Yes, Commander Graeme. I will attend to your order. She has just arrived. Reporting later."

Jessica was stiff with fright, yet she knew she must somehow brazen this out. If she only could get that terrible paper out of her bag. No matter what became of it, it wouldn't be in her possession.

But when she tried to fumble with the clasp of her bag the sharp-eyed keepers watched her every move, and there presently arrived a woman to search her, who seemed to miss nothing. The officers were at a distance, but she knew she could make no move without their notice. Now if only that woman would only pass by that paper and not notice it!

But no! She opened the bag at last and found the paper the first thing. A gimlet-eyed woman who knew every sign of official paper and knew what was important and what was not.

"Officer!" she called, and handed over the paper, also the handbag.

Jessica began to cry. "But I need that bag," she said, "and I need all those papers. Some of them aren't mine."

"That's right, they're not," said the officer coldly. "You took some of these out of the safe."

"No," she said. "No, I didn't. I only took out what I was told to take out. I'm a secretary, you know. I was sent to get them."

"Who sent you?" The sharp eyes of three officers were instantly upon her. They saw her flinch. They knew her guilt. The head one spoke a single word, and the others put handcuffs on her slender wrists and marched her away to a small room that was like a prison cell. More orders were given in low tones, and then she was left there with two women police, and one orderly at the door.

She cried a lot and begged them to send for her friends. She said she had many friends both in the army and the navy who would help her. At last she asked them to send for her husband, and she was frightened afterward when she saw a knowing look pass between the men who were guarding her. Also she remembered Carver had told her *never* to speak his name or he would be in trouble. But surely he didn't expect her to get arrested, did he? It was time he did something about this himself. He had no right to let her suffer. Even the blue diamond wasn't enough to pay her for going through a thing like this.

By night Jessica was taken to a place of safekeeping. She was fed and made comfortable, but she was definitely a prisoner, and from remarks she overheard now and then she gathered that there were a lot more suspects in this also. Oh, what was she in for?

At last she wrote a most piteous note to Rodney, telling him what trouble she was in and asking him to come to her at once, but though they took the note, they did not give it to Rodney. He was having trouble enough rounding up others of this gang and going over a mass of important papers that had been tampered with. Of course this was something that had been going on before Jessica had arrived on the scene, but she was definitely linked up with it, and he suspected that the honorable old De Groot was at the bottom of the whole matter, which probably originated out of the country.

So that night Rodney did not get home to the delightful dinner that had been prepared. Instead he telephoned that there was trouble at the plant and he must stay till things were straightened out.

Jeremy came later for him in response to his phone call, and they felt that the real work of their new labors had begun in earnest.

Jeremy frowned when he heard that Jessica was connected with the trouble, and he blamed himself. "I knew *some*thing was going on," he said, "but I didn't suspect it was as serious as this. There'll be a trial of course?"

"Sure," said Rodney.

"She'll try to get you to help her out," said Jeremy.

"No way," said Rodney. "They wouldn't allow it, even if I would, and I don't see getting into this. If she's guilty, she's guilty, and they'll soon find it out. And even if she didn't know any better, she has to learn her lesson. These people that play fast and loose with their country's honor are just as bad as our enemies and need punishment every bit as much."

"Certainly," said Jeremy. "But what do you think will happen to them? Will they be shot?"

"Some of them, perhaps, but most of them will be put in jail well guarded. Better off than some of the war prisoners, of course, but they'll not be able to carry on any of their machinations. They'll be out of circulation till they learn how to be decent. Some of them will be out of circulation for life. But that's the only way to make the world safe for the coming generation. Of course we can't make the world perfect, and it won't be, till the Lord Jesus comes, but it will help to have right living possible for everybody. They won't all want it, nor take it, but those who want it ought to be able to get it and not be under the domination of cruel fools."

So they talked it over, these two, who were sorely heavy-hearted over the world and the way that Satan had deceived the multitudes. But they went on, living near to God and trying not to bring their daily worries into their dear homes that were so precious to them.

A little later came the trial, for they had rounded up Jessica's husband and his gang and were sifting the whole matter down to facts, and later the names all came out in the paper. They had all been sent away to a safe place, Jessica with the rest, and poor Louella read about it in the paper and cried a great deal. She went off to a lonely little hotel in a far part of California and disguised herself, fearing that she, too might be rounded up with the criminals because of her close association with Jessica.

But the dear young people about whom all this trouble had circulated and tried to harm, went strongly on in the power of their Lord and were glad that they had found each other and found a Lord who could sustain them.

Saturday was on its way, and Rodney was very glad that he need not worry anymore about Jessica, nor have to deal with her in any way. He knew she was in the hands of right and just men who would find out the truth if anybody could and deal with her as she should be dealt with in order to teach her righteousness of a sort, and make her see that she could not play with sin and treachery and not take the punishment when a law of the land was broken.

CHAPTER 22

On Saturday, up in New York, Diana and Rodney walked into the Winters' apartment just half an hour after the arrival of the father and mother.

They found Diana's mother frantically trying to telephone her daughter back in Riverton.

It must be said that Mrs. Winters was at once impressed by Rodney's uniform, not to mention the stripes and other decorations, all of which she took in thoroughly, at a glance, even while she was standing by the telephone, receiver in hand, insisting that the operator ring Riverton again.

Then when she saw Diana, who rushed to embrace her at once, she hung up the receiver and turned to face her and the young lieutenant commander with such notable decorations and such a handsome face.

It certainly was incredible, she thought,

the way Diana always managed to attract the good-looking men, and high officers. This young man was almost better looking than Bates Hibberd. Where did she find him? Not surely in that little backwoods town of Riverton! Then she smilingly held out a welcoming hand and was introduced. Diana with pride gave Rodney all his titles, even the newly acquired one that he had only worn a day or two, and she had the great pleasure of seeing her mother look him over with eyes of approval.

Then she heard her father coming downstairs, and she called, "Daddy, come here! I want you to meet somebody I've brought home," and there followed another introduction.

I knew Dad would like him, I knew, I knew, she whispered to her heart as she saw the hearty grip he gave Rodney, and his smiling, interested glance.

Suddenly, as they all sat down and the mother was prepared to ask a few routine questions about their journey and so on, Diana burst in with her news. "Mother and Dad, this is a very special person I've brought home with me, because I am going to marry him just as soon as we can arrange it. We love each other, and we think that's all that matters. He has a good government job, so I won't starve, and I hope you'll approve. This is Rodney's place to say all this first, I know, but I wanted you to know where I stand before he begins, so there won't be anything said that you'll be sorry for afterward, because this is the man *I'm going to marry*!"

Then Rodney came to the front. "I didn't know she was going to do this, first, but I hope you'll excuse me for being slow. I came up here to ask your permission to marry your daughter. I've brought all my credentials with me, which you can examine at your leisure, but I sure hope you'll approve, for I love her a lot, and I'm going to make it my chief business to make her happy as long as I live."

Then Father Winters fell in line gallantly. "Well, young man, I don't know you, of course, but I like your looks, and I'm willing to take you on faith until I can know you better."

"Thank you, sir," said Rodney warmly, grasping the offered hand of the man whom he had been afraid was going to be just another enemy to be conquered, as he had conquered the enemies across the water. But suddenly he knew that the eyes into which he was looking seemed definitely to be friendly eyes, and his heart grew warm and happy. Then he turned to meet the mother whom he had been led to understand would be the hard one to please.

But amazingly Mrs. Winters was smiling, looking almost shy as she held out a lovely hand. "Well, I guess what Papa has approved, I will have to approve, too," she said in her most gracious manner. "But we love our girl a great deal, you know, and you'll have to measure up to the requirements if you're going to please us."

The mother gave him a scrutinizing look. Good heavens! Was he *religious*? Or was this just put on for the occasion? But Rodney was smiling and drawing Diana close to his side with her fingers squeezed tightly in his own, and he suddenly turned and gave her a kiss, so tender and genuine that the mother was won entirely over.

"And now," said Rodney, standing there with Diana's hand still in his, "we'd like, if you don't mind, to go right to the authorities and get a marriage license, for I have to go on duty at my new job on Monday, and I'd like to take my wife down with me just as soon as possible. Could we possibly have it the next Saturday?"

"But — but — *but*!" said Mrs. Winters. "We couldn't possibly arrange a wedding that soon. There are clothes to be bought, a whole trousseau, a wedding dress. It takes time to get clothes together to be married, my dears. Make it six months at least. Clothes take a lot of time!"

"Clothes!" sniffed Diana cheerfully. "What are clothes? I've got plenty for the time being, and even if you insist on a new one for the wedding, I can get that in an hour, I'm sure."

"But, my dear! You couldn't possibly get the invitations out in that time. A *week*! It's preposterous!"

"But why have invitations? We can call up the few people we like best and just have it a quick war wedding. I don't want a lot of stuff to put away in a trunk in the attic for the rest of my life the way you did with your wedding dress. I have it, Mother! I'll wear your wedding dress if you'll let me."

"Why, of course," said the father. "That would be great. It will fit her, I'm sure. You were as slim as she is when you were married, my dear."

But Mother Winters drew her fine proportions up and lifted her chin haughtily and said, "Now, Edward, I haven't changed so much."

"Why no, of course not, my dear. You're just as charming as when I first fell in love with you."

So great joy descended upon the two young people, and even the dazed parents began to think that life was pretty nice.

It helped a lot, too, when there came a telephone message from the other would-be bridegroom, saying he was to be sent overseas at once and wouldn't be able to come back to see Diana at present. But nobody was thinking anything about him, only Diana who wrote a nice little note of farewell and good wishes, and called that part of her life a closed incident.

They had a lot of fun and were very busy that week.

Of course Rodney had to get back to the plant early Monday morning, but as soon as the marriage license was arranged for, he had gotten in touch with his family at home and told them the good news so they could rejoice with him as soon as he returned. They were overjoyed at the news, and they all promised to come up to New York for the wedding, just for the day, of course. So Mrs. Winters had plenty to do finding rooms for them all and getting ready for a real house party, a thing she adored doing.

Diana tried on her mother's dress and found it needed very little alteration, and they simply eliminated all shopping for the time being.

It was a trial for the mother to give up all this delightful shopping, for the present, but she surrendered gracefully, with a resigned smile.

"I'll get you a lot of lovely things afterward," she said, "when we have more time to find what we want."

It was a goodly trainload of guests who came up the morning of the wedding day to see Diana and Rodney married.

Margaret Graeme wondered on the way whether Louella would ever forgive them that she should have started away only the day before the knowledge of the wedding came to the Graeme family. But Louella hadn't left an address where they could have reached her, and of course they were all just as well pleased not to have to have her.

And so it was going to be only the real families, Graemes, Sandersons, and a few very intimate friends and relatives of the Winters family. Though all their New York friends understood that they might come to the church if they cared to, as it was to be quite an informal affair.

The wedding was to be in the great stone church that the Winters family had attended for generations, and Mother Winters was having her own way about the decorations, costly, refined, and beautiful as any dream.

Lilies and roses and palms and great lacy ferns and masses of white azaleas. But then the decorations were only a matter of an order to the best florist of New York, so everything was fitting and beautiful, and everybody satisfied.

The reception was supposed to be private, for the families and *very* intimates, but that, too, was only the matter of an order to the best caterer in the city. Mrs. Winters had nothing to weary her naturally sweet temper. There were no hitches nor mistakes, nothing to show the difference between the quiet station of one family and the smarter station of the other, with the sensible, lovely Sandersons in between.

Jeremy of course was best man, and Beryl maid of honor.

The flowers were wonderful, and Diana's bouquet was as lovely as if she were marrying a millionaire. It was Rodney's one chance to show what he liked best for his dear bride. White roses, many of them, with maidenhair ferns, and smiling mistily in between, giving lightness to the whole spray, little waxen lilies of the valley. He enjoyed getting that armful of flowers for his dear girl. He had had so little opportunity as yet to show her how he loved her.

And even his new mother-in-law said it

was exquisite!

The wedding was in the early evening, and they were going away soon after the ceremony so they might have one whole beautiful day to themselves before they had to go back into the world and begin to live. Rodney regretted so that they might not have a regular honeymoon and go away somewhere together, but Diana only smiled and said that was the way most servicemen were having to do now while the war still lasted. And they were going to be together now in their own little home, a cottage at the upper end of the Graeme farm for the present, so it didn't matter.

Thank God Rodney didn't have to leave the next day and go back overseas, as so many war men had to do and leave their brides alone with an ocean and peril between them.

Besides, Diana was in a hurry to get home and get her house ready for her parents' first visit, when the Winters would really get acquainted with her dear Graemes.

And now, let's go to the wedding, all of us.

The organ was playing sweet hymns.

"But *hymns*! Darling! *Not* hymns for a *wedding*," protested Diana's mother. "*Just* hymns! I have never *heard* of such a thing!

You don't want to be outlandish. You *couldn't* really have such an innovation. It would scarcely be, well, respectable! Just hymns and no other music! I thought you were talking about that wonderful singer. Aren't you going to have him sing something? Yes, I thought so! And the 'Wedding March,' you know. It wouldn't seem right without that, of course. But hymns are not at all fitting at such a time of rejoicing. Hymns are so somber and gloomy."

But Diana was firm. "It's *my* wedding, isn't it, Mother? Well, that's the way I want it. That's the way we *both* want it. It's to be a kind of declaration of our faith!"

"What *nonsense*!" said her mother with a worried frown.

But the organ was playing sweet old hymns that meant very much to the bridal party. Softly, tenderly, the organ spoke, like a prayer breathed for the lives of those two who were to be joined in marriage. Some were lovely like the evening, some cheerful like the morning, and some triumphant, as when the words that belonged to their harmonies spoke of the coming of the Lord to those who understood.

Diana had compromised on having the "Wedding March" played just as she stood at the door ready to enter, for her mother had been so aggrieved and felt its absence so keenly that she could not seem to be comforted to have it left out.

So the great organist somehow was made to understand about these two with shining eyes who went to explain it to him, and so he made the "Wedding March" sound very far away at first, then drawing nearer, and nearer, till when the bride stood at the very door it melted into a triumphant note or two and went gloriously into another great sounding hymn.

Diana's mother frowned and caught her breath, turned quickly, and cast an anxious glance back at the door. What was the matter? Hadn't Diana arrived yet after all? How strange! She was all ready when she left home. What could have happened? Was she taken suddenly ill? But Diana was almost never ill! She gave another anxious glance back again, and there she could see by the door a vision of white, the wonderful old veil! A lovely vision!

The audience had caught its breath and looked back, too, saw her there, while that triumphant hymn went on for an instant, filling the church with its sweet glad harmonies, and then suddenly a thrilling voice took up the strains with wondrous words. They were new to Mrs. Winters. What did this mean? Wasn't the organist going to go on with the "Wedding March" while the bride came up the aisle? But then she had to stop her puzzled worries and listen as the great singer made the words of the song live.

And so when Diana walked softly up that richly carpeted aisle in the beautiful old white satin wedding gown, trimmed with rare old costly lace, her lovely face alight with joy that had a touch of real glory in it, it was not to the conventional "Wedding March" that she timed her footsteps but to the fine old hymn as that wonderful voice sang the words:

When He shall come with trumpet sound,
   O may I then in Him be found.
Dressed in His righteousness alone,
   Faultless to stand before the throne.
On Christ the solid Rock I stand,
   All other ground is sinking sand;
   All other ground is sinking sand.

Rodney, in his handsome uniform, with the glory-light on his own face, watched her come up the aisle to him, leaning on her father's arm, and said to himself in his heart as she came, "What a girl to come home to!"

ABOUT THE AUTHOR

Grace Livingston Hill (1865–1947) is known as the pioneer of Christian romance. Grace wrote over one hundred faith-inspired books during her lifetime. When her first husband died, leaving her with two daughters to raise, writing became a way to make a living, but she always recognized storytelling as a way to share her faith in God. She has touched countless lives through the years and continues to touch lives today. Her books feature moving stories, delightful characters, and love in its purest form.

The employees of Thorndike Press hope you have enjoyed this Large Print book. All our Thorndike, Wheeler, and Kennebec Large Print titles are designed for easy reading, and all our books are made to last. Other Thorndike Press Large Print books are available at your library, through selected bookstores, or directly from us.

For information about titles, please call:
(800) 223-1244

or visit our Web site at:
http://gale.cengage.com/thorndike

To share your comments, please write:
Publisher
Thorndike Press
10 Water St., Suite 310
Waterville, ME 04901